Roberta Latow has been an art dealer with galleries in Springfield, Massachusetts and New York City. She has also been an international interior designer in the USA, Europe, Africa and the Middle East, travelling extensively to acquire arts, artefacts and handicrafts. Her sense of adventure and her experiences on her travels have enriched her writing; her fascination with heroic men and women; how and why they create the lives they do for themselves; the romantic and erotic core within – all these themes are endlessly interesting to her, and form the subjects and backgrounds of her novels.

'Latow's writing is vibrant and vital. Her characters are much more than caricatures and she describes them in such a distinctive, dynamic way that you can't help but be swept along by them. Latow is a pleasure to read' *Books* magazine

'Her descriptive style is second to none' *Daily Express*

'It sets a hell of a standard' *The Sunday Times*

'Passion on a super-Richter scale. Roberta Latow's unique brand of erotic writing remains fresh and exciting' *Daily Telegraph*

Also by Roberta Latow

Secret Souls
The Pleasure Seekers
Forbidden
Objects of Desire
A Rage to Live
Love Chooses
Her Hungry Heart
Cannonberry Chase
Cheyney Fox
Three Rivers
Tidal Wave
Soft Warm Rain
This Stream of Dreams
White Moon, Black Sea

Only in the Night

Roberta Latow

HEADLINE

First published in 1997
by HEADLINE BOOK PUBLISHING

First published in paperback in 1997
by HEADLINE BOOK PUBLISHING

10 9 8 7 6 5 4 3 2 1

ISBN 0 7472 5568 7

Typeset by Palimpsest Book Production Limited,
Polmont, Stirlingshire
Printed and bound in Great Britain by
Cox & Wyman Ltd, Reading, Berks

HEADLINE BOOK PUBLISHING
A division of Hodder Headline PLC
338 Euston Road
London NW1 3BH

For Sarah and Leah –
friends who *have* stayed the course

Only in the night,
when kisses worship and
caressing hands liberate exquisite limbs,
passion burns brighter, hotter than the sun,
does my lust allow me to lay down my life for him.
Perfect bliss, the fulfilment of love.

The Epic of Artimadon

TUSCANY

1995

Chapter 1

It was a white horse, looking very much like a charger that Wellington might have ridden into battle, that David might have painted, or Napoleon might have commanded from: the muscled neck and mane of white hair, the swishing tail, the way he moved. He challenged her command with a spirit all his own that might be tamed but never broken; rearing up on his hind legs, straining at the bit, fiercely shaking his head from side to side. Mistress of the power and dash he displayed, his rider raced him through the olive groves ranging steeply down the hill. She wore no hat and her blonde hair gleamed like silver in the hot sun as she put the stallion through his paces, skilfully weaving him in and out of the trees. She was going hell-bent for the stream running through the bottom of the valley. Other than the rider and her horse among the trees there was nothing but emptiness, silence, a very special kind of loneliness; in the distance hill after hill, shading from green to pale blue as the sun moved across Tuscany under a soft sky bathed in streaks of yellow light.

'Sometimes I have the feeling that nobody looks at this view properly except us, Philip. The pointed green hills broken by poplars and cypresses; the ruddy farm-houses and patchwork of fields. The rushing streams, and nightingales that sing, the fruit trees swaying in a soft warm breeze and the scent of orange, lemon and peach blossom riding on the wind. The pale rider . . . They seem to be there only for our eyes.'

'That's a vain thought.'

'Yes, I suppose it is.'

'A self-centred fantasy that I too sometimes have. Most people probably do so, at one time or another. At least, the majority of the foreigners who come to Tuscany. And why do you call her the pale rider?'

'There is something ghost-like about her. Every time I see her riding off into the distance, I wonder about her. What sort of a life she leads. I imagine her as a woman with a past. There's something in the way she rides . . . a passion, a love of her sport and her animal, a love of herself. Is she young? Is she old? I can't tell from this distance. She's intriguing and so are those rides she takes. They seem to have a purpose – like riding on the wind, a race for the moon.'

Horse and rider were out of sight now and Philip stared out across the landscape. It was always the same for him, for both of them actually. At first fascination with the beauty and the people they knew in Tuscany: the wealthy and aristocratic English who had settled here in grand palazzos of stone or marble at the end of long avenues of cypresses amid formal gardens, and those artists and writers who had settled in houses such as theirs – large and elegant farm or manor houses or outbuildings saved by renovation that did nothing to distract from the beauty of the Tuscan hills. But that fascination would gradually be overtaken by an ennui that can descend on those who choose to live in beautiful places in the sun.

It was ennui that always drove them back to London. On the rare occasion when, as now, Philip was aware that he was content and seduced once more by one lovely day following another, and when there was nothing more to be seen or thought about but the texture of a landscape where nothing was vile, he was seized by a need to bolt back to England. Could it be, he wondered, that he couldn't bear to live too long in such perfection? And why couldn't he? What was missing from his life that he could not be content with the sublime? He broke into his own thoughts when he announced to Amanda, 'She must be Italian.'

'The pale rider?'

'Yes.'

'What makes you say that?'

'Just the way she is part of the landscape. I know why you're fascinated by her. It's because she is the Tuscany that has eluded us, that keeps us foreigners in a foreign land.'

Amanda wanted to ask, What are you talking about? But she couldn't because she did understand what he was saying. They loved their house and Tuscany and their friends who had houses and lives going for them in the area. But their years of meeting the same people, seeing the same paintings and sculptures in Florence, the architecture in Siena, the sunlight from San Miniato; the endless excursions to see yet another church or painting or fresco, to entertain themselves or one of their many house guests, like conversation with the other foreign residents that had declined into nothing more than gossip, seemed to be sapping rather than enhancing their lives.

It now occurred to Amanda that in the fifteen years

that Philip and she had had the house, which was their pride and joy and even now the place they would rather be than anywhere else in the world, they had not been befriended by any of their Italian neighbours. They had, in fact, been invited into the home of a local only twice. Where had they been? What had they been doing? And all the time they had thought they had been *living* in Tuscany.

It wasn't that she and Philip did not appreciate or that they took for granted every buttercup, wild flower, moment of scent or silence in Tuscany, they did; they just didn't give themselves up to those things any more than they gave themselves up totally to anything. The pale rider did, and that was why she fascinated Amanda. She appeared to be a woman at one with the world and every little thing in it. Amanda felt suddenly as if she had been missing something.

She unwound the patterned sarong wrapped around her body and dropped it on the marble floor as she walked from the terrace wall where she had been sitting towards Philip, lying on a wooden chaise. Naked save for her wide-brimmed straw hat and the antique ivory bracelets on her wrists, she looked sensationally sexy. Amanda had a glorious body, the sort of female figure that demanded sexual attention, adventures in the erotic. She and Philip were well aware of what they were to each other sexually, when sex was love. Were they perhaps emotionally crippled people whose sex life was the glue that kept them together? A question never pondered; a thought kept secret from friends, even themselves.

Philip rose from the chaise. Going to her, he removed her hat and spun it like a frisbee across the terrace. Her skin was warm from the afternoon sun and she smelled of jasmine and roses. They gazed into each other's eyes and he licked her nipples as he undressed. She had chosen her moment. The housekeeper was in the village, the gardener had long since gone, the maid was with the housekeeper, their house guests in Perugia for the night. Philip knew his lover well, recognised the hunger and recklessness in her eyes. She wanted to be riven and riven hard; she would be difficult to bring to orgasm and they would go to great extremes to achieve it for her. She would submit to anything, everything, sexual he would demand that might excite them and bring them both to their moment of ecstasy. He liked sex with her best when she was like this. It brought the dark side of their natures to the surface and gave their well-ordered and conservative lives a momentary fillip. Love would come into their sexual extravaganza only after the event. That was how it was with them, and how it always would be, and neither of them had ever been unhappy about that.

Did they know they were jealous of the pale rider? That what she had, that enigmatic something missing from their lives, was what they wanted? Yes, they knew, but buried it deep in their psyches with every thrust Amanda received from Philip, every pulsating, throbbing sensation he felt. The pleasure of sexual intercourse, the feeling of being whole and connected for a few minutes with another human being in the most intimate of acts – such bliss triggers forgetfulness.

It was several days later. Philip had gone to take their house guests to the airport in Pisa and Amanda was in the large, cool kitchen, sitting at the pine table, white and smooth from years of scrubbing with salt. She was shelling peas when Vittorio appeared at the open door. With the sun behind him, it took her some time to realise who it was. When she did, she invited him in for a cool drink. She liked the farmer who came to cut the grass in the meadow twice a year. There was never any fuss or bother with this handsome and rugged man; he arrived when he said he would and left when he had finished his work. The price never changed and what few words they had ever exchanged over the years were few and pleasant and always accompanied by a smile. Amanda's impression of Vittorio was that he was a man content with his lot in life, whatever that might be.

Maria, the housekeeper, arrived from somewhere in the house as Amanda was pouring Vittorio a glass of fresh lemonade. The bulky middle-aged Maria had been with them since they had bought the house, she was a treasure, had the measure of her employers and ran their house with ease and to perfection. There were never too many house guests, the work was never too much, she took a pride in the house and working for them, and was well liked in the village besides.

Maria pulled out a chair for Vittorio and produced a plate of Tuscan sweets which she had made earlier in the day. They were offered and the two of them joined Amanda at the table. Maria took up a copper bowl, removed the tea cloth covering it and got down to beating the makings of a polenta cake, Amanda continued shelling peas, and Vittorio, clearly the centre of attention, was enjoying his repast and gossiping with Maria. The two Italians laughed together over a bit of local news and Amanda mused on how much more handsome Vittorio would be after a few sessions with a Harley Street dentist. A sweet was forced on Amanda by Maria – not much of a hardship, she was partial to Maria's sweets. Amanda's Italian allowed her to eavesdrop on the local goings on, which unfortunately she did not find nearly as interesting as Maria did. But the kitchen was Maria's domain and she could entertain whomever she liked there.

After a short time Vittorio stood up and announced with some pride, in his not very good English, that his fiancée would be coming to pick him up – he would introduce her to Signora Dix. Amanda made all the right noises while thinking, How very odd. What a bore. Vittorio thanked Maria and Amanda, rather formally, thought Amanda for their hospitality, and made a hurried exit to wait for his fiancée on the drive.

Maria rose from the table looking quite cheerful at the prospect of having another visitor in her kitchen, and after pouring her cake batter into its ready-prepared tin and placing it in the oven, turned to Amanda and asked, 'Where would you like to have tea – on the terrace or in the library?'

'Tea? Do you think that's necessary, Maria?'

'Well, it's very English to have tea,' answered the housekeeper-cum-cook who was already getting down the best of the tea sets and placing cups and saucers on the table.

That was a typical Maria answer to a question, rather than say a definite *yes*. She quite clearly wanted to impress the farmer's girlfriend. Pride, Amanda supposed, and worried that it might embarrass a shy village girl who had most likely never had a cup of afternoon tea in her life.

'I think here in the kitchen will do,' she told her housekeeper.

There was a brief look of disapproval which Amanda ignored as she continued shelling the peas. She watched Maria remove her apron and tidy the hair in a bun at the nape of her neck before she went to the linen cupboard and chose a fine white linen cloth embroidered with raised yellow buttercups and napkins to match. From there she marched to the floor-to-ceiling bay window at one end of the vast kitchen where a small round marble table and four chairs overlooked the herb garden and herbaceous borders leading to the walled garden. This was Philip and Amanda's breakfast area, a place for informal lunches and dinners, their cosy eating place.

Amanda was on the verge of telling Maria that the best linen was not necessary for the farmer's fiancée but thought that might offend her sense of class distinction so gritted her teeth, feeling very put upon. Once more she was sorely tested when the Limoges cups and saucers, side plates gleaming white and banded with a wide border of yellow, were set on the table, the Queen Anne silver tea pot produced. But what could Amanda actually say? She had trained Maria well, and the housekeeper was doing what her mistress had always advocated: 'Any guest who comes to my house should be given the best.'

Maria whisked away the bowls of pods and shelled peas in front of Amanda and handed her a tea towel. Amanda washed her hands and watched with wonder as Maria produced a lemon tart and placed it on the Limoges pedestal dish. All Amanda could think was how sweet life could be in London if she had Maria there. By the time the two women heard the knock at the door, Amanda was quite resigned to impressing the farmer's fiancée and spending the next twenty minutes exchanging small talk in her moderately acceptable Italian with one of the locals. She did have the good grace to smile to herself as she thought, And all for PR to keep the staff happy.

There was a brief knock and then there they were standing together on the threshold. Vittorio had his arm around her waist, and not just he but both of them seemed to be beaming with happiness. Maria ushered them in and Vittorio proudly introduced his fiancée.

There was an air of gentleness about Eliza Flemming. She was soft-spoken and appeared to be a woman content with herself and life in general. It was like a perfume she wore or an aura that hovered around her. There was something else about her too, an infectious liveliness in her smiling eyes. Had it to do with their colour? They were dark blue, nearly violet. After Amanda overcame the shock of Vittorio's fiancée being a middle-aged, upper-middle-class English-woman, tall and slender with fair skin and blonde hair, she was able to assess her: a once great beauty, still highly attractive, sensuous, cultured, sophisticated – a woman not unlike herself. No wonder Maria had pulled out all the stops for tea. She had obviously heard about her.

'I hope this isn't an imposition?' suggested Eliza.

'Not at all. You will stay for tea?'

'That would be very nice.'

Then, turning to Vittorio, she asked him if they had time for her to stay for a visit. It was finally decided that Eliza would stop for tea and Vittorio would go to the village to do an errand and then return for her. While the couple discussed their plans all sorts of questions were running through Amanda's mind. Why had this woman chosen to marry this decent, hard-working but simple farmer with his rudimentary English and face darkened and roughened from work and weather? And when she did, what would become of her? What would be the consequences of giving herself up to such a simple man? Would he pull her down to his level?

'Tea would be a treat. I would like to stay for it but Vittorio cannot come back for me for at least half an hour,' she told her hostess.

'That's no problem, do please stay,' was Amanda's gracious reply.

She watched Eliza caress Vittorio's hand and listened to her thank him for arranging the introduction, telling him she would be ready to leave on his return. The love they had for each other, the care and respect, was as evident as their passion which could be read in their every gesture, seen in their eyes. Theirs was a true love story.

Vittorio gone, there was an awkward moment between the two women. It was broken by Maria who gestured with her hand that tea was to be served. 'Would you prefer to have it on the terrace or in the library? It's easily arranged,' asked Amanda, and received a knowing look from Maria.

'In here will do nicely. I like kitchens, always have done. And your table . . . how charming it looks. Afternoon tea doesn't happen very often for me any more.'

There was very little that embarrassed Amanda but she did find exchanging pleasantries with Eliza somewhat awkward. She didn't quite know whether to speak to her as an Englishwoman or a struggling Italian farmer's girlfriend. It was unreasonable but she nevertheless felt just a little angry with the woman for settling for a man such as Vittorio when she could clearly do much better.

The two women sat at the table talking about the herbaceous border while Amanda served the tea. But her mind kept drifting off into her own thoughts: wondering why Eliza had chosen to marry Vittorio. Sex! That could be the only reason for her stepping down to such a marriage. Amanda, having felt obliged to make an excuse for Eliza, was somehow relieved that it was something as simple as sex. She could understand that. Hadn't Vittorio always exuded a kind of rough and exciting sexuality that had made her, years ago, dub him 'our Tuscan Heathcliff'?

She was slicing into the lemon tart when she asked Eliza, 'Do you live close by?'

'We live about ten miles away, towards the sea.'

Amanda was curious about Eliza Flemming; there were so many questions she would have liked to ask her but could not. She had a sense that here was a woman who cherished her privacy, who did not gladly suffer intrusions into her life, most especially from the English colony settled in these Tuscan hills. Amanda had never heard Eliza's name mentioned, and she and her lover Vittorio would have been rich pickings for the gossips.

After a slow start conversation came easily. It was an amusing half hour, Eliza exuding simple charm and an intelligence that was winning without her trying to be so. The moment she heard Vittorio's lorry rattling up to the house, however, she rose from her seat.

'Vittorio's back,' she told Amanda, and a special light came into her eyes.

'It was very nice meeting you,' her hostess told her as she clasped Eliza's hand.

She smiled. 'Yes.' That was all she said before she went to Maria and thanked her, complimented her on the tart, and was gone.

'Well, that was some surprise,' commented Amanda to Maria, who was now clearing the tea table. The housekeeper said nothing but seemed quite pleased with herself.

'You've never met her before?' queried Amanda.

'No, but I have seen her many times in the village. I even saw her once in her robes.'

'Her robes?'

'She's a magistrate for this district, a good person to know. She almost single-handedly reorganised the hospitals in this district when she was attached to the Health Ministry. They say if she ran for Senator, she would win. But she'll never do that, she's not a woman for politics – she's a woman in love with her man and her freedom. And she has the Villa Montecatini.'

That bit of news was enough to take Amanda off her feet. She sat down, exclaiming, 'Then she's a woman of considerable substance! That explains a great deal.' Gigolo, sex, an older woman, were the thoughts running through Amanda's mind.

'No.'

'No what, Maria?' she asked.

'Not wealthy, not poor. Her salary, his salary . . . what the farm yields. They struggle like most farmers.'

'How do you know all this?'

'It's common knowledge.'

'But the Villa Montecatini is supposed to be filled with marvellous things! And its gardens, its farm . . . it's a place I have heard about, a legend. And that's hers? Are you sure? How did she come by it?'

'She's a Montecatini on her mother's side of the family.'

'But she's English.'

'There are English Montecatinis and Tuscan Montecatinis. She's an English one.' And with a shrug of her shoulders, Maria was quite finished talking about Eliza Flemming.

Amanda could not let it rest and approached her as she was washing the tea cups. 'You liked her, have respect for her. Why?'

'Because she has everything *and* a generous heart. You can see it when she is with Vittorio, or when at harvest time she has all the workers to the house for a feast. And the way she rides her white stallion.'

Only then did Amanda realise that Eliza Flemming was the pale rider.

Vittorio drove most all of the way home with one hand on the steering wheel, Eliza leaning against his chest, his arm around her shoulders. He asked so many questions. Was it a nice tea? Did she enjoy herself? Did she find Signora Dix agreeable? And then, finally, did she miss not having friends like Signora Dix in her life any more? Eliza did not miss the tremor of anxiety in his voice nor did she miss the sigh of relief and the smile that crossed his face when she told him she missed nothing in her life with him.

His stubble was rough against her cheek when she

grazed it with her own, and licked one of the deep furrows in his face with the tip of her tongue to emphasise to him she meant what she had said.

He was damp with perspiration and smelled of new-mown grass and the sun. All day she had been missing him, had wanted to be with him. She would have been quite content to have spent the day sitting in the shade and watching him cut the Dix-Markham meadow. Now that they were together again and intended to be so for the remainder of their lives, she missed him every minute of every hour they were apart. It was sometimes difficult for her to remember their age, that they were not the lovers they had been twenty-five years before. Today she felt exactly the same about Vittorio as she had back then. It was as if the intervening years and the tragedies had never happened.

After the conversation they drove in silence, Eliza caressing the inside of his thigh, occasionally lowering her head to kiss the bulge in his jeans, and admiring the hills and a sky still bright with light. Vittorio was concentrating on keeping the old and dilapidated lorry on the road and getting them home as fast as possible. Eliza thought only briefly of Amanda Dix and how attractive she was with that studied and very elegant casual chic. How stylish everything was about her; her kitchen, and most probably her life.

Eliza almost never thought of her first husband, John, but she did now: how very different her life might have been with him had she been more like Amanda Dix. How he would have loved a wife just like her, a woman trapped in being upwardly mobile, money and culture-oriented; jockeying always for a better place in the infrastructure of the 1990s quest for money and success. Briefly she remembered herself in those years she had been Eliza Hope-Quintin, and her struggle against who and what she was to make her marriage work. Eliza trying to be an Amanda for the love of her husband and children. A sense of overwhelming failure sent a shiver down her spine.

But mercifully it snuffed itself out as fast as it had flared up and she effortlessly let the past slip away from her. In her present life she was as happy as she had been as a child and young adult, before she had deserted Vittorio to learn about the cruelty man can inflict upon woman in the name of love; the disappointments that can twist and turn a life, make a stranger of one's self to one's self; and what profound loneliness and isolation can do to a psyche.

They pulled off the road on to the turning that led for several hundred yards up an incline to the gates. Eliza reluctantly abandoned the warmth of Vittorio's body to jump down from the cab of the lorry and push open the rusting gates, closing them after he had driven through. How sweet he was. Normally Vittorio would have used one of the side drives that would bring them to the farm buildings where he would deposit the lorry, but he had wanted to end her visit with Amanda Dix by bringing her home in style, through the main gate to the house they now shared. He loved her so very much.

The long drive twisted and turned through the avenue of cypresses bordering the helter-skelter of flowering shrubs and trees long since grown wild. More than a hundred years before they must have been well kept and impressive. A very English drive in a Tuscan landscape to remind the family of their other roots. The house, like the drive, had seen better days and more care but was nevertheless impressive, once a grande dame among the Tuscan houses and retaining an air of home, family and love.

Vittorio stopped directly in front of the entrance and cut the motor. For several minutes they sat there, listening. The heat of the day now on the wane, the birds were singing again, a symphony of several different songs. They watched the singers still on the wing coming home from their day's hunt for food as they swooped and pirouetted on the warm currents of air, then settled among branches heavy with bright green leaves. They looked plump and satisfied as they preened their feathers and made ready for night.

Vittorio slid from behind the wheel and, still holding Eliza's hand, pulled her along the seat and down from the cab with him. Their feet crunched the gravel underfoot as they walked across the courtyard, past the large white umbrella, chairs and table where Giacomo, the eighty-year-old retainer, who had been at the Villa Montecatini all his life, had left a jug of fresh peach juice with a tea cloth over it and two glasses.

The front doors, though closed, were unlocked. They pushed them open and the coolness of the house enveloped them as, together, Eliza and Vittorio climbed the grand staircase, two steps at a time, laughing. They made directly for their bathroom, a marble affair installed in the 1920s by Eliza's grandmother. Like so many other rooms in the house, it spanned centuries of design and house-proud ancestors. The whole villa reeked of a time when the family had had great taste, a passion for collecting all things Italian, most particularly antiquities and more money.

Eliza knew and loved every room, every object; it had always been her fairytale castle. Ancestors had lived in luxury; her nearer family more like gypsies than English and Italian aristocrats because for the last seventy years the family's history had been one of little money, more of a happy-go-lucky existence, living to the manner born in genteel poverty. For as long as anyone could remember the working farm had sustained the house just enough for it to remain intact. The pride of the Montecatinis had always been that they had a heritage, the house, their name, and had never sold one square foot of land or the smallest item from their villa. They had lived, as Eliza did now, in the splendour and sometimes squalor of the Villa Montecatini.

She bent over the black marble bath and turned the sterling silver Art Deco taps full on. Vittorio was bending over her, kissing the back of her head, the nape of her neck, and struggling with her dress. She fumbled with the buttons, anxious to help him. The sound of the water splashing into the tub was the only sound in the room except for Vittorio's heavy breathing. There was an urgency in the sound, a need, a desire, that matched her own. They wanted to bathe away the day's sweat but the pungent odour of earth and grass, the natural scent of a body in lust, was too raunchy. It demanded immediate sex, glorious base fucking.

There were whispers of love in her ear as Vittorio balanced her in exactly the right position over the marble rim of the bath to take her from behind, penetrating her deeply. She came on his first thrust and he moved in and out of her with a slow powerful determination that she should, they both should, enjoy every nuance of the sexual act. His hands on her naked waist for leverage, he screwed her down to her very soul with his sex.

There was something about sex with Vittorio that triggered multiple orgasms for Eliza, dissolving any sexual control she might have. She came and came again. She lost herself in her orgasms and was unable to stop coming. She became a living, vibrant, sexual vessel for Vittorio, and in that state knew sex as she had never known it with any other man. It was so easy to give herself up to lust with Vittorio, so exciting, so rewarding. Now, as always, he was in total command and the moment he sensed that she had submitted to her own lust, his only desire was to give her more pleasure. Several more thrusts and they came together. He pulled her upright and against him, and whispered love to her. Without even withdrawing he pulled her down to the floor and took her in another position. Lying over her body, his semi-erect penis in her mouth, his face now between her legs, he licked away their mutual lust for each other and nibbled like a gentle cannibal at her vaginal lips. Then once more they changed positions.

It was not very long before Vittorio and Eliza came together again and this time he had the pleasure of seeing her face as she came: a face filled with love and passion, lust for him. Their hearts pounding against each other for several minutes before he moved, Vittorio did what he always had to do to ease Eliza back from lust unbound. He kissed her lips, her eyes and chin, and spoke to her. 'Eliza, close your eyes. Sleep, my darling, for a few minutes.' And he rubbed their lust across her lips with his fingertips and she licked them and opened her eyes and sighed.

'Happy?' she asked him.

'More than any man deserves to be. And you?'

'I think you know how happy you make me.'

With that he scooped her up and carried her to the bath, now filled to the brim with water. He stepped into it, easing them slowly into the water to lie together in each other's arms. It caressed their bodies in ripples as sensuous as satin, as seductive as soft, warm, liquifying sex. They never talked at times like this. They merely lay there, bathing each other, caressing. It was usually possible, and was now, for Vittorio to take Eliza one more time.

He was the first out of the bath. Eliza watched him dry himself off. He looked so dark and virile. He was something rugged and rough, a man of the land, a hunter, a passionate man. One could never equate him with finesse; he was a simple man, without artifice. And that, and his animal passion for the woman he loved, was his power. Eliza was mesmerised by his body, so hard and muscular. To see him naked, as she was seeing him now, was to be reminded of his tremendous sexual stamina, the lengths he would go to give her sexual pleasure, how he cared for her when they were over the erotic edge into a world of lust and depravity where she was ready to die in his arms in sexual bliss.

She watched him lather his handsome face: the Roman nose, dark and sultry eyes under lashes long and thick, so very seductive for a man, sensual lips set in a square face above a jaw with a deep cleft in it. He always shaved before dinner and she watched him now, scraping away the day's beard, and marvelled that he should be hers, that they should be together in love and lust, and that no man or woman, nothing in the world, could ever change that. She raised the water-logged sponge from the bath and squeezed the water over her shoulders, never taking her eyes from the reflection of his face in the mirror. She was reminded of the many hearts he had unwillingly broken in his life: women, girls, men even, who had fallen in love or lust with him and whom he had not loved. She still saw many a head turn in his direction: women younger and more beautiful than she who wanted him, who could not understand how or why he had chosen to love her and only her. The Italians loved Eliza for loving Vittorio Carducci, for choosing one of them. Eliza and Vittorio were a Tuscan love story because of who and what they were. They embodied the romantic passion that the Italians thrived on and the English were embarrassed by and ran away from, or at best simply ignored.

She rose from the bath and he brought her a terrycloth robe and helped her on with it. 'I will go and have a drink with some of the boys. Dinner?' he asked.

'Nine o'clock.'

'Good.' He kissed her again and suggested, 'You look tired. Why not take a nap before dinner? You have time.'

He was right. He walked with her to their bed where she lay down and he placed an aged, lace-trimmed white linen sheet over her. They smiled at each other and he left the room.

Eliza fell into a deep dreamless sleep and when she awakened it was dark. Night had fallen, but it was bright with a sliver of moon and a sky studded with stars. She dressed and went down to the kitchen. There she found Giacomo, Amiata the cleaner, Francesca the cook and Paolo the gardener, sitting round the table set for dinner. These were old retainers who had been here most of their lives and who kept the forty-six-roomed house in running order.

It was the custom of Eliza's household that they all had dinner together at the long wooden table placed in front of the huge stone fireplace, unless specified differently by either Eliza or Vittorio. The evening meal at the villa never had less than the household staff and Eliza and Vittorio at table. The household had a reputation for simple hospitality and it was not unusual for other of the estate workers or a neighbour to drop in for a meal. The Montecatinis had always been known for their table. Their food, wine and generosity extended to open invitations to their Tuscan neighbours. And who knew who Vittorio might bring home?

Eliza looked in several pots, broke off a piece of bread and sat down at the table after greeting everyone. Giacomo served her a goblet of wine, Francesca sliced her a piece of salami. It was cosy, it was home. This was her family, and her life. She listened to Giacomo and the gardener discussing some work that needed doing in the conservatory and Francesca humming a song, and felt happy and content with the world. It had been another lovely day in her life.

Amanda Dix came to mind, and the tea party she had produced for the farmer's fiancée. It made Eliza smile. She'd liked Amanda and thought it too bad they could not be friends. But then, Amanda Dix's curiosity might make them friends. She seemed to be the type of woman who would have to know what had brought Eliza to her downfall: marriage to a near-illiterate farmer. She sipped her wine and laughed aloud as her mind ranged back over the life she had had to live to get here tonight, drinking in her kitchen, waiting for the man she loved to come home for dinner.

TUSCANY,
THE COTSWOLDS,
LONDON

1968–1987

Chapter 2

Julian Forrester commanded respect in just the way his father and grandfather had, as indeed had all his ancestors living for three hundred years in the Cotswolds. They were county people. In his quiet, unassuming way Julian had power, the kind of power that gets things done, and it was that power, and the prime tracts of land that had been in the family for generations and made him an important landowner, that gained him and his family entrée into the best manor houses and stately homes within a seventy-five-mile radius of Little Barrington where he and his family lived.

The Forresters were land rich and cash poor; it was the history of their family and everyone knew it. The family did not so much work their land as conserve it. It meant their income was paltry but other equally important landowners, who had for generations been trying to buy Forrester land, had nothing but admiration and envy for the family's ability to say no.

Everyone liked the Forresters, who were quintessential English eccentrics: they should have been aristocrats but were bourgeois; they should have been snobs but for the most part found their own company more amusing than society and crossed all class barriers in their friendships. They rode with the local hunt, a family passion, and were a formidable sight when they went out: mother, father and five daughters. Theirs was the best pheasant shoot in the area but none of them shot. They all fished their trout streams, and they all travelled. Everyone considered them colourful rather than exotic, because they remained so very English in spite of the family's speaking several languages and Dulcima Forrester's having been born in Italy, the youngest daughter of the English branch of the Montecatini family.

From July to mid-September the Forresters were never in Little Barrington. They packed up and transported themselves to the Villa Montecatini, between Bagni di Lucca and Barga in Tuscany, where they lived and played with life much as they did in England. They were barefoot summers where everyone did much as they chose to and the house received a multitude of visitors and relatives. Where everyone pitched in at harvest-time or cleaned and polished the house on Dulcima's insistence that a spring clean was better than an inventory; it gave everyone a chance to appreciate what they had.

They half-heartedly groomed the overgrown gardens and repaired the summer awnings, even though the Forresters preferred the rundown condition of the Monetcatini estate. It reeked of time and heritage and suited their streak of inverted snobbery. They rode their horses cross-country to visit their neighbours or to swim in the sea – when they chose not to swim in the lake, or the still-elegant pool installed on the eve of the first world war. There were fierce games of tennis played on clay, croquet on the lawn, and every year there was a cricket match. They made endless fun, touring the countryside in vintage cars inherited from the family and kept in running order by a neighbour in exchange for his racing them in rallies. Money was not very important to the Forresters who in Tuscany relied more on a barter system than anything else. In fact, not one of the family had the least understanding of how to make or keep money. They were actually disinterested, thinking money something not quite vulgar but close to it.

Summer romances seemed to be always in the air. The five Forrester girls were very good-looking and popular. Boys came from England; the local lads courted them. The more prosperous and worldly young Romans, summering in their own family villas, were besotted by the blonde and incredibly unrestrained sisters. The many Tuscan cousins who adored the English branch of the family were always falling in love with them. There was never a time without one or two romances on the go for the family to tease the girls about.

Dendra Forrester's constant summer time companion was the saddler's son until, much to her mother's and father's horror, she fell in love with the heir to an Earldom and left the bosom of her family to marry well and live a more grand life. Constanza Forrester was swept off her feet by an American and one July they held a wedding at the villa before she left them for West Virginia. Eliza was in love with the farmer's son, Vittorio, and had been since she was six years old, and Clara with his brother. The two sisters dreamed of how one day, when they were old enough, they would marry their handsome young Italians and live together happily ever after in the villa six months of the year then bring them home to Little Barrington for the other six months. Effie Forrester declared she would never marry but have many lovers and adventures and travel as a photojournalist, which she did in fact do.

This then was Eliza's immediate family, her legacy, and what gained the Forresters their reputation for being both solid and frivolous, interesting and amusing. Except for Effie, none of the girls was ambitious nor were they career-minded. They were really country girls: excellent horsewomen, lovers of the countryside, who thought that their lives would go on forever as they had started. They were all well read: tutors lived with the family, teaching the girls English literature and languages, Italian, French. For several summers there had even been a Greek tutor, but higher education was not a priority, any more than marriage was, which was why when the girls did fall in love and marry, it was always a shock to the family.

Vittorio's father was a tenant farmer on the Montecatini estate, and yet the Forresters depended on him because what he made from the farm he shared with them. That was the only income that kept the Carducci family and the Villa Montecatini going. Vittorio had the run of the house as a friend of the children and their cousins, and later as the boyfriend of Eliza. It was more of a surprise *not* to see him there than it was to see him. The years rolled on. Eliza and he became inseparable and displayed their love for each other openly. It never occurred to any of the family, except Eliza, that the sweet love affair which they all enjoyed watching would not one day die a natural death by merely running its course. The couple were after all worlds apart, with not much in common.

It therefore came as a surprise to Julian Forrester when his wife Dulcima said on the evening of Eliza's sixteenth birthday, 'Do you think they know love is running out for them? It will be a terrible blow for Vittorio. It always is for the one that's left behind. I'll not be happy to see the boy badly hurt.'

That night Vittorio and Eliza did not realise that their life together was threatened. Nor did they realise it the following summer when sex came into their lives.

Vittorio, three years older than Eliza, had been having sex since he was fourteen years old. Women as well as girls had always pursued the boy. He had a sexual aura about him that triggered lust in those who were ready and willing for an uncomplicated sexual affair. But sex for a poor farm boy in a sexually repressed society was no easy thing, especially one who was in love. Of course he wanted sex with Eliza, he had an erotic passion for her as well as love, but she was too young. He prided himself on his ability to wait for sex with her until she was old enough, ready enough, had a hunger for it. He promised himself he would be the best lover in the world for the girl he loved and wanted to make a life with.

It was his luck and one of the tragedies of his life that when he was sixteen he was hired by a beautiful lady, a famous French writer, who lived in a farmhouse several miles from the Villa Montecatini to do odd jobs for her. She seduced the boy and for several years they were secret lovers. It was she who taught him how to channel his sexual energy into becoming a quite remarkable lover. Their erotic life was adventurous and since both had very strong libidos they were well matched in their desires and the amount of sex it took to keep them content. Through their sex life they became friends and he confided in her his passion for Eliza, their love for each other, their dreams that one day they would consummate their love and marry.

Since Eliza was fourteen years old she and Vittorio had been kissing and petting, lying naked in each other's arms, exciting each other. They were able to set each other aflame: masturbating, coming separately and together, declaring undying love. But never did they have intercourse. As Eliza awakened sexually, she wanted to know everything about Vittorio's sex life and was astounded to know that he had one, though he did not tell her with whom. Eliza found it more fascinating than anything else that he should have sex with a woman who had nothing to do with their lives. It actually excited her to hear him tell of the delights sex could bring, how it would be with them. By the time she returned for her seventeenth summer in Tuscany they both knew they could wait no longer, they simply had to have each other.

The family arrived from England around eleven in the morning on a very hot day in late-May. Off came Eliza's shoes and she was out of the house looking for Vittorio. No one thought anything of it; she had been doing exactly that same thing for ten years. He and several men were working in the peach orchard when he heard her calling and saw her running down the hill through the trees towards him. Vittorio dropped the spade he was working with and broke into a run uphill towards her. They crashed into each other's arms. It had been nearly ten months since they had seen each other. She always wrote, he rarely, though sometimes he would call. Not a word needed to be said. They knew it was time for them to express their feelings with their bodies as they had never done before.

Their hearts were pounding as he swung her up and into his arms and began kissing her. 'I missed you, I love you, I want you, I need you,' she whispered huskily in his ear as tears of emotion and anguish from months of pent-up frustratration ran down her cheeks. He carried her over to where his horse stood tethered under a peach tree heavy with blossom. Placing her on the horse in front of him, he leaped into the saddle and pulled her against his chest. His arms went around her and he caressed her full breasts and pinched her nipples. He sensed the tremor that went through her body and bit into the side of her neck, sucking her flesh into his mouth. She unzipped her blue jeans and, taking his hands from her breasts, placed them over her mound of pubic hair. Then she slipped the knot and took the reins in her hands and led the horse from under the tree.

With one arm tight round her and holding her hard against him, Vittorio eased the horse into a canter and then a gallop out of the orchard, to the sound of the men he had left behind hooting and hollering joyously for the lovers.

They had a private place they liked to think of as being all their own and that was where they rode to. The lovers left their clothes strewn on the grass. Eliza climbed into his arms and, wrapping her legs tight around his waist, began kissing him: his lips, his eyes, his cheeks. She bit into his neck and licked and sucked his flesh, and in between her kisses and caresses she begged him, 'Vittorio, please fuck me. So many nights of imagining and yearning! I keep coming just thinking about you, about us. I'm coming now but I feel empty, alone, and always will until you take me.'

He leaned her naked back against the rough bark of their tree and placed the palm of her hand against the carved heart with their initials inscribed in it, which years ago had made it *their* tree. 'You are my life,' he told her, and pressed a deep and passionate kiss upon her.

Without further ceremony he raised her by the waist and impaled her on himself. She screamed with pain, shock, excitement. The thrill of feeling a man taking possession of her for the first time, ridding her of what had become burdensome virginity, was an act more violent than she had expected. It left her breathless. Only his deep kisses, the hunger for her that made him bite into her lips, and the manner in which her body submitted to his assault on her cunt, allowed her to go with the thrustings, take them for what they were. It was a matter of minutes before she experienced multiple orgasm. Her body stiffened, she felt hot and flushed as they flowed. With Vittorio she was able to drift off into a special kind of ecstasy that she had never experienced before. In his fucking he was transporting her to a place she had never been; a place that was as sublimely pleasurable as it was painful. She sensed that the pain would vanish and that there were to be unimagined pleasures in sex just waiting for her to discover them.

For Vittorio, this first sex with Eliza was a discovery. His love had sexual needs and demands to be fulfilled. He had learned from Janine about natural eroticism, and though he was thrilled to learn that the girl he loved possessed it, he was at the same time surprised to find her such a sexual being. Eliza, though sensuous-looking, had a manner that was soft, a sweet nature, simple and never demanding. And now this discovery! He had never imagined that beneath those traits was a fiery need for sex and a man.

They lay in the grass, wrapped in each other's arms, for nearly an hour before they spoke and then it was not with words but their bodies yet again. It was dusk before they dressed and mounted the horse to ride home. During those hours they had had sex several more times in new and thrilling ways, and Eliza began to understand that sex with Vittorio was to be better, more thrilling, with every act of submission on her part. All she had to do was give herself up to sex and the rewards would be special moments of intimacy that led to a kind of oblivion unique to sex, the erotic, and relating to a man.

The house was ablaze with lamplight. Eliza was aware that everything looked the same but nothing would ever be the same for her again. A new world had opened up for her and Vittorio. She had mixed feelings: sadness that they would be leaving something of themselves behind, their youth, their innocence, but excitement too for a future of sensations and experiences she had never thought or dreamed of. Her thoughts were broken when Vittorio asked, 'You are happy about what happened today? You have to be happy!'

'Yes, I am,' she told him, and while still on the horse and leaning against his chest, turned to kiss him and prove to him that she was.

'I've marked you for life now. You're mine, and will never be anyone else's as much as you are mine.'

'I believe that's true,' she told him, and she did believe it. And she realised by what he had told her and the tremor of passion and urgency, a strange inflection of fear in his voice, that there was something very serious and grown-up about what he was saying, how he was feeling. Something sombre and binding that made her look at Vittorio with new eyes, those of a budding beauty with a whole world laid out for her to discover. It frightened her to think that there might be more to life than being in love and lust with Vittorio and running free and wild with him in Tuscany, so she blocked that thought from her mind and swung her leg over the horse to slide down. She kissed Vittorio's hand and told him, 'This has been the most glorious day of my life.'

'Tomorrow then,' he told her.

'Meet me at the lake before you go to work. I'll bring breakfast.'

'No later than six o'clock.'

She agreed and turned to walk away from him, whereupon he dismounted and grabbed her. Holding her close to him, he asked, 'I didn't hurt you, did I? I couldn't bear it if I'd hurt you. It will be easier tomorrow, and more exciting. I love you, you're the most glorious woman I have ever had, and there will never be another for me again. You do understand that that's the way it has to be for me, for us? We'll marry as soon as I can afford for us to.'

Their kiss was deep and full of passion. Vittorio's control and concern for her vanished and he rushed her into the shadows and down to the grass where, on their knees, he took her in a rage of lust. They came together almost instantly. Then he adjusted her clothes and caressed her hair but they said nothing, merely parted. Sex, the thrill of sex, the excitement and danger of their lust, filled their hearts and minds. More was all they could think about; more of what they had had and what they would have tomorrow.

Tomorrow came and all the other tomorrows of that summer, and lust took over the young lovers' lives. Not for either of them could there have been or would there ever be a more glorious summer. And then one day there were no more tomorrows left for Vittorio and Eliza. It was over. Janine le Donneur, Vittorio's secret lover, made the fatal mistake that many women of a certain age who take on a young and inexperienced lover do. She had, without realising it, fallen hopelessly in love with her sweet sexual partner and could not bear to lose him.

She had wrongly assumed that he and Eliza would have their sexual fling and it would make little difference to her own sex life. She could not allow herself to believe that an inexperienced girl could satisfy Vittorio. It never occurred to Janine that he would do other than return to her. But he didn't return to her for sex, and in his honesty and innocence made a fateful mistake that was to change the course of his and the two women's lives. Only days after he and Eliza had consummated their love, he went to Janine and told her their sexual liaison was a thing of the past. She was an intelligent and mature woman, worldly in the way of men and sex. She believed Vittorio's words were no more than youth talking and was not unduly concerned. Janine gave them six weeks at the most and was certain Vittorio would return to her. He did, but to do no more than his chores. He stayed away from her on any more intimate level.

At first she was amused and believed he was making a concerted effort to be faithful to his girl, but after several visits she saw a change in Vittorio, sensed that he was repelled at the very idea of sex with her now when once he could not get enough. The pain was intense. It was anguish at the loss of a man who had insinuated himself into her life, given her passion, goodness, kindness, and created in her an erotic revival that had instilled new life into her whole being. She approached Vittorio about this, believing she could talk him back into her bed and a relationship that had worked for both of them. Again she tried to reason with him, and again, and then it was a matter of reproaching him, and after that came ultimatums and threats. Unkind words from him that cut her to the quick and destroyed her sense of self, her joy in life.

It was a woman scorned who approached the Forresters and Eliza and told them her story of love and abandonment, how she had kept Vittorio all those years. She was even graphic about his stamina as a lover, describing a young man with a rampant libido who had a voracious appetite for sex and women. If it were possible for it to be worse it was because this miserably unhappy woman, who admitted her passion and folly in loving a near-illiterate young man who would never be any more than he was, was soft-spoken and articulate rather than raging in her despair. In front of her parents, Janine pointed out to Eliza how impossible it would be for her to marry a Tuscan farmer with no future when she was so young and lovely and had her whole life to live.

Eliza had never seen such pain in another human being. She felt despair for Janine le Donneur as she would have felt it for herself if Vittorio had abandoned her. To be the cause of another woman's pain, as she felt she was, was unacceptable. That Vittorio should have carried on such an affair in theory had not worried her, but faced with the reality she was appalled.

Julian Forrester, disconcerted by what he had heard, returned from seeing Janine le Donneur to her car. He was embarrassed by the incident which, he pointed out to his wife and daughter, would never have happened had the woman been an Englishwoman. He poured himself and his wife a sherry, and then seeing how disturbed Eliza was, poured one for her as well. They sat in silence, trying to make sense of what had happened, what if anything was to be done about it. They were not a family for scenes or grand gestures. They were a family for peace at any price, fun, life without embarrassing complications. They did not quite know how to handle them.

This was the 60s and promiscuity, the Age of Aquarius, had burst into everyone's life to enchant and amuse, so they were by no means surprised that Eliza and Vittorio's was no longer a childish summer romance. They were simply embarrassed at having been confronted with the fact, and confused as to what they were supposed to do about it.

After Julian had poured a second sherry for them all he sat down once more to stare through the open windows leading out to the courtyard and a view of the hundred-and-fifty-year-old maze. Beyond that were the hills and he listened to the light, hot breeze rustling the leaves, the birds singing, the sound of water splashing in the marble fountain.

It was Dulcima who finally broke the awkwardness of the moment when she went to Eliza and sat on the arm of her daughter's chair to stroke her hair. 'I'm sorry you had to experience that scene, Eliza. It's very disturbing to see a woman of such intelligence fall so low as to behave as she did here today. I'm afraid she's desperate. A scandal is quite likely. I don't want you hurt by it.'

'A scandal may not happen, Dulcima! Let's not look for trouble where trouble may not exist.' The first sound of annoyance could be heard in Julian's voice.

'I think I would like to go home as soon as possible,' announced Eliza.

'Do you want us to talk to Vittorio, Eliza?' asked Dulcima.

'No. I will, Mummy. You do know that I love him with all my heart?'

'Yes, dear, I do.'

'And he loves me the same way.'

'Yes, dear, I know that too.'

'We are the love of each other's life, Mummy.'

'Then you mustn't hurt each other, Eliza.'

'We would never do that!'

'Maybe not intentionally. I'm sure that Vittorio did not want to hurt Madame le Donneur, intentionally, but look what happened. She made some valid points about your youth and there being a world out there you are yet to discover, didn't she?'

'Yes.'

'Under the circumstances, time and a little distance

can be no bad thing for either you or Vittorio. You both have a great deal to do if there is a future for you together, surely you are both able to see that?'

'But you don't see that for us, do you, Mummy?'

'Frankly, no, dear.'

'After having had Madame le Donneur draw you such a candid picture of the differences in your lives and the hopelessness of any future together, can you honestly say you do, Eliza?' asked her father, speaking to her for the first time.

'But I love him, Poppy,' she told him, tears trickling slowly from the corners of her eyes.

Julian Forrester went to his daughter and sat down next to her. Very gently he placed an arm around her and slid her on to his lap. Then he told her in the softest, most kindly manner, 'I'm not asking you to stop loving Vittorio, Eliza, only to leave him, for each of you to see other people for a year, and then see how you feel about each other. And you must do this as much for Vittorio as for yourself. He must work something out with this woman to avoid a scandal, and needs time to make a life for himself so that he will be able to support a wife and a family one day.

'There is too a basic need for the young man to be free, to run with his friends, be wild with his youth, before he settles down to loving and making a permanent commitment. And you are stopping all that because you have made him exclusively yours. You must give each other a chance. I think your instinct was right. We should go home. Let's say we leave in three days' time?'

Eliza remained on her father's lap for several

minutes before she stood up and told her parents, 'I think this is the worst day of my life.'

'Oh, darling Eliza, can I do anything?' asked her mother.

Julian found the entire incident too sordid to cope with. Though he felt sympathy for Eliza, he somehow felt more sorry for Vittorio because he could see no happy solution for the young man of whom he was so fond.

'No, Mummy, I just need to be with Vittorio. We need to have these next few days together to make some plans. And I have to tell him what happened, don't I?'

'Yes, you do, Eliza,' answered her father.

She went to him first and kissed him on the cheek. 'I love you, Poppy, for helping us and not being angry with us.'

Then she went to her mother, and kissed her, and said, 'You too, Mummy. I hope I will do what's right.'

But as she ran from the room in floods of tears something in her heart told her that not only was she unsure what to do about loving Vittorio but that they were star-crossed lovers, paying for the years of happiness they had already had.

They had planned to go to the village with Clara and Vittorio's brother Alessandro, and from there to the lake. But that seemed utterly impossible now. Eliza knew Vittorio was dredging a stream on the far side of the estate and that was where she would find him. She hopped on her bicycle, feeling quite desperate to see him, and pedalled furiously in that direction. From a distance away she saw him standing in the stream. Stripped to the waist and wet, he seemed to gleam in the sun. How handsome and sensual he was. A girl deeply involved in her newfound sensuality, she could think of nothing but his taking possession of her, of his rampant penis penetrating her again and again, of the sensation of such utter bliss when he came and she was awash with his seed. She whimpered and bit into her lower lip, trying to keep control of her need and desire to be lost in sex with Vittorio, and for the moment forgot that they were so very soon to be parted, possibly for ever.

She saw him place a hand on his forehead, using it to shield his eyes as he watched her approaching. He smiled and waved to her to come to him. He unzipped his wet jeans and caressed his already erect penis, tossing back his head and laughing. She dismounted from her bicycle and let it crash to the ground as she jumped into the shallow stream. He took her down with him into the clear, rushing water and tore at her clothes. There they fucked, the mountain stream cold and caressing as it washed over their entwined bodies.

Throughout the sexual delights he was bringing her to, Eliza kept wondering how she was going to be able to give up sex with Vittorio for a day, never mind a year. He had taught her to enjoy a man's sexuality and her own sexual desires. She wanted him and sex as a part of her life now, and yet she found that an impossiblility in the light of the scene Janine le Donneur had played out before her.

She tried not to be angry with Vittorio, but she was,

for having made love to a woman so old. Forty, no matter how beautiful and well preserved she looked, was old to a seventeen-year-old girl. And for Vittorio to indulge himself with an old woman was somehow obscene and nasty. And, worse, he threw the woman aside when he was finished with her. Even worse than that, he had never loved her. She, Eliza Forrester, had been the cause of this woman's misery and she felt guilt, something she had never felt before, and did not like it. Yes, that was how she saw it: Vittorio's lust had placed guilt at her feet. She wanted that washed away. She wanted assurances he would never do to her what he had done to that woman.

She scrambled out of his arms and struggled through the water to the bank, dishevelled by lust and the stream, her clothes wet and clinging to her. Half naked, she climbed up the bank and lay in grass burned golden by the months of hot Tuscan sun. Vittorio lay down next to her and with great tenderness removed her wet blouse and wrung it out, and then her skirt, spreading them out to dry. He shrugged out of his jeans and flung them away and then he sat up and pulled her head into his lap, offering his semi-erect sex to her.

He had taught her oral sex and how to enjoy it. She had mastered the act, one she found thrilling for the power she felt because she could excite such pleasure in Vittorio. She came and came again in spite of knowing to the very core of her being that she had to give up Vittorio, that such delights as this were already very nearly a thing of the past for them. How, why, she should have decided that at this very moment she would never know. But quite suddenly she felt heartbroken that fate should have dealt them such a blow.

She eased him from between her lips with one last caress, one last kiss, and sat up. 'This is no time to stop, *cara mia*,' he told her.

'Maybe it is, Vittorio, just the time,' she told him, a light in her eyes he had never seen before, a catch in her voice that concerned him.

'Is something wrong, Eliza?'

She chose not to answer his question but to tell him, 'You know I love you more than life itself? You do know that, Vittorio?'

'Yes, and you know that's how I feel about you. What's this about, Eliza? You're frightening me.'

The tears were cascading down her cheeks now. He reached over and took her blouse that had, even in those few minutes, dried somewhat in the baking sun. He helped her into it and began doing up the buttons. 'Janine le Donneur came to the house and asked to see my parents and me. She told us everything, spared us very few details.'

'You mustn't believe anything she says. Anyway I'm through with her.'

'But I *do* believe everything she said. And I know you are through with her and that she is suffering as I want never to suffer at the hands of a man, not ever, Vittorio.'

'I will never leave you.'

'How do you know that? You left her and broke her heart.'

'You don't understand, it was sexual with no commitment, no love, involved. There were no promises and she always knew that I loved you. Men can do that, have a sexual life with someone and never let it touch anything else in their lives. That's the way we were. It was convenient.'

'All those years, all that sex, and you had no feelings for her? You're right, I don't understand.'

Eliza was crying again. She felt as if her whole world was collapsing around her. Nothing made any sense to her, not her and Vittorio nor a beautiful woman shunned. And, worse, she could not get a picture of Vittorio in flagrant sex with Janine out of her mind.

He grabbed her by the shoulders and shook her, telling her, 'Stop this, I'm no monster. Of course in time I grew to have feelings for her, if I hadn't I would never have stayed. Life is a matter of choices. Once you and I had fucked, whatever was going on with Janine died. It would have been an act of betrayal to you both and to myself had I carried on having sex with her. Why can't you see? She just doesn't want to let me go, and I won't go back to her, so she is driving us apart.'

'I love you, Vittorio, and these last weeks have been the happiest, the most thrilling, we have ever shared but this awful scene I have been put through by that woman has opened my eyes. We need some time apart to look at ourselves and how we can find a way to be together in love the way we want to be. She pointed out that we have nothing in common and I know nothing of the world, any more than you do. We have nothing but our youth in common. I'm going back to England the day after tomorrow.'

Vittorio felt ill. His voice was broken when he told Eliza, 'I'll go right now and talk to your father.'

'It is I who asked my father to take us home to England. My father and mother are concerned about us. They love you very much and have said not one word against you. But Poppy said he thought we owed it to each other to spend a year apart and see other people. Normalise our life and see what we want to do with it. I hate the idea, Vittorio, but maybe it will protect us from hurting each other as we have hurt Janine.'

'You're speaking like a child.'

'No, I'm speaking like a woman in love.'

All those sensible ideas she had just uttered had been interspersed with sobs and Eliza still could not tear herself away from Vittorio. The young lovers were beaten though they hardly understood why. And, despite despair at their plight, their intense attraction towards one another remained strong. Almost without realising it, they were peeling off their clothes again. Eliza was soon writhing with sexual delight at the sensations she was experiencing as Vittorio sucked on her nipples and beat himself into her to a rhythm so perfectly tuned to keep her coming in a series of orgasms that they left her breathless and exhausted.

They remained together for the rest of the day but never spoke of Janine again. They were home in time for dinner. That evening a long table had been set under the trees in the kitchen garden and sitting at it was the family and the girls' various boyfriends, several neighbours and two of the farm workers. As they'd expected, Dulcima and Julian Forrester received

Vittorio as they had always received him in their house and it was a jolly and delicious meal that lasted late into the night.

When Dulcima and Julian left the table to retire to their room, she told her husband, 'Vittorio and Eliza seemed very happy, but did you see the sadness in their eyes? It was almost too much for me to bear. Julian, our Eliza will not have the easy time in life our other girls will. Thank God we gave her these years here in Tuscany, I pray that they will sustain her.'

The following day Eliza and Vittorio saddled up the horses early in the morning. Eliza raided the kitchen to put together a picnic for them and they rode several miles from the house to a wood where Vittorio had many years ago built them a marvellous tree house. It was there they kept their treasures, all the bits and pieces from their childhood. It was furnished with table and chairs and a bed, all made by Vittorio out of branches, wood from slender trees he had felled, and willow reeds. On the floor was a red carpet; on the bed a colourful patchwork quilt. There were candles of all sorts and sizes and even gingham curtains at the windows which were odd-shaped and askew.

They spent the day in their tree house lost in sex, trying new depravities they had never experienced before which Eliza found thrilling if not a little frightening. But she was a young woman possessed, wanting to be dominated sexually by Vittorio, wanting to go to the edge of life itself in lust with him. It was a strange day for them, a day of pure eroticism that had to it an edge of base lewdness that Eliza thought, with utter indifference, she might die in. It was a desperate sort of day where like people condemned they confessed undying love for each other for ever, no matter what was to happen to them.

Chapter 3

The Forresters were not worriers, they believed in getting on with things. Effie was working and living the way she wanted to live; Dendra was getting on with living in a grand house in Derbyshire, being groomed to be a Countess; Constanza was in West Virginia getting on with America; and Clara, who was much more demanding of her life and the men who wanted to be a part of it than her sister Eliza, was getting on with finding a replacement for Alessandro. She, unlike Eliza, had always known that her Italian lover was just a summer romance. Because the Forrester girls had been so close and happy in their home life, they remained in contact by telephone or occasionally post. What that meant to Eliza, who was getting on, albeit very slowly and not very happily, with discovering life anew without Vittorio, was that though the family was there for her, it was at a distance. That created in her a sense of deep aloneness, an isolation she had never known before she had parted from Vittorio. It seeped into her psyche, took her over.

Other than that, life went on as it always had for Eliza in Little Barrington. Her friends, whom she had known all her life, were there for her to ride, walk the woods and fish with, and help to organise the

Forrester shoot. Often she accompanied her father on official business. They had always been close but on this return from Tuscany Eliza and Julian Forrester seemed to be seeing more of each other, talking about the world and how it turned. The one thing they did not talk about was what had happened in Tuscany and how she had left Vittorio behind.

If Eliza didn't realise that she had changed, her family and friends did. Upon her return they saw that she had changed. She was, though it was almost imperceptible, somehow more sensually attractive, and now looked at men in a different light, less as a child, more as a woman. She seemed drawn to them, and as a result seemed to bloom in their presence, yet she made no overt moves on them. If anything she was less flirtatious than she used to be, even a little aloof. Men who had been once amused by her pretty and childish flirtatiousness were no longer amused by it; they were more interested in her budding sexuality. They sensed that she had been had by a man since that virginal bloom, that puppyish look she had had only months before, had vanished. Here was a young woman who had discovered sex and would never run away from it again. Yet she puzzled the young men who tried to date her. It was not that she showed disinterest, more that she showed an indifference which made them all the more keen to be accepted by her.

As the months passed, Eliza realised that she was seeing the world, people, places, things, differently now that Vittorio was no longer the centre of things. She still wanted, tremendously, her happiness with him and could not really understand why he and the simple life he'd offered her in her beloved Tuscany was not enough to ensure a full and rich life. That both shocked and pained her. Her desire to have Vittorio as the centre of her world remained, even with all the questions as to whether it was right for them. There was not a day that passed when she didn't want him sexually, nor when she didn't remember how good it felt being in love with her best friend. He had awakened her to the beauty and excitement, the thrill and bliss of a sexual life, and she missed it desperately and wanted it badly. To be riven by a man who could incite lust without boundaries in her, and one whom she could excite by her sexuality, give pleasure to as Vittorio had taught her to, was what she yearned for but did nothing about finding. And so her sexual frustration kept building, and her love for Vittorio breaking down. And in her confusion it was inevitable that, almost unknowingly, she should slowly be relegating him to the back of her mind.

Eliza was not wholly to blame for that. Vittorio's months of silence had much to do with it. She kept waiting for him to do something, to sweep her away from Little Barrington and into his arms for ever. Every day that didn't happen was a blow to her, evidence that he couldn't or wouldn't make the effort to do whatever it took for them to be together. A Forrester cousin, having returned from Tuscany with news from the Villa Montecatini, reported that Vittorio was well and sends the family his best regards. That he was being seen often with a famous French writer, an attractive older woman, which had taken everyone by surprise. When Eliza received the note brought to her from Vittorio by the cousin, she read: 'Nothing about my love for you will ever change.' There had been no more than that, another crushing blow.

It was those mixed signals she received from Vittorio – his professing love for her and being seen with Janine – that finally drove Eliza into the arms of another man. The very idea of his having a sexual life with his older woman again crazed her with jealousy. She found it nearly impossible to think of anything but their erotic trysts; all those marvellous sexual experiences she and Vittorio had had, were now going on between Janine and Vittorio. Eliza's sexual fantasies took flight and nearly made her wild with lust and frustration. In the silence of her room she would often cry and wish she had never discovered sexual ecstasy, and moments later that was all she wanted. It was better than love. That and separation were too painful.

John Hope-Quintin came to hunting quite late in life, but when he did find his sport he took to it with a passion. So much so that he bought a house in Coln St Aldwyn, kept a stable, and swiftly became a presence in the Hathrop Hunt and the neighbourhood. Mr John Hope-Quintin was much sought after in society, a tall, handsome, urbane surgeon of some renown, a forty-three-year-old bachelor, well born and well connected, with a reputation as a ladies' man.

It was known that he had a penchant for young nubile maidens who invariably succumbed to his charming, suave and very flirtatious manner, but that the women he dated were beautiful, sophisticated, intelligent and usually titled. Married women adored his gallant manner, his roguish sexual reputation. He was one of the few really eligible catches because he sat well not only on a horse but in so many different social circles, the perfect spare man at any dinner table.

He had always admired the Forrester girls. In the field it was a joy to ride with them. Excellent hunters who rode well, they were pretty, fiercely independent, sexy, and played with him the way a cat does with a mouse. John found Dulcima and Julian agreeable and enjoyed their eccentricities, the way they were able to be in and out of society at the same time, but he did rather despise their preference for being bourgeois. He had had Effie several times in his house in Coln St Aldwyn after they made a pact to keep their sexual encounters a secret, for the sake of both their reputations. She had been seventeen at the time. They parted friends, agreeing that they were not made for each other. Ever since John had had a secret fantasy: to seduce, one at a time, all five Forrester girls and their mother as well. But a fantasy it would remain because none of them except Effie had taken his passes as serious, or if they had they found him too experienced and therefore too dangerous. They were actually quite unsophisticated, innocent and conventional young women. His fantasy was marginally revived when one day he saw Eliza.

Shortly after she returned from Tuscany, John met her and Dulcima in Burford at The Bay Tree where they were having lunch. In the few minutes he sat down to have a chat with them before he went on to his table and the lady waiting there for him, he recognised a change in Eliza. There was a scent of sexuality about her; she looked ripe, ready for plucking. There was more to entice him: she looked at him as she had never looked at him before, with undisguised interest. She was relating to him as a woman who has had a man and saw him as a potential second.

Several days later they had occasion to meet again. The sexual attraction was evident to them both. Eliza felt excited, full of life and hope for the first time since she and Vittorio had parted. This older man, experienced in life and women, was taking a keen interest in her. He made her laugh and the twinkle in his sexy blue eyes promised much. There were several other women hovering around them, as keen for him as he was for Eliza. It was a boost to her ego, the way he was charming to them but made advances to her. They were horse people, talking horses and riding, and when one of them spoke of the enchantment of riding through the Forresters' wood, John seized the moment and asked if one day he might be granted that privilege?

Two days later they were doing just that. It was a day of dazzling light, crisp but not cold. They rode over a carpet of brightly coloured leaves under a canopy of trees where the sun's rays filtered down at steep angles, lending enchantment to the place. They enjoyed the company of small animals and several deer, and saw pheasant in abundance that scuttled in front of their horses and flew up into the trees. The acres of forest at one point thinned out at the top of a ridge where they rode over nearly a mile of ancient Roman road. The land sloped steeply to either side to valleys far below, with streams and bright green meadows where flocks of sheep were grazing.

They said very little to each other because the ride and the views occupied them. Most of the time they rode side by side, occasionally glancing over to acknowledge their joy at being together, with a smile. This was only the second man Eliza had felt sexually attracted to, and it felt different. Though not exactly a stranger, he was someone she had no history with as she did with Vittorio. It was on that ride that she realised that sex for her was a matter of trust. With Vittorio she could submit to everything sexual because she trusted him with her life.

The stolen glances on that ride? In every one of them she was taking the measure of John Hope-Quintin for sex, working out how far she could trust him.

He, an experienced seducer of women, used to them falling at his feet, knew exactly what Eliza was doing and was flattered that she should have chosen him.

They rode for nearly two hours and in that time experienced something between them that finally exploded into a *coup de foudre*. They were struck like a thunderbolt with love for each other. There was no rhyme or reason to it and it quite stunned them, so much so that they said nothing of it to each other but simply wallowed in their own delight that such a thing might have happened to them.

The Roman road continued into a wood and then was lost among the trees. Riding on for another half an hour to a small clearing, they came upon a shack with a veranda all around it, set under an overhang of stone tiles, the same as on the roof.

'It was the woodsman's cottage, built at the turn of the century. We can light a fire and have tea here, if you like?' Eliza suggested.

'I'd like that very much,' he said.

The door was unlocked, and as soon as they entered it felt to John as if he had stepped back in time and into another world. It was a two-room shack. There was one very large room with a massive stone fireplace at one end, wooden floors covered with worn and torn carpets and animal skins. Broken-down sofas and rustic furniture obviously cut from the woods and roughly put together by some woodsman generations ago were scattered throughout. There were mounted animal trophies on the walls and faded framed photographs of shoots, from Victorian and Edwardian times right down to the present day. The second room was a small bedroom with a large brass bed in it and a chest of drawers.

All day John had been enchanted. Now, as he was building a fire, he realised he was besotted by a very unusual girl, such as he had never met before. She was a beautiful, budding young woman, passive, childish, a very natural creature, and at the same time sexy. She was exciting because of her openness, her sensual ripeness, a hunger to be sexually taken over by him. With barely a word, hardly a gesture, she had made those things clear to him.

The fire flared up and the logs caught almost at once. For some time he stared into the fire, enjoying this state of being in love. He was feeling relaxed, at ease with life and his condition, one which he had experienced several times before. He was a man who liked the anticipation of taking a young girl and exciting her lust, introducing her to all the facets of sexual experience, teaching her how to enhance his own sexuality.

He felt her step up to him and lean against his back, place her arms around his waist and press her cheek against the rough tweed of his jacket. He covered her hands with his. She broke the silence when she asked, 'Was the ride everything you expected it to be?'

He turned around to face her and told her, 'I think you know it was, and so are you.'

Colour came to Eliza's cheeks and she lowered her eyes, somehow afraid to look into his. With a crooked index finger, he raised her chin and demanded, 'Look at me.' She obeyed, and delighted him with the edge of nervousness and at the same time the lusty fire that showed in them. 'Are you afraid of me?' he asked in a husky voice, an edge of surprise in it for her benefit.

'Yes,' she told him.

'Why?'

'Because they say you're a devil with women.'

'And you are afraid that I will be a devil with you!'

'Not so much afraid, as I don't want you to be.'

'Ah, then you assume we are going to be together?'

'You're playing games with me, John, and you mustn't do that. I have only been with one man in my life and he loved me and did not know how to play games, in love or in sex.'

'Ah, sex! Then you know how much I want you, admit how much you want sex with me. That, my dear girl, is the first and most important thing for you and me. Not that you had puppy love and sex with some immature young boy. And, just for the record, I have wanted you in that way ever since I saw you in The Bay Tree. Frankly, I've been thinking of little else.'

What exciting words and sentiments these were for Eliza. Her heart was racing along with her mind. This handsome older man, who could have his choice of women, wanted her for sex, for love. They were still in their riding jackets. He worked on opening the buttons of hers and sensed the shiver of excitement she experienced at such a simple act. He liked that, enough to lean forward and place a light, sweet kiss upon her lips. She caressed his face with her hands and he was surprised that that little gesture should mean so much to him. He slipped her jacket from her shoulders and let it fall to the floor. He raised the thick turtleneck black jumper up over her head and saw her naked breasts for the first time. The nimbus circling her long nipples was dark against her fair flesh and already puckered from the sexual excitement she was experiencing. There was a flush of pink on her chest. She had had a light, sweet involuntary orgasm. It delighted him to learn that she had no control over her lust.

She looked exceptionally seductive, naked above her tight riding breeches and shiny leather boots. He looked at her for a considerable time before he pulled her into his arms and caressed the ample swell of her breasts, licking the nimbus with his tongue. The kettle sitting on a small gas burner cut the silence of the room with its shrill scream. John picked up her jacket from the floor and held it for her to slip into, then buttoned it. The disappointment showed in her eyes.

After tea they lay on the floor against old and dusty flower-patterned cushions and talked about his life. She wanted to know all about his London world, his work. He wanted to know nothing about her: her thoughts, her dreams. Those things meant nothing to him, only her sexuality, seducing her to his will, and her being hopelessly in love with him did.

He knew how much she wanted sex with him, then and there, but made no further advances on her. Not that he wouldn't have delighted in fucking her but for the moment he gained more pleasure from the chase to win her love for him alone.

Eliza, a girl without artifice, bold in her sexuality, innocent of how to behave with men, surprised John, quite took him aback, when she slipped out of her jacket and rolled on top of him to drape her breasts over his face, swing them gently back and forth over his eyes, his lips, and then slip down his body slowly whilst undoing his breeches, gathering his erect penis and his scrotum in her hands and gently setting them free from the restricting riding clothes. She dazzled him with her expertise in oral sex, the manner in which she sucked and tongued on his genitals. He groaned with pleasure, was lost to all else but the delights of being had by her. He placed his hand on top of her head, ran his fingers through the very blonde hair and pulled hard on it. After he came in an astoundingly forceful and copious orgasm nothing could have seduced him more than the joy she displayed in swallowing every last drop of his seed.

He held her in his arms and kissed her face, eyes, breasts, told her how sublime she was and asked her if she had come. Many times during her act, had been her answer, and he loved her even more for that, that she should delight in pleasing him, be able to find sexual satisfaction in giving him pleasure. His hand went beneath her breeches to search out the slit beneath her mound of pubic hair and found her wet with come. For several minutes he delighted her with his fingers and when he removed them and had her lick them he could see that he had introduced her to a new and erotic experience that excited her. John was overwhelmed by her ability to enjoy sex so freely. For the first time he wondered with some jealousy what man had had her, taught her how to be passionate in her lust and so very giving of herself.

Never could Eliza have imagined sex with anyone but Vittorio, or that she could be satisfied by the sexual attentions of a near stranger, but she had been. It had been thrilling and thoughts of Vittorio never came into it. She was too inexperienced to realise that some of the excitement of being with John was that she had sexual control over him. Now, lying in his arms, she wanted him to take over and possess her with rampant fucking until she was driven into sexual oblivion, that place where she had transported him.

She whispered in his ear, almost fearful to ask him aloud, 'John, fuck me. Please. I want you so much.'

He could tell by the catch in her throat what it had cost her to ask him that, and was somehow touched by her desire to be riven by him. He kissed her and told her, 'Not now. I want you to be sure you want to get into an erotic life with me. I'm jealous and possessive and besotted by you. Think about us, and come to dinner tomorrow with me. I'll take you somewhere special.'

The following morning she received three dozen white roses. No one had ever sent her roses before. The family was impressed. They knew him and were delighted that he should be smitten with Eliza, seeing it as the boost she needed to launch her into a wider world of new people and places, and because it might curtail her unhappiness over Vittorio.

When he called for her at her house he brought a box of marrons glâcés. She liked receiving gifts from him, being spoiled by a handsome, dashing older man.

They dined at an excellent restaurant in Oxford, and he was further charmed by her lack of sophistication, this time in dress and choice of food. But she had the look of a young woman in love and heads turned when they entered the dining room. After dinner he took her home and they sat in his car at the bottom of the drive to her house and talked for some time. It was, as always, about him, his career. He explained to her that surgery, a life in medicine, was his great passion and pride. That it would always come first in his life. To an eighteen year old that sounded noble, glamorous even. Finally he told her, 'I'm going to London for several days. Why don't you come and stay with me? We'll have fun.'

'I don't know that my parents would approve of that,' she told him, a naughty twinkle in her eye.

'Don't tell them. Surely you have a girlfriend? You can say you will be staying with her and that I've invited you to the opera. I will take you to the opera, if you come.' To entice her further, he whispered in her ear, 'And come will be the operative word because it's there in my house that I'll give you what we both so desperately want from each other – unbounded sex. Yes, a great sexual adventure.'

He had made it impossible for her to refuse him. To Eliza this sounded like a great adventure, something just a little wicked and different for her. London, and a fascinating older and sophisticated man to be squired around by and who wanted to have sex with her – these were experiences she had never envisaged for herself but which now seemed somehow exciting and right.

She was not a girl who knew how to tell a fib to her parents, or anyone else for that matter, never mind an outright lie. None of the Forrester children had ever had any need to tell lies with such open and liberal parents as Dulcima and Julian Forrester. And in the morning, when she did ask to go to London and stay with John, they gave permission, believing that such a serious, well-respected man as Dr John Hope-Quintin would never take advantage of her. In addition there was their understanding of how well Eliza could take care of herself. Somehow the doctor's reputation as a ladies' man did not seem to apply here. He was making most proper advances out in the open. They were in fact quite pleased about John Hope-Quintin and their daughter.

John had explained to Eliza that he would be leaving for London at five in the morning because he had a very busy day in the operating theatre of King Edward VII for Officers hospital but that she should call his rooms and leave a message if she intended to be on the train arriving at Paddington at five o'clock. If he could, though he would not promise and it was unlikely, he would be there to meet her. If he did not appear, her instructions were to take a taxi to the address he had written for her on a piece of paper, having assured her there would be someone there to let her in. John knew that she would be there on exactly the train he wanted her to be, that she was incapable of refusing him.

Eliza watched the countryside seemingly fly by the train window and listened to the hum of the wheels on the tracks. She could think of nothing except the fun and sensual excitement of being with John. Half a dozen times she opened her handbag and looked at the address he had written on the piece of paper: 56a Ennismore Gardens, South Kensington.

When the train pulled into Paddington Eliza did not even bother to look for John because she simply could not believe that he would find the time to be there for her. It therefore came as a surprise to her when, as she was walking with the crowd of other passengers along the platform towards the vast concourse, she felt a tap on her shoulder. When she turned a smiling John presented her with a camellia which he pinned to the short, sadly worn grey rabbit fur jacket she was wearing over a grey wool skirt that covered the tops of her black suede boots, dulled and shabby from age and wear. Her tall figure, the fresh young face framed by long, very blonde and silky hair, the swing to her step, made up for her less than stylish clothes. She looked to John every bit the country girl, out of her depth, being swept along by big city people in a rush to their destinations. It quite surprised him how delighted he was that she was there.

Walking through the terminus to his waiting black Jaguar and driver, Eliza chatted about how excited she was to be with him, John about where he would take her. There were promises of surprises to come which he refused to reveal but guaranteed she would be thrilled with. Only after the driver had tipped his hat to her and she and John had slipped into the back seat of the car did he kiss her, slip his hand beneath her skirt and kiss her again. It quite thrilled him how she was unable to hide her delight in being handled by him. She actually squirmed. He laughed and she was immediately embarrassed that he should find her out and laugh about it.

Eliza pulled away from him and said, 'Laughing at me – that's not very nice.'

She looked so hurt and vulnerable his heart went out to her, for her youth and inexperience. They excited his own lust for her. 'I'm not laughing at you but because you delight me so much.' And he smiled at her, kept the distance she had put between them, and did not touch her until she returned his smile and then broke into a giggle.

'I didn't know you had a driver?' she whispered.

'I almost never drive in the city – too preoccupied with my work. I do nothing very much for myself when I'm here except work and make love to beautiful women.'

'You're teasing me, trying to make me jealous,' she told him, rather pleased with herself for being on to what he was doing.

'Am I succeeding?'

'I refuse to answer that,' she told him, delighted by his interest, assuming that he wanted her to be jealous.

'Ah, so you are a woman who could be jealous of other women in my life? I like that. That's a good thing for me.'

'How so?' she asked.

'Because,' and now he pulled her roughly across the seat and tight against him before he continued, 'you will have to work very hard to satisfy me, so that I don't wander, will not want to have sex with anyone but you. See to it that I remain besotted and want only to love you. And you, you amusing, very sensuous, very young lady, how do you expect to accomplish that?'

He could see in her eyes how flattered she was, enchanted by his seductive charm. She flushed pink with embarrassment and was searching for a way to tell him: in lust, in bed, in sex. He had to hold back, laughing with the pleasure of her predicament, and told her, 'You can whisper how in my ear.'

But she whispered nothing in his ear, merely licked it and sucked on his ear lobe. She felt a rush of excitement, a yearning for him that was almost impossible to hold back. She sighed deeply and it said more than words.

'Ah, good, that's a beginning.' He teased her lips with the point of his tongue and kissed her on the side of the neck. Then he continued, 'And this girlfriend's house where you told your parents you were staying – we don't have to call in there? I can assume you were clever enough to see your parents won't be calling to check up on you?'

Eliza instinctively felt that it would be a mistake to tell John that her parents knew exactly where she was staying. She heard herself replying, 'I think that would be a fair assumption.'

She was deceiving John as he had asked her to deceive her parents and she did not feel good about it, but somehow feared that if she had told him the truth it would make a difference to their few days together. A difference that would not be conducive to the romantic tryst she was so looking forward to.

He used his key on the entrance door to the building and then another to the ground-floor flat where he lived. They were no sooner inside than they were greeted by his housekeeper who was on her way home for the day, but having been introduced to Eliza, stopped long enough to show her to her room and unpack her overnight bag. While that was being done John gave Eliza a tour of the rooms he lived in, after he had opened a bottle of champagne and poured them two glasses.

They were large rooms and furnished with eighteenth-century furniture and fine paintings, all of which meant nothing to Eliza who knew nothing less than large rooms and beautiful objects that had been passed down the many generations of her family. The thing she was most impressed by and found slightly intimidating was the sparkling cleanliness of the place, the perfection of the restoration techniques applied to everything. The Forresters lived in a muddle in both Little Barrington and Tuscany and repaired only when it was absolutely impossible not to: the grandfather clock's case was tied closed with a piece of clothes line; bits of loose marquetry work were always Scotch taped in place so as not to be lost; broken chair legs had temporary metal staples applied; anything chipped remained chipped. There were various boxes around the Forrester residences marked 'Bits and Pieces'. Their draperies had a disintegrating quality about them. They were not house-proud people, just a family who lived hard among their things.

John's large and beautiful Chinese vases were filled with marvellous flowers: Casablanca lilies, lilac, tulips, branches of dusty green eucalyptus and camellia leaves. They delighted Eliza. An impressionable young girl, she was thrilled to think that he had made an effort with flowers for her. She watched him put a match to the well-laid fire and all her body and soul focused on this very special man who was courting her.

As if reading her mind, he turned from the fire. Walking up to her and placing an arm around her waist he told her, 'I can't court you with a housekeeper here.

Usually she stays to serve me dinner if I'm entertaining or dining at home alone, but I wanted you all to myself, for us to be free to discover each other without anyone hovering around us. Do you mind if we help ourselves to the dinner she has prepared for us and stay in tonight?'

Her answer was to kiss him. Once more John was delightfully surprised at the power and passion of Eliza's hunger for him. Her giving nature, the lack of sexual inhibition, excited him. He sensed untold possibilities to a sex life with this young charmer who hardly knew what or who she was.

'You suit me perfectly. We are going to be very happy together,' he told her as he removed his jacket and dropped it on a chair then began undoing the buttons of her blouse.

They stood naked in front of the fire, just gazing at each other's bodies for several minutes, as if they wanted to etch them and this moment in their minds for ever. For John, she was lovelier, more purely erotic, without her rather shabby, cheap clothes. Naked, she was all young firm flesh with an edge of voluptuousness to her that elicited lust. She was at the same time obviously innocent of how thrilling sexual debauchery, the depraved side of sex, could be, yet with a body and a psyche ready and waiting to be mastered by sex with him. Eliza, a giving soul, was just as ravenous to give him pleasure in sex, affection, adoration, as much as she craved to have those same things for herself. He would teach her well how to love him, groom her for a London life. The very idea was enough to make him fall in love with her that little bit more.

John carried her to his bedroom and the four-poster

bed and laid her down on the bronze silk damask coverlet. He switched on the lamp on the table next to the bed and then lay down next to her. He was no rough-and-tumble, highly sexed farmer. Here was a man who seduced Eliza with finesse, by exciting every one of the more sensitive areas of her body. In no time at all she was willingly submissive, he her sexual lord and master. And when he did penetrate her for the first time, she was as if flayed, every nerve end exposed, ready to be set alight.

They missed their dinner that evening and dined instead on lust. By morning *she* was hopelessly in love with this very sexy and exciting man, *he* more than just smitten with her. They had breakfast together in bed, served by the housekeeper, Mrs Fanshaw. Eliza was wrapped in one of John's silk Turnbull & Asser dressing gowns, he had no more than the bed clothes to hide his nakedness. After breakfast they bathed together and he made her confess that she was in love with him. They made love in the bath and Eliza was more surprised than shocked when he turned her over and made her take a position on her knees facing him. He caressed her breasts, even more sensuous and tantalising to caress in the slippery smooth warm water with one hand while using a rather beautiful sexual object to fuck her with. He explained he wanted to watch her come, concentrate not on his pleasure but on giving sexual ecstasy to her. She was both excited and moved by his selflessness.

After her bath, Eliza went to her room where she dried her hair and dressed. She felt somehow as if she were floating on air, that she had been transposed into another life. From her room she went back to John's room, then to his impressive library, then the drawing room – looking for him in the vast flat. This was the first opportunity she'd had to really look at his home, absorb the things she was seeing. The many silver-framed photographs on the piano in his music room, the others on a table or a desk: beautiful woman, famous statesmen, one of Princess Margaret, several recognisable actors, many hunting scenes – the Beaufort, Belvoir, the Vale of the White Horse, and his own Hathrop.

Unable to find him anywhere in the flat, Eliza went to the kitchen where she found Mrs Fanshaw, who offered her another cup of coffee. Eliza accepted and then sat down at the large wooden table in the middle of the room and asked, 'Where is John, Mrs Fanshaw?'

'Oh, he's gone off to the hospital. Mr Hope-Quintin asked me to tell you that he's sending the car back for you to take you wherever you want to go.'

Eliza tried to cover her disappointment, but there had been so few in her life that she did not actually know how to do that. Mrs Fanshaw could not help but feel sorry for her. John Hope-Quintin was a marvellous man and she enjoyed working for him, but he was a devil with women. He seduced them to his bed and his heart, he was kind and generous to them, but for only for as long as it amused him and did not interfere with the life of work and intense pleasure he had designed for himself. Even when, as Mrs Fanshaw suspected now, he was in love, he was what she termed a natural philanderer who never could resist a pretty young face whom he would seduce behind the back of the number one girl of the moment.

There had been so many Elizas and older, more

sophisticated beauties who believed they would be the one to grab the title '*wife of Mr John Hope-Quintin*'. How many times had she, without being disloyal to her employer, tried to warn the women off, most especially the young girls whom he tended to ruin for life with his seductive charm? They never listened or wanted to believe that here was a man they could not change, for he was quite straight with them about one thing: he was not looking for marriage. Mrs Fanshaw asked Eliza if she could sit down and have coffee with her?

'Oh, please do. In our houses the kitchen is the heart of the house for everyone. Not so much in Little Barrington where I live now, but at our summer house in Tuscany there is always a pot of coffee and lovely things to eat.'

Eliza suddenly thought of Vittorio and felt a pang of love for him. She still missed him. Their love felt strange because it was drifting away from her so swiftly. It felt so different from the love she was feeling for John, this strange new world he was introducing her to.

She abandoned all thoughts of the past and Vittorio when Mrs Fanshaw asked, 'Do you have something nice planned for the next few hours? It's only until half-past one, you know, because the car will pick Mr Hope-Quintin up at the hospital.'

A light came into Eliza's eyes at the mere suggestion that in a matter of hours they would be together once more. It was not missed by Mrs Fanshaw. As concerned as she was for the girl, the housekeeper did know that the doctor would give her a grand time for as long as he was smitten. All she said to Eliza, as she rose from the table with her empty cup in her hand, was, 'You go out there and have the best time you can because good times don't last for ever.'

Immediately after she'd said it, the housekeeper sensed that Eliza hadn't heard, because she was struck deaf by love. More's the pity because she is the best of them I've seen for a long time: no gold digger, no social aspirations, too young to think of marriage, ruminated Mrs Fanshaw.

Eliza never left the house that morning. Life outside the flat held no interest for her. All she wanted was to be enveloped by the flat and *his* things, that spoke so strongly of *him*. She discovered his enchanting garden with its sculptures and trailing ivy, its late-autumn flowers and the long flight of iron stairs that led up from the basement garden to the much larger communal Ennismore Gardens, enclosed by an iron railing. The deserted garden was open only to the few of the residents living in the several blocks of flats surrounding it who had a key to the gate. Everything Eliza looked at she could only relate to as John's. John's flat, John's garden, John's neighbours.

A pattern emerged on that first day they had together in London but Eliza was too dazzled by love to recognise it, let alone do anything about it. The car, with Eliza waiting impatiently in the back seat, picked John up at precisely half-past one. He issued instructions to Banberry to take them to Wilton's where he had booked a table for lunch, then took the back seat to sit next to Eliza whom he thought looked prettier and more seductive than ever. His kiss was deep and passionate. He stroked her hair and was surprised at how enchanted he felt to be there with her.

'Now then, what did you do with your morning? Where did you go?'

'Nowhere. I just stayed at home.'

'Weren't you bored?'

'No, not in the least. Quite happy and content,' she told him, and was surprised at the look that came over his face, as if he were disappointed. She was relieved when he said no more on that subject.

Instead he whispered in her ear, 'You look delicious today but you were sublime last night.'

A flush came over Eliza's face. She answered him with difficulty, choked with delight and pleasure that this older, exciting, experienced lover had found her so. Flattered, she told him, 'Oh, I'm so glad you think so.'

He opened the rabbit fur jacket and was disappointed to see that yet again she had not dressed to his liking. She had shrouded her sensuality with a beige silk dress that had seen better days. John realised that she simply did not have any dress sense. He undid three of the small white mother of pearl buttons to expose some cleavage and then, taking the navy blue and white polka dot silk square from his pocket, meticulously folded it into a narrow band and tied it round her neck to finish it in a minute bow. It suited her long slender neck and she looked instantly more enticing, even a little chic. He found her quite irresistible and kissed her again, slipped his hand into the dress and caressed a naked breast.

After lunch he took her to South Molton Street and Brown's where he introduced her to the proprietor who was given a directive: 'Miss Forrester is coming out in London and needs some fashion advice. I would like you to guide us today with some things for day wear, dinner parties, the opera. And I'd be grateful if, in future, you would be available to her.' The next stop was to Church Street and Manolo Blahnik for shoes where a similar directive was issued.

Eliza did try to resist his generosity but several turns in front of the mirrors in the shops and the look of pleasure on John's face made it difficult to keep up her protests. She was finally defeated after she told him, 'You know I cannot afford these clothes nor can I accept them as gifts, how could I explain them to my parents? Actually they would be offended on many counts.'

His answer was quite simple. 'Don't tell them, or else find a clever way to explain them. I simply cannot squire you around London dressed as you are.'

And the subject was closed.

Chapter 4

All the Forrester girls knew how to rise to an occasion, that was the way they had been brought up. Eliza rose admirably to a London life with John, and a sexual life with him that kept her on the edge of lust very nearly every waking moment they were together. He had the measure of her. She was malleable, dizzily in love with her sexuality and with him. He could mould her any way he pleased and that excited him, kept him interested, even hungry to play with his young thing. It was flattering to him that she had no ambition but to please him, add something light and frivolous to his hectic life. And he did enjoy enormously that ability of hers to rise to the occasion, whether it be in bed or enjoying food she had never tasted, seeing a play she had never heard of, an opera, a ballet, even wearing with style a dress he had bought her.

Eliza, for her part, was not so much dazzled by John's lifestyle – elegant, cultivated, a crammed social calendar – as fascinated by it, and by how important all those things seemed to be to his happiness. In her heart she thought, as her parents did, that there was something just a little shallow and unnecessary about it all – but love can dictate to the heart. She believed she could get used to John's life, that it might be a valid way to live for her just as much as it was for him. She was aware, but pretended to herself that she wasn't, of how his friends and colleagues, the endless stream of shop girls, hairdressers and beauty therapists that he instructed to groom her, viewed her: as John Hope-Quintin's young thing, an inexperienced country girl who had fallen into a good thing.

Eliza was having great fun, she was in love with a man who was besotted with her and all she had to do was lie back and enjoy being a part of his life. She truly didn't give a fig for what people were thinking or saying. Part of the excitement of their love affair was that they spent every weekend in the country. She lived at home and sometimes John would be invited to stay over. Otherwise he lived in his house several miles away, which she visited for sex, a meal, but never to stay the night. That had been John's rule, not Eliza's. She was too besotted to think about rules of propriety, too anxious not to lose Mr John Hope-Quintin. In a matter of weeks he had seduced her away from her adolescent first love. He had opened worlds for her that she had hitherto never even contemplated.

But this was no one-sided love affair. John was, for him, very much in love with the pretty girl who had flowered into a beauty in his hands. He saw his Eliza as an uncultivated country girl who enjoyed the excitement of the new and the different world to which he was introducing her. Until John, she had not been ignorant of but indifferent to a cultivated existence because nature had taken precedence. John could appreciate that, it was part of her charm. She was after all no more than a light distraction, an amusement in his life, and she was a natural libertine in bed, something he had not come across in the many women who had in the past been able to keep him interested, except of course the rare prostitute whom he did on occasion enjoy. He had no doubt that part of the excitement of Eliza and her sexuality was her youth; that she was totally his, in her inexperience and eagerness ready to follow him down any erotic path he wanted to take her.

In a matter of a few weeks after they had met it was obvious to them both that sex had a grip on them that was binding them closer and closer together. There was one little incident which should have been a warning to Eliza, but unfortunately was not. They were returning to his London residence one afternoon, standing at his front door, John placing the key in the lock. Eliza was momentarily distracted by a young man assembling scaffolding on the house next to John's. He was dark and handsome, without a shirt and in tight blue jeans, rough and common-looking, sexy. She suddenly felt her heart skip a beat, not for the young man but for Vittorio. What was she doing here on a doorstep in London? Her beloved Tuscany and Vittorio, was that not where her happiness lay? A shiver racked her body briefly and was gone as soon as she felt John's arm around her waist. She was snapped back to the here and now, the reality of her life. She was after all very happy with John, very much in love, and forgot the young man on the scaffold and Vittorio in Tuscany.

However, John did not. In that moment when he turned round to usher her through the front door, he had caught her looking at the young man who to John looked no more than a common stud. He was quite shocked at how jealous of the fellow's youth he was, how disgusted he was that Eliza should even find him attractive enough to give him a second look. Together they walked into the building and then into his flat. They went directly to his bedroom and once in the room he helped her off with the suede coat she had had been wearing and tossed it on a chair. He shrugged out of his own black cashmere double-breasted coat and, spinning round, pulled her tight into his arms. She laughed and kissed him all over his face.

'At the front door, you seemed a million miles away. Tell the truth. Would you rather I paid that young tough out there a hundred pounds to come and fuck you?'

'Are you mad? What are you talking about?' she asked, quite horrified that he should even think such a thing.

'I saw the way you were looking at him.'

A blush rose immediately to Eliza's face. Taking his hands in hers, she kissed them and told him, tears of emotion in her eyes, 'I was looking at that man because he reminded me of the first and only man I loved before you. I used to think about him all the time until I met you, and then he vanished from my life, my every thought.'

John swept her off her feet and into his arms. Carrying her to the bed, he whispered huskily, 'Prove it,' as he urgently tore the clothes from her body.

There was a certain intensity – was it anger? Could it be deemed violence? – in John during the sex they had together that afternoon. Even when lust took them over, and during the many times they professed their love, they experienced a new thrilling, yet dangerous, kind of erotic togetherness that set them free to experience the darker side of sex. Much later, when they were dressing to go out to dinner and Eliza was covering a bruise on her neck with small scarf, John asked her to sit next to him on the end of the bed. She obliged and when they gazed into each other's eyes he asked her about her first love.

She hesitated for several seconds before she told him about her love for Vittorio, and her life with him in Tuscany. She told him everything, held nothing back, it never occurred to her that she should, that there could ever be a reason not to be honest and tell it as it had been, as it would always be. It was after all her history, a part of her life. In the telling she was relegating it to the past but she felt no sadness about that. There was no room for sadness in an eighteen year old who had just been transported to sexual oblivion by a man who claimed to love and adore her, who was able to reach down into the depths of her sexuality, her erotic fantasies, and bring them to the light, expunge any guilt for the lust she enjoyed in herself and in him.

John had marked her with his lust and she would remain branded his for ever. She sensed in her heart and soul that he would see to that, which Vittorio had not done. From that day on their sex life progressed into another realm of erotic bliss. Sex was unbound for them. They had set themselves free to experience everything, anything, and that sexual freedom bound them together as nothing else ever could or would. Eliza in her innocence called it love, thought of it as marriage, believed it to be for ever.

In all the time she was living in John's flat she remained a guest. She had her room and slept in his. Otherwise her clothes, or any of her possessions, were forbidden to be left around the flat. She had been amused when he had set down the ground rules though they in fact suited her: she was never to move anything around, not a chair or an ashtray. The kitchen and any cooking were off limits, except to make the odd cup of tea when the housekeeper was not there to do it.

She considered John too neat, too meticulous, he considered her too sloppy and slovenly, so the ground rules suited them both. In his house he was the master, she the slave. Everyone seemed to recognise that fact except John and Eliza. And by the time they did it was too late to do anything about it. How they lived suited John, and what was good for him was right for Eliza.

The Forresters loved Christmas, they made a big thing of the holiday whether it be in Tuscany or Little Barrington. This year Christmas was to be in Little Barrington and all the family and friends were expected to drift in and out of the Forrester house as it suited them except on Christmas Day. The Forrester girls and their families or partners invited friends, were expected to open presents under the tree at seven o'clock, attend church at ten and be at table for Christmas dinner at one o'clock, to hear the Queen's Speech before pudding and raise a glass of champagne to Her Majesty. That was about the only structured day Julian and Dulcima ever demanded of their children. And every Christmas the girls all turned out from any corner of the world where they happened to be. This year would be no exception and Eliza could talk of nothing else but the fun of their all being together for the holiday.

John had what he considered more interesting invitations than the Forresters'. But as the time had drawn near when he was obliged to make his choice several unexpected problems arose, the main one being Eliza.

She had not been invited to Christmas at one of the grander stately homes of England, his first choice as to where he wanted to spend his Christmas break. Nor had she been invited to a house party in Barbados which he also intended to accept. England for Christmas Day, New Year in the Caribbean.

Eliza had expected him to stay with her and her family in Little Barrington. As far as John was concerned, it was all quite simple, straightforward even – he was quite prepared to disappoint her, but in the nicest way. Eliza would accept his decision. She was too much in love with him not to. He had only one small problem: he would have quite liked to have taken her with him for Christmas. John had grown used to Eliza on his arm, and in his bed. To sleep without her would be a wrench. The very thought of being away from her sexually for ten days irritated him. He was further agitated that she should have penetrated so far into his life that he might actually miss her.

'Why are you so grumpy with me, John?' she asked one morning when they were having breakfast in bed.

'Because you keep talking about Christmas, making such a fuss about us being in Little Barrington with the family.'

'You don't want to come to us for Christmas?'

'I have other plans.'

'But you know I want to be with the family for Christmas dinner!'

'Then you must be.'

'I thought we were together.'

'We are, but not joined at the hip, Eliza.'

'It's three weeks away. You might change your

mind,' was her only reply, and she poured herself another cup of coffee.

John was surprised at how calmly she took her disappointment. He had expected a scene of some sort. At the very least tears. But nothing. Eliza did have a way of presenting him with the unexpected, and he liked that in her. But this morning he was somehow annoyed with her for thinking he even might change his mind and spend Christmas with the bourgeois Forresters.

John disliked complications and all day long, except for the several hours he spent in the operating theatre, had the distinct feeling that complications were somehow at work in the background of his life. That evening at dinner Eliza looked enchanting in a short, black crêpe-de-chine dress. She seemed to glow with happiness, sparkle with vivacity. He was delighted with the progress she had made in her big city life with him. A catty former girlfriend had told him, 'You wear that young thing on your arm like an old soldier wears his medals on his chest – with too much pride and not enough thought, dear boy.' Jane had been right. That was one of the great attractions of Eliza for John. He didn't have to think about her, only enjoy playing with her, controlling her, moulding her to satisfy his needs.

They were at Mr Chow's dining off a stream of tiny white plates proffering succulent tidbits – dumplings, fried seaweed, tiny lacquered spare ribs, fried wonton, sesame prawn crackers, tiny bowls of pungent sauces – that kept arriving at the table in the hands of smiling oriental waiters. It was this glorious bloom he saw in Eliza's face that seemed to John to be something special – and yet, enjoying it as he was, he sensed complications were taking over his very uncomplicated life. And they were not manifesting themselves just in his plans for Christmas.

Eliza had told John she had had a craving all day long for Chinese food; the day before it had been oysters, and the day before that for Indian curry. He watched her as she forked a dumpling into her mouth and could not help but smile. Life for Eliza Forrester was nothing more than eating, riding, fucking and sleeping. All of which she did very well. Never one to put herself about much in the city while John was at work, in the last two weeks she had been doing less than her usual little and more sleeping. He disliked that lazy, sleepy, unstructured side of her. He actually found the uneducated, unambitious side of her distasteful, especially so since he was an overachiever. Yet he kept quiet about that, never addressed what he saw as the flaws in her character, although he knew, when the time was right, he would have to.

Eliza asked him, 'May I have another order of dumplings?'

'The main courses are yet to come,' he answered.

'But I crave more dumplings,' she told him a smile on her lips.

'This is something new. You keep craving food and sleep.'

'I know, isn't it strange?'

'Not so strange if you're pregnant.'

The moment John said it, he knew he was correct. That was what was different about her looks, her behaviour. And now the complications really began.

He was both furious with her and overwhelmed that she might be carrying his child. The couple gazed into each other's faces, trying to assess what had just been said. But the shock of such a possibility had struck them silent. Eliza was very white. John placed a hand to his forehead as if suffering a blinding headache.

A waiter arrived to sweep away empty serving plates and place a bamboo steamer in the centre of the table. That broke into the storm of emotion each was silently experiencing. 'I can't be pregnant, John!' exclaimed Eliza as soon as the waiter was gone from their table.

There were tears brimming in her eyes and her lower lip trembled.

'I don't think that's an answer, Eliza. I think that's more of an exclamation about something you don't want to be true. Now calm down, no scenes, and answer me: are you pregnant?' he asked her in his best bedside manner.

'I honestly don't know, John.'

'Eliza, are there signs that it might be a possibility?' he asked, while reaching across the table and taking her hand in his.

'I have to think,' she answered, still looking frightened and shocked at the mere possibility.

'Then think, Eliza. It is not a difficult question.'

'Don't be angry with me, John. I couldn't bear that.'

'I'm not angry. Just answer me.'

Eliza lowered her head and placed a hand over her eyes. She remained like that for several minutes, and then when she took her hand away and looked across the table at him, she answered, 'There are signs, but I never thought anything of them. It never crossed my mind that such a thing could happen. There's the coil . . . and I thought the delay was because of our having such an active sex life, and then the excitement and passion and being in love. Oh, tell me you don't think it's so, John? I'm too young, still a child myself. What if it's true?

'I can't have it, if it's true, you know. I'm not ready for such a commitment. I'm not good at commitment.'

John was very good with Eliza. He calmed her down and insisted she should put all thoughts of pregnancy out of her mind. He would take her to a doctor in the morning and they would soon know and then deal with the problem accordingly. He called for a bottle of champagne, insisting that a celebration was in order either way. John Hope-Quintin was a most charming seducer and managed to save the evening for them. By the time they were in bed and making love, all thoughts of what might be a monumental problem for Eliza had vanished from her mind. Not so from John's. Taking a wife was not something he'd ever contemplated, but to have children had always been on the agenda. That night he made the most exquisite tender love to Eliza, a night of bliss to die for, to have a baby for. Before morning he was certain she would do whatever he decided for them.

His colleague told John that his 'friend' was thirteen weeks pregnant, and very healthy. He saw no complications. John actually laughed at that last statement because he knew that there may not be with the birth of his child but there would be for him for the rest of his life. But still he felt some excitement at having created a human being out of lust, pure pleasure, with this enchanting girl whom he would now take for his wife. He was surprised by how delighted he was that a child was coming into his life. He knew he would make a good father, and of course he would mould Eliza into being the right kind of mother for his children, the right kind of wife for him.

As they left the hospital she asked, 'John, what did the doctor say? Do I have anything to worry about? It's not true that I am going to have a baby? Oh, please, let it not be true.'

'Let's wait and talk about it when we get home.'

'Oh, no, it *is* true! I'm too young! My parents will be very shocked!'

He began to laugh, 'You're such a little hypocrite, such a bourgeoise.' And he ushered her into his waiting car. After telling the chauffeur to take them home, he slid across the back seat to take her in his arms and kiss away her tears. He could not help but laugh at her distress, then said, 'Now let's talk about Christmas.'

'I don't think this is the time to talk about Christmas, John!'

'What do you say about a Christmas wedding? Very small and discreet, in Barbados. I get the holiday I want and you get the husband you want. You do want to marry me, don't you? I am a very good catch.'

'I don't know what to say.'

'Yes will do,' he told her, kissing her several times on her face and the side of her neck.

'And what about my little problem? You're not asking me to marry you only because of that, are you, John?'

'No, not only because of that. But I would be less

than honest if I didn't tell you it has everything to do with it.'

For the remainder of the day and all that evening Eliza tried in vain to make him understand that she had no maternal feelings for the child she was carrying; that it was not so much fear of having a baby as that she simply was not ready to be a mother when she hardly knew who and what she was herself. But by morning she had been seduced once more by John into believing that his happiness was her happiness, what he wanted was what she wanted. That evening he dominated her thoughts as he did her body, her very soul, with lust. Only one thing marred his decision to marry Eliza: she was such an innocent, so easily seduced, weak in character. She would take some looking after vis-à-vis people who might drift in and out of their lives: her family, his friends, men who would be attracted to her, those Tuscan relations she was always going on about, someone she might take a momentary fancy to as she had the scaffolder. The moment John asked Eliza to marry him, in his mind she became his possession and he was a possessive man.

The next few days were the happiest of Eliza's life. John was magnificent with her: loving, generous, kindness itself. He bought her a diamond to celebrate their engagement and the family was told of the betrothal and invited to a dinner at his flat along with a few of his closest friends and several of his cousins the following week. Dulcima and Julian knew that Eliza was making an advantageous marriage, one that would give her wealth and status, but those things mattered little to them, her happiness everything. Was she happy? Deliriously so, she had assured them, and that was enough for her parents. Dulcima did however suggest to Eliza that she should not rush into anything. Actually what she advised was that time was a leveller.

Eliza was too happy at the thought of being Mrs Hope-Quintin not to grant John a few wishes: her pregnancy would be kept a secret, as would their wedding plans. She was swept along as if floating off the ground on some magic carpet.

But then, in the midst of her euphoria, a most incredible thing happened to jolt her back to earth. Vittorio arrived in London only days after she had agreed to marry John. When the telephone call came through to Eliza at the flat, John was at the hospital. Initially it had been Eliza's cousin getting in contact with her. He had discovered the telephone number from her father. Eliza was overjoyed to hear from him. Suddenly Tuscany, the Villa Monetcatini and the sweet bird of youth began singing for her again.

'What are you doing here, Federico? I know how you dislike London,' she said, laughter in her voice.

'I've come as a second, so to speak. Hold the line, someone here very much wants to speak to you.'

Eliza sensed at once that it was Vittorio and her heart began to race. He had come after her. Just hearing his voice was enough to knock her off kilter. She hardly knew what to say. He was there but the pain of their separation was there too and it still hurt, more than she'd imagined it ever could now that she had John. She had difficulty listening to what he was saying because she could not get that woman, Janine le Donneur, out of her mind. Finally, numbed by surprise and intrigued that he should have left his beloved Italy for her, she agreed to see him and gave

Vittorio the address, saying he should come round as soon as he liked.

Once Eliza had put down the phone, she panicked. There was simply no other word for it. She began to hyper-ventilate and felt as if she wanted to be sick. She was afraid to see Vittorio, afraid to fall in love with him again or find out that she had never fallen out of love with him. She didn't know which and it didn't matter because all she wanted was not to feel the pain of losing a man or her happiness again. Her hands were trembling while she freshened her make-up and combed her hair. Looking in the mirror at herself, she suddenly let out a scream of anguish. What was the point of seeing him, loving him or not loving him? It was over for them now that she was pregnant. It suddenly seemed wrong that she should be carrying John's child. 'Vittorio,' she said aloud.

Eliza heard the doorbell and Mrs Fanshaw ushered someone into the drawing room. She was actually trembling with the fear of seeing Vittorio again. What if their meeting was to prove to her that she loved him more than John? Was John an escape, someone she'd chosen on the rebound? The anguish she had suffered over loving Vittorio and wondering whether he was the right man for her suddenly returned. John had made all that go away. What bliss it had been not to feel that pain of loving Vittorio and not knowing what to do about it any more than he did. She gazed at the large diamond on her finger, placed the palms of her hands on her still flat tummy, and tears came into her eyes. She took a deep sigh and hardened herself to face Vittorio, who had come too late.

He was standing by the fireplace staring into the

leaping flames when she entered the room. He turned to face her and they gazed into each other's eyes. Eliza felt quite sick with nervousness and was trembling. Vittorio looked handsome and young but so terribly nervous and tense, very out of place, dressed in his badly chosen and ill-fitting suit, standing in this elegant London drawing room.

'You've taken me by surprise,' she told him in Italian, and then sat down in the nearest chair, feeling too weak-kneed to remain standing. Her fragility was not so much from love but the anguish she felt at seeing Vittorio now, in this place, in her new circumstances.

He sat down next to her and told her, 'You look lovely, so elegant, beautiful and grown up. I've come to take you home to Tuscany. I want to show you off to our friends, to the world. For us to wed and make each other happy again.'

Then they fell silent. The tension in the room seemed to swallow them up, put them on edge, to kill all the things in their hearts they might feel for each other. They were unable to express in words or by the smallest gesture their sentiments. Even to make mundane conversation became impossible for them. Vittorio's eyes were filled with love for Eliza, she could see that and it unnerved her rather than drew her towards him. The former lovers did not fall into each other's arms and weep with joy, though they were aware that that was what they should be doing. Instead the fear that was gripping them created an enormous chasm between them.

Finally Eliza could bear the silence no longer and broke it by telling him, 'I don't know what to say.'

'Don't say anything. I'll go away and come back later to take you to dinner. We can talk then.'

She knew by the tone of his voice that he was as emotionally overwrought as she was. Did he understand that too much time had passed, she had been through too much without him, that he should have never let her go? For a moment she despised him for that and herself for having been too weak to listen to her heart and nothing else back then in Tuscany. He looked like a displaced person out of his environment, not so much lost as no longer belonging to her life, this new London life, a very English life where he would never fit in.

'Eight o'clock. You'll see, it will be better for us then. It's as much of a shock for me, this meeting, as it is for you.'

'Yes, eight o'clock.'

She rose to walk with him to the front door. His scent was familiar, his walk. She felt herself weakening, feeling the things for him now that she had felt for him in the past and that frightened her, traumatised her actually. It was too late, she had moved on. In the past she had always succumbed to Vittorio until the very day they had parted. Now that was no longer even a possibility. She was afraid that Vittorio and the love they had once had for each other might yank her away from the new life she was creating with John. Now, when fate had taken over their lives, he was here for her, trying to give her the life she had once wanted.

After Eliza had closed the front door she leaned back against it and was astonished at how very much afraid of Vittorio she was. His cruelty to Janine, his wanting her in his life, in his country, that he might discover she was carrying another man's child. She only just made it to John's bathroom where she was violently sick. John . . . if only he had been there. She lay down on his bed and clung to a pillow, trying to calm herself. She would of course have to tell him she was going out to dinner with Vittorio.

It was very nearly half an hour before Eliza felt calm enough to call his rooms. She was astonished that John was available to speak with her. As soon as she heard his voice she felt undone again. It was clear to her that she was far more emotionally confused than she had thought she was, but she did manage to control her voice.

Quite calmly she told John, 'Something unexpected has happened. My friend from Tuscany – Vittorio – he's in London. He wants to have dinner with me, do you mind?'

It was the anguish in her voice that gave Eliza away and made John hesitate for not one second before he answered, 'Of course not, we'll take him somewhere nice. Obviously not Italian.'

Eliza's anxiety did not vanish but it immediately subsided when John took over the situation. Like a knight in shining armour he had come to her aid. He would give her the strength to keep Vittorio at arm's length. They could instead be together as friends until the end of their days. It was settled, there was only the evening to get through, and though Eliza was not looking forward to it, she was at least in control of herself, had a direction to follow now.

'He will be here at eight. When will you be home?'

'In time to answer the front door,' was his answer.

When John did arrive home he behaved no differently from any other evening. He asked nothing about Vittorio, and made only one comment when she joined him in the drawing room for their evening drink before going out. 'I think you look just a little underdressed. How about changing to your black crêpe-de-chine, the St Laurent we bought last week.'

'I thought I should dress down for Vittorio. He's a simple country man, John.'

'As you like. This is your evening, but I should have thought you would want to dress up for such an old friend, honour the occasion.'

Eliza was wearing her St Laurent and looking every inch the elegant young beauty, sophisticated and desirable, when Vittorio rang the doorbell. Eliza all but shot out of her chair, and looked very embarrassed and sat down again hurriedly as John rose from his and went to let their guest in. She heard him introduce himself as a friend of Eliza's and say he was joining them for dinner and hoped Vittorio did not mind.

It was not a successful evening. Several times Eliza wondered if she would even be able to live through it. Vittorio could understand English very well but did not speak fluently, and John made capital of that. He embarrassed the young man at every turn he could by asking Eliza if he had understood Vittorio correctly practically every time their guest opened his mouth. They went to The Ivy for dinner and it was far too grand a restaurant for Vittorio, showing up his table manners.

John never stopped talking, and when he was not talking he was making considerate and affectionate overtures to Eliza. Several times she tried to change the subject by asking Vittorio about the Montecatini farm and the villa and their friends, but John would deflect her attempts by talking directly to Vittorio, asking him about his life, his background, politics, the state of the Italian economy – all of which Vittorio was not forthcoming about or else was relatively ignorant of.

Several times he made brave attempts to ask Eliza about her life and the family, even to ask how soon she would be going to the villa. It was at that point that John said, 'We will be going to the South of France long before we go to Tuscany. There is so much of the world outside Tuscany that Eliza knows nothing of. I hope to show her some of it. You would like that, wouldn't you, Eliza?' And he took her hand in his and squeezed it.

There it was, out in the open. John had made his claim on her. Only a blind man could have failed to see that he was telling Vittorio there was no chance for him with Eliza. There was nothing that she could say or even wanted to say. She was somehow relieved to have John openly claiming her, taking over her life and constructing a future for them with that takeover. She was feeling too young, too inexperienced in love, to make such important life choices. Eliza was numbed, as if she had been anaesthetised by John. He made it so easy for her to take what appeared to be the easy option without even considering the state of her heart or what she really wanted.

It was then that Vittorio called for the waiter to bring the bill. John insisted the three of them go home to his flat for a night-cap. Eliza tried to get out of it gracefully as did Vittorio but John was insistent, he had control of the situation and was not letting go. He stood up and handed Eliza her evening bag.

'We must wait for the bill,' suggested Vittorio.

'There is no bill, it's been taken care of,' John told him.

'But I invited you. I insist, John,' Vittorio said, the anger he had hidden so well throughout dinner now audible in his voice.

'It's too late, it's done, and I was delighted to have done it. Now do let's go home for that cognac.'

It was all quite unbearable for Vittorio. He stayed for no more than ten minutes before he insisted he must leave. 'I'll let Eliza see you out, if you don't mind. It was an interesting evening and I am glad we met,' John told him, and the two men shook hands.

Eliza walked Vittorio out into the street. 'Are you still with Janine?' she asked, somehow hoping that he did have her or someone else in his life as she now had John. 'If so then maybe we can all meet next time you come to London?'

'I do not expect to come to London again. And, no, I don't think you will ever meet Janine.'

Eliza was quite taken aback by the anger in his eyes, the venom in his voice. It dismayed her. She asked him, 'Please, Vittorio, we can be friends? I'd like that, it would mean so much to me.'

'That's impossible. Walk away from this house with me now and never look back. You and I, that's all there is for us.'

He never touched her, merely looked at her. Her mind was spinning and she felt as if frozen to the spot. It was only a matter of seconds and then he was gone without another word. She watched him walk away from her and knew she would never forget the pain and disappointment in his eyes. She was aware of how cruel she had been to him, how much she had hurt him. She had until that moment never hurt anyone and the realisation of what she had done shocked her into a dislike of herself that she knew would remain with her all her life. Something hardened in her heart.

Returning to the drawing room she was surprised not to find John there. He was in his bedroom undressing. 'Oh, there you are. I hope you didn't get a chill.'

'Did you have to be so cruel to him? Show him up so badly. Humiliate him at every turn. He was like a fish out of water here in London, away from Tuscany.'

'I was jealous, that's my only excuse.'

'You had no need to be.'

'I know that now.'

John went to her and began undoing her dress, kissing her with great tenderness on her lips and face. 'He was only a peasant. He will never be any more than a poor Tuscan, quite uneducated, farmer. And you, my beauty, were not cut out to be a poor farmer's wife.'

'Now we can never go back for summer with the family at the villa, it would hurt him too much. And I will never hurt him again with your snobbery, John, and my new lifestyle.'

There were tears of anger and frustration in Eliza's eyes but John kissed them away. He finished undressing her and then carried her to the bed. He loved her tenderly until she came once, a second time, and when she was lost in her ecstasy and he was still in the act of exquisite fucking to bring her to orgasm again, he told her, 'I don't want you ever again to expose me to such a stupid and boring evening as we have just had, do you understand? Never!'

Chapter 5

The Forresters never did have Christmas dinner in Little Barrington; they had it instead in the form of a wedding luncheon on a large and luxurious yacht off the coast of Barbados because that was what John wanted. They were all there, mother, father, all four of the Forrester girls and their husbands and lovers. Eliza had been emphatic: she would not marry John unless her family was invited to the wedding. He relented on one condition: she was to leave all the arrangements to him, everything must be a surprise to her.

It was all frightfully elegant, as were most of the guests whom the bride hardly knew. Glamorous and social enough for the *Tatler* to fly a photographer and columist out for the event. But that hardly seemed to matter because Eliza was swept along on a tide of happiness. John was responsible for that: besotted still by his young bride-to-be and by becoming a father, he courted her in an even more attentive and loving manner in public, and in private quite simply could not get enough of her sexually. Eliza was dazzled by his love for her, the attention and the gifts which never seemed to stop coming.

It was several days before the wedding when John took her quite by surprise. They were in bed in the early hours of the morning, lying wrapped in each other's arms, when he asked, 'What are you going to do with your life, darling?'

The answer that she gave him was immediate and exact, before she even contemplated the question: 'I'm going to marry you.'

'That's marvellous but not enough.'

'I'm going to be the mother of your children.'

'A wife and a mother, admirable, but in this day and age that is still not enough. Have you ever considered going to university?'

'No,' she answered him, but this time unwound herself from his arms to sit up in bed and look at him. At last she understood that he was trying to tell her something.

'I think you should,' he told her, while brushing strands of hair away from her face.

'What's this about, John? If you have something to say then just come out and say it.'

'Frankly, much as I love and adore you the way you are, I think I need more from you, that you should be better educated. I see a big life ahead of us and a dim wife . . . well, not good for you, your husband or your children. You have a good mind which you don't use. If you will forgive me, darling, you have a lazy mind, and that's not very interesting and difficult to build a life on. I have my career, I think we should find one for you.'

'You astound me, John. Run your home, care for a baby *and* go to school?'

'Well, you won't be running the home or cooking the meals – we have staff for that. There will be a live-in nanny for the baby. There's our hunting and riding, but that's not a career, that's not developing your mind, doing something for society – all of which you are capable of but are not doing. What did you think was going to happen when we returned from Barbados? That you were going to lie around the house waiting to give birth? No, I expect more from my wife than that.'

'What do you expect, John?'

'For you to be my wife, my delicious whore in bed, the mother of my children, the hostess of my home – and for you to do something with your mind for yourself. I hoped you would like my suggestion. I can pull a few strings and get you into London University after the Christmas break. We can get you tutored for the first half of the year you've missed. You can go to classes while I'm at the hospital and we can live as we have been these last few months as lovers, then a family when the baby arrives, and have a wonderful life. You're so young. You'll get bored by domesticity, which you're hopless at anyway.'

'What you're really saying, John, is that it's you who is worried about getting bored with me.'

'Well, there is that possibility if you don't grow as a human being, stretch yourself outside our intimate life. Will you think about it?' He teased her with kisses and caresses to soften the impact of his suggestion until she agreed to take it under consideration. He had Eliza obedient to his will by the sheer power of his sexual possession of her, and delighted in her weakness.

Eliza was standing with her father and Effie under a canopy garlanded with flowers in the stern of the yacht owned by a Saudi prince who was hosting the wedding in gratitude for John's having saved the life of his favourite wife. Eliza was still feeling haunted by the memory of that morning several days before when John had all but declared that he did not want an uneducated wife. Not for the first time she was offended by him and his expectations of her, but love and fate tend to make a young woman rationalise away offences and make compromises.

Only an hour before when Effie had been helping Eliza to adjust her wide-brimmed straw hat banded with cream-coloured satin and embroidered with seed pearls, the two sisters had caught a reflection of themselves in the mirror. For a second they had gazed into each other's eyes and Effie had remarked, 'You don't have to do this, Eliza. Even now it's not too late to pick up your skirts and run. The family will support you, you know that.'

She had replied, 'But it is too late.' Nothing more.

Had Effie been reading her mind? Only then, minutes before she was to marry John, she had felt unsure as to whether she had made the right choice. Was opening a new world for her, giving her a grand and glamorous life, one that offered security, being the woman John had chosen in lust and love above all others, not enough for her? Was not the fact that their erotic togetherness, so extraordinarily sublime for her, had created first a bond to tie them together, and then a baby, not sufficient for her happiness? John had made it clear to her in so many ways that he loved her for those things as much as he loved her for herself – was even that not enough? She felt spoiled and foolish for her misgivings, ungrateful for the rich and full life he was offering her, even though she had never been looking for such a life, and so she had laid her doubts aside.

She had stood up and Effie had taken Eliza's hands in hers. 'Just remember, Lizzy, John Hope-Quintin will never be better than you. You're the best.' And the two sisters hugged each other and, arm-in-arm, left the stateroom.

As Eliza had walked down the aisle on her father's arm, smiling, looking around at so many people looking joyful at the occasion, she felt a degree of relief that it was too late for doubts, in spite of thinking, I wish all this and my new lifestyle were more important to me than they are and less of a burden to be dealt with. But then John had taken her arm and she had once more been seduced by how handsome, sexy and exciting he was at that moment, as he always was to her. They were together, and Eliza had once more felt thrilled and full of hope for them.

She snapped out of her thoughts as her father slid an arm around her shoulders and touched her cheek with his hand. 'You look the loveliest of brides but you seem very far away.'

'I was thinking about my new life and the future, Poppy.'

'I think John will take very good care of you materially, dear, better than I ever did my wife. But then there were compensations: we had a very good time, lived the way we wanted to live, were very happy. And we had Tuscany.'

'I feel a long way from Tuscany, Poppy, but it will always be my spiritual home.'

'You of all the girls loved it best, understood it most, respected the land and beauty of the place. The house loves you as it doesn't the other girls. I always think it's you that will be the next custodian of the villa. Your mother says that and she should know – it did after all come down through her side of the family. Yes, maybe you're more of a throwback to the Montecatinis than the other girls. Oh, dear, I'm getting sentimental, missing you already, and I've only just given you away. Well now, you and John and the children that will come can add to its history, be a part of its divine grace.'

Eliza knew in her heart that that would never happen, John would never settle in the villa or ever appreciate it as she and her family did. But she somehow could not bring herself to say that to her father. She merely kissed him on the cheek and said, 'I need you to do something very important for me, Poppy.'

'Anything I can, Eliza.'

'I want you to beg some favours on my behalf. Come over here where it's quiet and I'll explain. You too, Effie.'

The father and his two daughters only had a short time to themselves as the guests were milling all around them, but Eliza was quick and made her point with clarity: 'Poppy, John thinks that I am not very well educated, and he is going to do something about that. I don't want him to. *I* want to do something about it. He may be my husband and think he is in control of my life, as he is, but only to a degree. He thinks I should go to London University. He can think what he likes. I know I want to go Oxford, to your old college. John thinks he will choose some impressive career for me. I know he won't because I would like to follow in your footsteps and study ancient and modern law.'

'Eliza, you take my breath away, you *are* full of surprises. That's right, you give John a run for his money,' said a smiling Effie.

'I knew you were interested by justice and the law but I had no idea you were committed enough to make a study of those subjects. I am of course delighted and will do what I can for you, but this isn't a spur of the moment thing, is it?' asked her father more soberly.

'No, Poppy. I'm sure that if you can get me in, I'll make it to graduation. But, Effie, Poppy, I want it kept a secret until I'm accepted. Promise?'

It was then they were interrupted by John and their host: there was champagne to be drunk, guests looking for the bride, cables of congratulations to be read, the appearance of the four-tiered wedding cake, a gift from Robert Carrier. The three Forresters, full of the joy a wedding can engender, rose admirably to the occasion.

It was not a good marriage. But like so many flawed marriages there were interludes of short-term happiness: Eliza and John's sex life and the birth of their children, Alexander, the elder, and Olivia, born just one year later. Horses and ponies for the children, and riding with the hunt for them all. Eliza, a young mother of two, achieving a first at Oxford. John's work. A busy social life that was a burden Eliza bore with fortitude but was on occasion interesting to her. She and John enjoyed holidays for just the two of them to exotic places round the world, usually taken to save the marriage for another few months.

John was a good lover but a bad husband to Eliza. He had to be in control, have the power in their relationship. She was passive in the face of his controlling nature. That was quite easy for her because she really did not understand control, it meant nothing to her. She had come from a household that didn't believe in domination or manipulating people, and only when it was almost too late did she come to understand how evil such things could be.

John's domination of her caused Eliza to be a guest in her own home: being replaced by interior decorators, party planners, florists, a cook, cleaner, live-in nanny, chauffeur – and always with John at the helm of their lives, making all their decisions, directing every detail of their marriage. Even his nurse and receptionist were brought in on occasion to accomplish some task that Eliza had been excluded from.

Though she had not been happy about having a baby so young, the moment she took Alexander in her arms she fell in love with him and motherhood – only to have her son taken away from her because John did not want her to have to deal with the hard work and mundane tasks of bring up a baby. Like some Victorian upper-class mother, a kiss in the morning and an hour at teatime was pretty much the extent of her rearing of her children. Even when they went on family holidays, the staff went with them.

John wanted her always to be young and beautiful, his child bride. He wanted no encumbrances that might keep him from taking her out and playing with her as and when he wanted to play. He gave her roles in his life to act out but not to live. She went along with him but did on occasion surprise him. Oxford had been a case in point: her insistence that they gear their lives to her time there as much as she geared hers to being wife and lover to the famous surgeon, and mother of his children. John was proud of Eliza and her accomplishments; he considered them his.

She had been shocked and upset that she should become pregnant again so soon after giving birth to Alexander. John had been delighted. He liked her pregnant. It did nothing but excite his lust for her and she made beautiful babies whom he loved. The years seemed to fly by, Eliza and John living in separate worlds when she was in the role of student and he was working in the hospital. The world of husband and wife, where she neither felt he was a husband nor she a wife and mother, was a play worthy of the West End. What they were both aware of was that he was a more considerate father than he was a husband. This was made even more evident by the contrast with Eliza's behaviour with her children: she was awkward, never quite knowing how to behave with them. They simply did not take to her in the same way as they did to their nanny, Mrs Fanshaw or their father.

Alexander was four when Eliza discovered that John had other women, many and often, that he had always had them: that it had begun when they were lovers and had never stopped. They were a part of his life as much as being married was. That he had never been particularly discreet about his affairs had made it common knowledge. Eliza was devastated by the discovery and that she should be the last to know. The deceit, that she had been cuckolded and had never seen a sign of it, was shattering enough but the very idea of John with another woman made her insanely jealous as well. She had believed that she was everything to him, that their sex life was too good for him to crave another woman. Her ego took the blows badly, her self-esteem plummeted. She was now twenty-two years old and her life was inextricably entwined with John's in lust, in love, by children. She was no more equipped to handle disloyalty than she had been a marriage made by circumstances. Over and over she kept asking herself, How could he deceive me? Have I been deceiving myself?

It was not a case of a friend telling her. Nor even overheard gossip. She saw them with her own eyes. She was walking down Harley Street on her way to John's rooms when his car passed her. She raised her arm to wave and get his attention when she saw him kissing someone in the back seat of the car. She was so shocked by the sight of John in the arms of another woman that she stopped in the middle of the pavement, dropped her arm and very nearly convinced herself that she had imagined it. Taking several deep breaths and feeling very foolish she walked on, her eyes still on the Jaguar ahead of her. John's car stopped, and so did Eliza. The chauffeur opened the door and discreetly turned away, then John emerged and helped a beautiful, very well-dressed and groomed woman from the car. The lustful look in his eyes, his body language with the woman, showed a togetherness with her that Eliza recognised. She had not seen that look directed at her for a very long time – years, in fact. Had she ever seen it as acutely as she saw it now for this woman?

She watched her husband, quite clearly besotted, raise the woman's chin with an index finger and kiss her on the lips. His arms went around her and drew her to him. Eliza slipped stealthily into a doorway so as not to be seen by them. She felt guilty for having caught them like this. Had John ever been so obviously affectionate to her? She watched him raise the woman's hands to his lips and kiss them. She could feel his reluctance to let her go and wanted to die right then and there.

Someone opened the door to leave the building behind her and Eliza, who had flattened herself against it, slipped into the silent entrance hall. It was one of those elegant Harley Street buildings where doctors had their consulting rooms, looking much the same as John's building, as all the others on this street famed for its doctors. The elegant eighteenth-century rooms were always furnished sparsely but in good taste: the right chandeliers in the entrance hall, Chippendale chairs and settees in the reception room, usually filled with quiet people dragged down to silence by worry about their condition or a friend's or relative's.

A sigh escaped Eliza. Deceit played out before her very eyes had quite unnerved her, made her weak-kneed. She sat down on one of the Chippendale chairs facing a line of brass nameplates of the doctors in the building, the tears trickling down her cheeks. She heard a muffled sound, the whirr of a small lift hidden somewhere at the rear of the hall. A nurse appeared, white-clad, a small pristine cap pinned to the top of her head. The nurse's rubber-soled shoes hardly made a sound on the white marble floor as she walked to the reception room to summon a patient.

Eliza jumped when a few minutes later, after the lift had whirred its way upward in the building, the same nurse came and stood before her. 'Are you feeling unwell?' she asked.

'Yes,' answered Eliza, who was just barely able to speak.

'Who are you waiting to see?' asked the nurse.

Eliza raised her eyes. The brass plates on the wall caught her attention. She felt not so much saved as relieved to see Robert Flemming's name. He was the children's paediatrician, the nicest and kindest of men, one of the few of John's colleagues whom she really liked. Enough to use his name as a reason for her being there but certainly not enough to confide her distress in him.

'Mr Flemming.'

'I'll send his nurse down to see you,' said the good Samaritan nurse.

'No, please don't do that! I'll be fine and wait my turn.' And Eliza very nearly choked, trying to hold back a sob.

The nurse left, vanishing somewhere into the recesses of the building, and Eliza closed her eyes and made an effort to compose herself. Her eyes were still closed when she heard Robert Flemming's voice, husky but kind, and felt his hand raise her chin.

'Oh dear, Eliza, you're not very well, are you?'

'No, Robert,' she answered, and burst into tears.

He helped her from the chair and walked her to the small lift hidden behind a wooden panel. She trembled so much he had to steady her. Once on his floor he asked, 'Eliza, shall I call John?'

'No, please don't do that!' And then once again she burst into tears.

Robert Flemming walked her past his nurses to his consulting room and sat her down on the leather settee. After bringing her a glass of water he sat down next to Eliza and placed an arm around her. It was several minutes before she was able to calm herself and when she did she leaned against him silently.

They remained thus for a considerable time, until Eliza was able to sit up and tell him, 'How embarrassing.'

'Do you want to tell me about it?'

She gave him no answer which caused Robert to suggest, 'A cup of tea? I could do with one.'

The nurse was called in and Robert let Eliza be and attended to some case-reports on his desk until Nurse Keely returned with a tray. It was placed on the table in front of the settee where Eliza had remained, dry-eyed and staring into space. Robert returned to sit next to her and pour.

Quite calmly she told him what she had seen. Robert handed her a cup of tea and replied, 'Drink this, it will do you a world of good.'

Eliza sipped from her cup and almost immediately felt revived by the hot smoky taste of the Lapsang Souchong. She sighed. Gazing into Robert's eyes, she asked, 'I suppose, like so many other wives, I'm the last to know?'

'Marriage never changed John. We all assumed that when you married him there was an understanding between you.'

'An understanding?'

'That he would be devoted to you, love you best, more than any of his other women.'

'We! Who's we?'

'His colleagues, your friends.'

'And why would they assume such a thing, Robert?' A certain anger was coming into her voice now.

'Because though he never flaunted his women in front of you, he was not particularly discreet.'

Eliza was astounded. Trembling, she placed her cup and saucer on the table and then her hands over her face. Several minutes went by before she removed them and told Robert, 'I feel such a fool, so humiliated. How could I not have known, not seen it coming, or even thought he might want another woman? I didn't, you know!

'I was once loved by a man who was devoted to me, I was his world, and I assumed that John, who had won me away from him, felt as that man did. I thought we had given our lives to each other. The life I held back from that young man. I'm afraid I don't understand deceit and disloyalty.'

'I've known John for a very long time, Eliza. Maybe he doesn't see his philandering as disloyalty, just sex. This isn't in defence of him, just to point out to you that it is a possibility you must contemplate before you confront him with what you've discovered. Now you wait here and drink your tea. I have two more patients waiting and then I'll take you home.'

'You don't have to do that, Robert.'

'I think I do, and besides I want to. I am after all your friend and have been for many years. But then, maybe you don't know that any more than you know your husband.'

That last remark gave Eliza something more to think about. Had she been so blindly in love with John, so self-involved, that she'd never realised Robert had always been there for her as a close friend as well as being a colleague of John's and her children's paediatrician? Suddenly his many kindnesses to her, the way he'd supported her against John in little things about the children, the many quiet talks they had had together during those social occasions she detested, came to mind. Only now did she think about those things and realise that she had taken Robert's affection for her, his friendship, for granted.

In the car on the way home she asked, 'Robert, I think I have been blind, naive about more than John's infidelity. I have been so busy getting on with being John's wife, and the mother of his children, I have no idea who or what I am, how John sees me . . . how *you* perceive me.'

'I can't speak for John.'

'Then speak for yourself.'

'Are you sure you want to hear this now?'

'Yes, very sure.'

They were riding through Hyde Park. Robert pulled the car to a halt and cut the motor then turned in the seat to face Eliza and took her hand in his. 'I have always seen you more as a victim than a wife. A willing victim: young and naive, not at all a match for John and his charm. The bearer of children rather than their mother. Not that you would not nurture your children but rather because you don't know how to. That natural mothering instinct is not there in you, it has never developed because you're still undefined, still a child yourself. John delights in keeping you as his young thing. It's very appealing for a man, that child-woman quality, but it doesn't make for particularly good mothers.'

'And that's what you think I have?'

'In abundance. It's very sexy to some men.'

'And to you, Robert?'

'When I first met you I found you a refreshing,

sensuous young beauty. That John was besotted with you told me a lot about you, what an erotic delight you must be. I liked you then, but as the years went by I liked you more: for having beautiful babies and returning to university to do your own thing, for being so devoted to John and still being able to retain something of yourself apart from him. I think I've loved you for a long time from afar. Now you're not going to get upset about that, I hope?'

'I never guessed you had any feelings for me,' answered a stunned Eliza.

'You weren't meant to. I would not have spoken about my feelings for you even now but you did ask. I don't think this is the time to talk any more about them. For now, the best thing I can do for all concerned is to take you home.'

In front of her house Eliza and Robert stood for several minutes gazing into each other's eyes, taking the measure of their friendship, seeing one another in a new and more intimate light. 'I'm sorry you had to learn about John in such a brutal way. I meant to say that before, in my office, but to be sorry for you was not so important as being honest with you.'

She was very much aware that he was not saying, Call me if you need me. I'm here for you. You have a friend. He didn't have to. The look in his eyes, the stance he took next to her, told her he was all those things and more. She also liked the fact that he didn't ask her what she was going to do about John and her marriage. He took it for granted that she was capable of dealing with her philandering husband, and now that her eyes had been opened could correct the mess she had made of her life.

Nothing would ever be the same for Eliza after she had discovered how conveniently she had blinded herself to the reality of her life. Her first inclination as she entered the house was to grab her two children, put them in her car and flee to Little Barrington or the Villa Montecatini, her mother and father, home, the only home she'd ever really had. But once in the entrance hall and being confronted by Mrs Fanshaw with a message from John, she realised that to flee would be an act of panic. It would be to lose the life of sorts that she had worked hard at. If not the right life for her and John, it was still the only one she had. In an instant she knew that she would not flee, she would deal with the mess of her marriage and her own weakness. She needed time to sort herself out and get a life for herself and her family that worked for them all. But her brave thoughts did not stop her from bursting into tears once she was out of Mrs Fanshaw's sight.

Eliza felt a stranger in her own house, lost and adrift. She went directly to the nursery. It was empty, the children were with Nanny in the park. She was shocked, not because they were gone but because she could at last face the truth: love them as she did, she was relieved she didn't have to deal with them. She felt as much a stranger to them as she did in her house. In her bedroom John's dinner clothes had been laid neatly across the bed: dress shirt, studs, silk bow tie, suit, socks, shiny shoes. She stared down at them and thought: John.

Only to him did she feel a sense of belonging, only with him was she not a stranger. Her heart raced. She hugged herself, imagined she was in his arms, that he was comforting her. She yearned to hear his voice, for him to tell her how sublime a creature she was, how divine she was in bed, to feel his lusty penetrations take her into an erotic nirvana. She collapsed on the bed and, crushing the shirt to her face, wept into it for some time before she calmed herself and remembered he was a deceiver, disloyal, had abused the life she had entrusted to him. He was making love with, fucking that woman she had seen him with. And other women too.

Dry eyed now, she left the room to go to John's upstairs study and when she returned it was with a pair of long silver paper scissors, a favourite possession of his. Very calm now, Eliza sat down on the bed and quite deliberately and methodically cut his evening clothes into small squares. She was amazed at how much pleasure she was deriving from this desperate act. So much so in fact that when she was finished with his clothes she attacked his custom-made Lobb shoes with two tubes of toothpaste and an electric toothbrush.

Eliza looked at her handiwork which she had assembled in a neat mound in the middle of the bed topped by his Crest-polished evening shoes. Delighted with what she considered a job well done, she ran a bath for herself.

A couple of hours later she was dressed in a long silver lamé Versace dress, silver sandals, with her face and hair looking young and fresh. She looked exactly the way John liked her to look when he took her out on his arm to a grand dinner party: sexy, provocative, almost untouched, and all his. A date rather than a wife.

She was sitting on the bed, legs crossed at the knee, leaning against the pillows, the bedside lamp casting a lovely soft light on her, the silver lamé shimmering, when she heard his footsteps on the stairs and his voice calling out, 'I hope you're ready, darling, we don't want to be late.'

Seconds later he burst into the room, looking happy and sexy and handsome as he peeled off his jacket. He saw her before he did the pile of swatches that had once been his clothes for their evening at St James's Palace. She was amused that she could still dazzle him, stop him in his tracks.

'You look marvellous, and you *are* ready.'

'I certainly am,' she answered. It was the tone of her voice that made him realise something was amiss. He took only two more steps into the room before he saw the mound that had been his evening wear. He gazed at it but briefly then turned away from it and her to close the bedroom door.

He was very calm when he asked her, 'Are you all right, Eliza?'

'Yes, I am now.'

'Have you destroyed my other evening suits?'

'No, just one gave me enough satisfaction.'

'You do know that it is too late to cancel this dinner invitation? We must go.'

'Oh, you don't have to worry about that, John, I'm quite ready to go,' she told him as she rose from the bed and walked from the room.

When they returned that evening it was gone midnight and still they had not spoken a word about what she had done or why she had done it. In fact they hardly spoke at all throughout the evening and when they did they were polite. John looked in on the children as he usually did whenever they returned home from an evening out. Eliza did not. She went directly to their room.

'Thank you for not ruining the evening for me,' he told her as he removed his jacket and went to stand next to her in front of the long mirror where she was removing the dress's short ermine jacket banded in silver lamé. He placed his hands on her shoulders and kissed the side of her neck then took the jacket from her hands.

She wheeled around to face him. 'Everything in its time, everything in its place. One of your dictums, I believe? Well, this is the time and the place, John. No woman, not even one as young and naive as I have been, likes to be made a fool of. And what a fool, what a laughing stock, you have made of me! Do you love her, that woman I saw you with in front of your office this afternoon? The way you looked at her told me that you do. You're a pig and a cheat for deceiving me with that woman. Disloyal and dishonourable for leading me on to believe *I* am the love and passion of your life. I gave everything up for you, to make you happy . . .'

John interrupted her. 'No, my dear, you did not give everything up for me. You have that quite wrong. You never had anything to give up. Now we are not going to have a hysterical scene. Instead we are going to talk this out like the two civilised people we are, people who love each other.'

And that was exactly what they did before they eventually went to sleep wrapped in each other's arms. Two days later they flew to Fiji in the hope of healing Eliza's marital wounds. It was more like a second honeymoon than a holiday because she was still sexually besotted with John and he was loving and charming to her, but the holiday did not heal their damaged marriage. Instead Eliza was made to understand that John would never change but that he intended to love her better than any other woman who might enter his life. His confession that marriage was not much to his liking but children, and having a family were, that he tried to think of her as someone he'd seduced rather than a wife, was hurtful to Eliza, too painful was the picture he drew for her of why she could not leave him. He would not give up his children to divorce. She must face the fact that she had no money of her own, had never earned or saved a penny so was dependent on him to take care of her. But the most tormenting thing for her was when John told her she could never leave him because she was too much in love with him and the life he had constructed for her, because she had given herself completely to loving him and the erotic life he had addicted her to. It was all true. Eliza knew at that moment that until she was strong enough to walk away from John she would remain with him in her unhappy marriage.

It was to take four more years, a master's degree in law, a not very rewarding spell of working with a firm in Lincoln's Inn, and falling in love with her best friend, Robert Flemming, before she walked out.

Chapter 6

The last three months before Eliza walked away from her marriage were quite desperate times for her. Completely alienated from her home-life from the moment John left the house until his return, and having resigned from her job, she spent most of her days window shopping on Bond Street and having long coffee breaks at Fortnum & Mason or Richoux and afternoon tea at the Ritz or Claridge's, occasionally with a sister or a friend but mostly alone. She spent hours sitting in Farm Gardens off Mount Street chatting to strangers walking small dogs, and lunched alone in small out-of-the-way restaurants. Observing, always observing, strangers, imagining the lives they were leading, measuring their happiness.

Those friends who did join her had no sense that anything was wrong, Eliza was as jolly and charming as she could be. The first few days spent creating this new pattern to her life seemed strange and yet somehow extremely pleasant. After a week she was amazed at what a good time she was having on her own.

She was always home by five in the evening when she would look in on the children, who treated her more and more in the same way as John did, as if she were an awkward child rather than a woman, their mother. They loved her and dismissed her as her husband did for being a pretty, silly mummy. She would bathe and change and wait for John to return from the hospital, his office, or some liaison she could only guess at because in all the years since she had caught him in his infidelities he had been careful not to offend Eliza by being at all obvious about them in her presence.

Dawdling her days away, she was always ready and waiting for her evenings out with John, and to spend her nights sating her erotic appetites with him in bed. In the morning she would wake hungry once more for sexual delights. Eliza felt as if she were regressing in time: back to those early days when John had first seduced her, had whetted her appetite for sex.

It was several weeks before she realised that the only life she was having with John was one where she was sexually there, seducing him, baiting him to take her down a more thrilling sexual road while at the same time she was distancing herself from him as the love, the great passion, of her life. She was living in a strange kind of limbo that was both pleasurable and disconcerting, almost schizophrenic.

Then one morning, after a particularly exciting night of debauchery, John told her, 'My darling, lazy Eliza, you're such a delight because sexual satisfaction is all you think about. Having you for a wife has one most delightful advantage. You don't fuck like a wife, more like a whore. You were and still are, after all our years together, value for money in the sex game.' And he kissed her passionately, used his hands to caress her naked body.

It was instantaneous, struck her like an unexpected

blow to the head. His words not so much knocked her *out* as *into* her senses. She removed his hands from her body. He was having no protest. They caressed her breasts again and once more she removed them, not with anger nor with any suggestion that there was something wrong. She pulled herself up against the bed pillows and reached out to run her fingers through his hair. She felt him relax under her stroking.

She told him, 'You know, John, before I met you, a simple Tuscan farmer who loved me and who was gentle and kind, appreciating everything that I was and respecting it, taught me how to enjoy sex as part of loving. It took you and your seduction of me to turn me into a whore, just a lady who gives sexual services for a price. How flattered I was to be your whore, without ever realising until this very morning that that is what I am to you. About the only thing I will be able to pride myself on about this marriage is that I never cheated you. You got what you wanted. I have *always* been value for your money.'

This was just the sort of talk that excited John's lust. He broke into peals of laughter and made a grab for her. The joy of forcing her to submit to the power he had over her and watch her dissolve in endless streams of orgasm was one of the pleasures of his life. He missed and had to watch her slip away from him and off the bed.

Eliza knew when his lust was up and how to tantalise him. She had reached for her silk dressing-gown, rubbed her body with it and tossed it to him. Once more he laughed while he watched her move around, naked and provocative. Every step she took, every stance she struck, was a pose to tease him with. She knew well his erotic thoughts, the things he would be planning for them: that light sting of his belt on her flesh to excite a touch of fear, issued to teach her who was master of their erotic games; the elegant sexual toys that he used for her pleasure, to reduce her to begging to be riven by him. She could feel his eyes eating into her flesh but didn't turn around to face him. Instead she slid the painting on the wall opposite their bed away to expose a wall safe where her jewellery and any spare cash was kept.

'Put it all on. I like to see you naked and glittering with jewellery. It's so decadent, erotic as hell, and fun to fuck you looking like that.'

For the first time since they had been together, she found his husky and yet smooth and seductive voice no longer irresistible, merely ridiculous. She did not obey him. Instead she took a stack of banknotes held together by a rubber band and walked with it to the bed where she sat at the foot facing him, striking the most open and lewd position. One that decadently exposed her sex to his eyes.

She waved the stack of bank notes in front him and asked, 'You think I'm value for money? Would you say as good as a very good lady of the night, a first-class hooker?'

'Most assuredly,' answered an amused John. He liked this new game she was playing with him.

'How much would you have paid such a woman for a night of sex such as we had last night?'

'It's the woman who sets the price, Eliza.'

'I set it at two thousand pounds. Would you say that was a fair price?'

'OK, done at two thousand pounds,' said a by now rampant and amused John.

Eliza peeled off exactly two thousand pounds and tossed the remainder of the bundle of notes to John. He caught them with one hand and, smiling, told her, 'Eliza, as usual you shortchanged yourself. I would have paid three thousand for a night like last night. Now come and kiss me and see what you can earn for this morning. Maybe a bank note at a time placed strategically?' he teased.

She slid off the bed and walked to the bathroom and on through to her dressing room. An impatient John called her back several times before she returned to him. When she did she was dressed in a pair of jeans and a cashmere polo-neck jumper, a leather jacket over her shoulders matching shiny riding boots. She was carrying a small Louis Vuitton overnight case, the money held in one hand. Eliza stood at the foot of the bed facing John, who was stunned into silence.

She placed the case on the floor and as she stuffed the money into her pocket, said, 'John, I'm leaving you, taking this money for services rendered last night which you declared to be a bargain. My solicitor will be calling yours. I would like a divorce without scandal as soon as possible.'

'You're being ridiculous!'

'Maybe so, but let me tell you – it feels terrific.'

'You will never get custody of my children.'

'Not a problem, John. You took them away from me a long time ago. You can keep them.'

'You can forget money or alimony!'

'Calm down, John, I'm taking my car and my horse. There is nothing else I want from this marriage. Not your houses or possessions, only to see *our* children whenever they want to see their mother, for them to know that I am there for them. And that will be made clear to them through the courts, not you.'

'Why are you doing this?' he asked, now wrapped in his silk dressing-gown and standing only inches away from her.

'Put it down to being tired of being your whore or perhaps growing up. It was never a marriage. Pick anything that satisfies your ego, you always do.'

'If it's another man, Eliza, I'll get you for adultery!' he told her, anger in his voice.

'John, infidelity never appealed to me. I never considered another man for one minute from the day I met you until now as I walk out on you and the miserable, honey-coated life you dealt me. You were an evil prick to have done what you did to me.'

'And you were a willing masochist, remember that.'

'Or an inexperienced, naive girl who fell in love with you on the rebound. Goodbye, John. No scenes. Remember how you deplore them. Not now, not ever. You pride yourself on being a civilised man and I expect you to be that way to me when, and if, our paths cross in the future.'

'You can't have the BMW.'

'Fuck off, John, and keep your BMW. Do you begrudge me a few bits of my clothing as well? Yes, I suppose you do.'

With that Eliza dropped the keys on the carpet and walked from the room, leaving her case standing where she had placed it. John followed her out and in a more controlled voice, speaking quite softly, told her, 'I don't want you waking the children, not even to say goodbye.'

'I never really had a chance to say hello, did I, John?'

Those were her last words to her husband as she walked past the nursery door and out of the house to take a train for Little Barrington and home, having left behind eight years of her life.

She was, as she had expected to be, received by her mother and father with barely a question. Surprised but not shocked that she should have left her husband and children because she found them and her life intolerable, they rallied round her as did her sisters with affection rather than sympathy, though it was evident to the family that Eliza was deeply upset by the failure of her marriage.

After several days at home she brought her horse from John's stable and spent hours riding through the countryside, easing herself back into the Forrester way of life. Old friends who had been abandoned by her when she married John made her feel as if she had only been away a day. But when Tuscany time came around, much as she wanted to go to her beloved house with Julian and Dulcima, she somehow could not face a return after eight years until she felt emotionally more stable. Everyone guessed, and Eliza knew, that she simply was not ready to face Vittorio.

So instead she lived between Little Barrington and the woodsman's cottage, and because she had no money, took a job as a roving Justice of the Peace for the Cotswolds. There were lawyers to be paid for. The divorce never got messy because Eliza wanted nothing from her marriage and allowed John to sue her for divorce on the grounds of desertion. It moved along quickly without his even suggesting a reconciliation. Another blow to her ego, another indication of how little she'd meant to him.

In the year that followed her walkout there was much soul searching into her role as bad mother, bad wife, her being in love with John, her selfishness, how very shallow a life she had led, her sexual desires. She had been seriously damaged by the dark side of John, and had consequently lost confidence in men and love and most certainly herself. She had been burned by man's inhumanity in the guise of 'A Better Life-Love For Another'. Her family, good people, and Robert Flemming, who was a genuinely kind and loving human being who truly cared for his fellow man, were her healers.

After a year alone in which she remained celibate, Eliza married Robert Flemming. It was an easy marriage if not a passionate love. She found in life with Robert a respect for her as an individual that she had never received from John. They did everything together, including buying and furnishing a large cottage by the pond in Westwell which was close to Little Barrington and not very far from John's house in Coln St Aldwyn. It took several years for him to come to terms with Eliza's walking out on him, their children and their marriage, but since they were country neighbours and rode in the same hunt, knew the same people socially, he was never less than civil to her.

Robert lived in London during the week and Eliza took the train in on occasions to spend a night there with him. It was always the country for weekends.

Eliza and Robert had a child together, Samantha, and her birth helped to bring Eliza's children with John back into her life. Robert had remained the Hope-Quintin children's doctor and it was he who always maintained a good relationship with John and the children, he who broke the news to them that he was marrying their mother, and he who told them they had a little sister. At first it was no more than curiosity that brought the children back into Eliza's life but several years later there was a genuine love for their half-sister and Robert, a newfound respect and affection for their mother, between them all that brought them together in an easy-going and friendly relationship. However, their real love and devotion would always remain for their father who could do no wrong in their eyes, whereas they felt their mother could.

What was evident to both Robert and Eliza soon after Samantha was born was that she would be no better or no worse a mother to Samantha than she had been to Alexander and Olivia. Robert and Eliza had thought she would bring the baby up on her own but she simply did not have the disposition to handle that. The will was there but the reality was that John had not so much damaged as killed her mothering confidence. A live-in nanny was found soon after Samantha's birth and together Robert, Nanny and Eliza raised Samantha, and Eliza learned how to love and nurture her child, and even those from her first marriage.

That Robert and Eliza had a deep affection and respect for each other, loved each other for who and what they were, that they were each other's best friend, was finally not enough to keep the marriage together. There was no shock, no despair, only a little disappointment for them both when on the night of their eleventh anniversary, while they were dressing to go out to dinner, Robert approached Eliza who was sitting at her dressing table combing her hair. They gazed at each other in the mirror and he said, 'I somehow don't think we are going to make a twelfth anniversary, do you, Eliza?'

There was a long pause as she reached up to offer her hand over her shoulder to Robert who had remained standing behind her. He took it and lowered his head to kiss her fingers then resumed eye contact with her through the mirror. 'Are we that unhappy?' she asked her husband.

'No, just not happy enough to go on, Eliza.'

'You're saying we deserve better than what we've got, is that it?'

'Yes, I think we need a chance to go out and look for the passion, the adventure, that's missing from our lives. We married each other because we were friends who cared about each other. We had Samantha and she bound us together, gave our marriage stability and contentment.'

'But it hasn't been enough?'

'We're still young enough to try again for more, be alone for a while, get used to ourselves again, discover a wider world and a more thrilling way to live and love. The way I feel is not just for me. I sometimes see a yearning for something I'm not giving you, there in your eyes. I've never been able either to fathom or satisfy that yearning. You're unfulfilled and I have caught that sense of unfulfilment from you.'

'I never knew it was so obvious. Oh, Robert, I

haven't hurt you, have I? I simply could not bear it if I have.'

'No, no, never think that. I wouldn't have missed these last eleven years with you for the world, nor having Samantha, but it seems to me that it's time for us to move on. We will always have what we have had, a deep and abiding affection and friendship for one another.'

Ten-year-old Samantha was thrilled at the prospect of living with her father in London. She was made to understand her parents' divorce to be a necessity so that they might all remain together as family and friends, and took her mother's decision to settle in Oxford alone as part of a new life that Samantha would eventually be part of.

Eliza refused to be kept in any way or form by Robert. She left the marital home empty-handed for the second time, with the exception of a ten-year-old BMW, a suitcase of clothes and a loan of ten thousand pounds from Robert so that she might begin another life.

Detached and free was what Eliza wanted to be, and to find her place in the sun – something she felt she had not done since she had left Tuscany all those years ago, never to return. Tuscany . . . how happy and uncomplicated her life had been there, the wonderful innocent years in love with Vittorio. They were on her mind often, they were her companions during those first lonely days on her own again. Returning was an option but one she somehow felt she was as yet unready to take. She had things to do in her life before she could honourably return. And for Eliza to return to her beloved Tuscany honourably meant saying she was sorry for the pain and humiliation she had caused Vittorio when she rejected him for John. Still unmarried, Vittorio had remained loyal throughout the years. He was the tenant farmer working the land that kept the Villa Montecatini going for the Forresters, having inherited the job after his father's demise.

Alone in Oxford in a rather shabby bed-sit Eliza was unable to settle. She had drifted too far away from herself. But she did accomplish one thing: she came to realise she had spent more years of her life than not serving husbands and trying to serve her children. They had been years without thought for her own desires and needs, years of lost youth and dreams. Effie, Constanza, Dendra and Clara, all married now with families of their own, remained supportive of her, understanding and sympathetic towards their sister in spite of their being, except for Clara, geographically apart. Dulcima, living with Clara and her husband at Little Barrington since Julian's death several years before, remained close to Eliza, seeing her more often than the others. It was Clara who pointed out to Robert that of all the Forrester girls Eliza had always been more of a European than an Englishwoman, mentally and emotionally. Abroad suited Eliza, and it was Clara who influenced Robert to do something to help her find herself in another country, away from her Englishness and her past failures.

As chance would have it, it was only a few days later that Robert was approached by an old friend and colleague for help. Doctor Cousins recruited doctors to give some of their time gratis to work in third-world countries where his small organisation established hospitals and clinics. Doctor Cousins was in England looking to hire someone to run a provincial hospital being established on the banks of the Nile in Upper Egypt. That person had to be someone who was quick to learn languages and could speak Italian, because it was an Italian and Egyptian collaboration being funded from Rome.

While they were looking for someone efficient, even more important was the need to have someone who could relate to people: mostly poor, uneducated, wary of hospitals and doctors, modern medicine, modern anything. A woman, the right woman, could achieve something worthwhile by serving a large community of remote villages that thrived, at considerable distances from one another, along the banks of the Nile between Luxor and Aswan and from the river inland among the stony hills and desert. These were impoverished people from a remote part of Egypt who had to be won over to a better health care system.

Robert knew instinctively that this was the job, the place, for Eliza at this time of her life. Doctor Cousins could hardly believe his luck once he met Eliza. That she was fluent in Italian was such a bonus since most of the supply system and administrational red tape were dealt with in Italian; that she had studied law and had been a Justice of the Peace indicated to Doctor Cousins that she would know how to settle the endless squabbles between the Italian and Egyptian authorities. The patients would see in her a woman who would not take sides against them. Forty-eight hours after Eliza met Doctor Cousins, at the age of thirty-seven, with two broken marriages and three children left behind, she was gone from England.

* * *

Eliza wanted to feel that surge of excitement that a new life, travel, strange people and their customs, can bring. She sensed it was all there somewhere beneath the surface of her life but she was too worn out from failure, the mechanics of survival and a just-adequate love, to feel it. But if excitement didn't happen on that flight something else did. As soon as the wheels of the Boeing 747 left the Tarmac at Heathrow and they surged at a steep angle up into the sky, Eliza experienced a fluttering sensation in the pit of her stomach and felt her heart race. Beads of perspiration appeared on her upper lip. Then, as suddenly as those sensations had appeared, they vanished. She wiped her upper lip with her fingers and sighed with relief as she sensed her past begin to drop away: the husbands, bad marriages, children, life in the Cotswolds and London.

By the time the cabin speaker announced the white cliffs of Dover could be seen through the windows of her side of the plane, Eliza had gathered sufficient strength to smile and wave farewell as the chalky cliffs receded to no more than a slim line of white slashing the blue sky and the sea.

Several hours and a bottle of champagne later, the heat of Egypt and a hot wind blowing in from the Western desert wrapped themselves around Eliza as she walked down the steps from the plane into the chaos of Cairo airport. It was difficult to work out whether it was the heat and dust, the sights and sounds, or the sheer volume and vibrancy of the people that triggered in her something that made the past recede and become no more than history leaving her feeling young and fresh, ready to experience everything Egypt had to offer. As if from the depths of her soul that surge of excitement and adventure she had yearned to feel when she had been in flight surfaced, and a longlost Eliza, from before husbands and children, domesticity and lost-self esteem, was reborn. She was filled with enthusiasm, amused by her fellow passengers complaining of the heat and dirt and disorder on the Tarmac before they even entered the terminal. Unlike them Eliza embraced the mayhem and immediately became a part of it. She felt as if she had come home from a very long and boring journey.

She was to have been met by a representative from the Italian Embassy but no one claimed her. She had travelled light, with one large piece of luggage, and sat on that outside the terminal surrounded by people laden with all sorts of bundles and suitcases, pushing past her to enter or leave. There she waited at what should have been a taxi rank but was instead a jumbled traffic jam of cars and taxis. The travellers and luggage carriers dashing between cars, to deposit baggage in car boots, on roof racks or shove it into the automobiles, appeared to be taking it all in their stride. The din of honking horns, shouting, and policemen's whistles, the clouds of exhaust pumped from creaking pipes, was pure theatre of the absurd but deliciously Egyptian, an introduction to the Cairo to come.

Two hours later, having tried several times to catch an empty taxi without success, Eliza was still sitting on her luggage, resigned to waiting to be claimed. Eventually she was, when the embassy's car arrived, Italian flags flying from stainless steel poles mounted on the well-polished fenders. The embassy representative, a man a few years younger than herself, dressed impeccably in a white linen suit, emerged from the fifteen-year-old Rolls-Royce and rushed into the terminal, obviously in search of someone. Eliza guessed she was that someone and so, after handing her suitcase to the chauffeur, she followed him.

After profuse apologies, not for being late but because he had not recognised her, they settled in the rear of the car. Eliza was amused at how many times she had to tell the young aide that, yes, she was Eliza Flemming, and yes, she was going to run the Nile Hospital and Clinic. They spoke in Italian as if they were great friends and he beamed with pleasure at the idea of being the one to present her at dinner at the embassy that evening, because as he explained, 'You are not what we expected.'

Eliza bathed and changed into the one long evening dress she had brought with her for just such an occasion as an elegant dinner at some foreign embassy, which Doctor Cousins had explained she must at times take the opportunity to attend in the cause of good public relations. She left her Nile Hilton room for the lobby. There waiting for her was the same young man, Mario Derotti. All the way to the embassy he beamed at and flirted with Eliza. She was charmed, amused, and not at all interested, although for the first time in many years she felt stirrings of desire such as she had known with Vittorio and John and it felt good.

Eliza had had a good sex life with Robert, better than good, but the wild passion she had experienced with Vittorio and John, the obsessive yearning to vanish into sexual oblivion, had never been there. She had given up those things for kindness, a good heart, admiration and love from a man who did not know what it was to be cruel to her, did nothing to denigrate her as John had done. Robert had seduced her with friendship, not sex, and they had both made the mistake of believing it had been love, could eventually be passion.

Mario placed a caressing hand on her knee and gazed into her eyes. His voice had dropped to a sensual whisper. She gazed back into the young man's eyes and found it hard to believe that she had only had three men in her life. Mario was tempting. Effie's words to Eliza, backed up by Constanza and Clara when they had seen her off at Heathrow, came to mind. 'Eliza, I think you did it in reverse – the marriages and babies before you had your fling. Now's the time to have your men.'

'We mean it, Eliza, you've had marriage, had your children. It's a case of been there, done that. Now go for sex and romance without the strings,' advised Constanza.

'At least for a while. But, darling, don't, I beg you, this time round mix them up with love.'

A smile crossed Eliza's lips and Mario took that as a sign of interest. 'I never expected anything like you,' he told her, awe in his voice as he raised her hand and lowered his head to kiss her fingers.

'What did you expect, Mario?'

'Middle-aged, unattractive, bulky and dressed from Oxfam. A worthy woman, a do-gooder not so interested in men as she might be in women, although that can be interesting to watch.'

'Mario!'

'Have I shocked you, Mrs Flemming?' he asked, a twinkle in his eyes, obviously delighted with himself.

'No, but you are hardly being discreet, giving yourself away as to what a liberal sensualist you are with someone you've only known for a few hours.'

'I can't help it, you're a very foxy lady.'

Eliza playfully slapped the hand that was holding hers and told him, 'Forget it, Mario. As attractive as you are, it's not going to happen.'

'I had to try, you understand?'

'Of course, it's the nature of the Italian man,' she answered, and knowing smiles appeared on their faces before Mario hunched his shoulders and looked for a moment just a little sad.

They were inching along in the evening traffic on the Sharia El Nil and it was fun for Eliza to be flirting with this young man. She liked him, his Italian charm and flattery. He seemed to fit in perfectly, this 'wanting to be decadent' young foreign diplomat in residence, with the heat and the pungent smells: garlic and jasmine, desert heat, dust and carbon monoxide. The black sky was studded with a myriad of stars and besides a bright white crescent moon, yellow lamplight hissed from Kerosene lanterns, highlighting exotic fruits, tired-looking vegetables on the flat carts parked on the Nile side of the road, and the river flowing darkly, ridden lazily by lateen sails in the soft warm breeze that looked like winged creatures from another age.

The Italian Embassy was exactly what Eliza had expected: a marvellous, extremely elegant, stone and marble mansion designed by a French architect at the turn of the century. It was surrounded by high walls and had a handsome iron gate and beautiful gardens overlooking the Nile. The Ambassador was charming, his wife as elegant and chic as only Roman aristocrats can be. The other dinner guests, of which there were twenty-seven, were a dazzling array: the women all without exception beauties and dressed in the best French and Italian couture, jewelled and groomed to grace soirées such as the dinner Eliza was attending. They flirted discreetly, the Greta Garbos of the Nile. Eliza thought she looked extremely English with her blonde hair done in a French twist at the nape of her neck, her fair skin, and smart lipstick red crêpe-de-chine evening dress that looked little more than a long underslip cut on the bias with garnet straps over her shoulders and no jewellery. A Versace left over from her social life with Robert.

The look of surprise on the other guests' faces made Eliza believe that they had been warned of having to dine with a frump of an administrator on her way to organise a hospital in Upper Egypt. Mario looked like the cat who had swallowed the canary, he was so pleased with the surprise he had given them.

Aside from being dazzlingly good-looking and well turned out as a group, they were a fascinating collection of people: French, Italian, Swedish, Egptian, a Saudi Prince, and a former American Secretary of State. Eliza was a new face in a small but elite social set, who adored welcoming any interesting stranger, especially if they were attractive, into their midst. The women were just as charming as the men to Eliza, and once they learned of her Italian-English lineage and the estates in Tuscany and the Cotswolds, as being her background, London her city, that she spoke both Italian and French as fluently as she did English, that she adored horses, they embraced her as if she was already a part of their circle, thinking her an adventurous spirit for taking on a job in such a remote place.

It was with a happy heart that she left the embassy with several of the guests, who took her on to another party on a house boat on the Nile. Not only had she had a good time, she had managed to impress several of the guests with her reasons for giving up the good life she'd been living in favour of one of isolation and hard work. Few would forget the way the attractive, sensuous and still young at heart Eliza Flemming had told them, 'I needed a job and to create a life of my own, just for *me*.'

Few listening had missed the pathos in her voice, the real hurt in her eyes. Several of the women had been there too, had wanted to do as she was doing, and were aware that they had not had the courage of Eliza Flemming, that touch of English eccentricity needed to do as she was doing nor the will to conquer a strange country as well as find a new and better life. They offered admiration and friendship as well as the calling cards they gave her, telling her to call on them if she was in need of help. The Ambassador looked pleased with her and whispered, 'Well done.'

The incessant ringing of a telephone brought Eliza out of a deep and dreamless sleep. 'Mrs Flemming, are you ready? The earlier the start, the easier the ride.'

'No, I am not ready. And who are you? And ride to where?'

'My name is Antonio Rinaldi. I am the doctor in charge of the Nile Hospital and Clinic. I'll explain everything once we're on our way. I'll pay your bill and check you out to save time.'

'Coffee?'

'OK, I'll get someone to organise that. How long?'

'Twenty minutes,' Eliza told him.

'Faster if you can. I hate begging favours and I had to, to get us a flight,' he told her, his voice already fading as if he were about to put down the telephone.

She was quick. 'Stop! Don't hang up. How will I know you?'

'Oh! You're quite right. Six foot two inches, slim, wearing bone-coloured linen trousers, white shirt, a tan linen jacket. You won't miss me, I'll be waiting at the bank of lifts in the lobby.'

When Eliza stepped out of the lift she saw a man with the looks of a mature cinema star talking to an Egyptian while casually leaning against a column, his eyes on every person leaving the lifts. Eliza was quite taken aback by how very attractive she found him. It was a purely physical attraction as she felt that sense of sensual desire for a man other than a husband which had laid dormant in her for so many years suddenly rekindle. It was such a good feeling, like an old friend come home, it made her smile. She was thoroughly enjoying getting in touch with herself again.

Eliza was amused when she saw Dr Rinaldi straighten up and take several steps towards an aggressive-looking, somewhat sour-faced woman in her fifties dressed in something from a catalogue of safari wear. A look of relief crossed his face as the woman took one glance at him and passed him by. Eliza, who was quite used to admiring gazes, received one from the doctor but he made no move towards her.

Feeling much too tired from travelling, partying and the excitement of being in Egypt, she had no inclination to play games with her employer. She went directly to him and the man standing with him, and introduced herself.

'Well, you're certainly not what I expected,' he told her as he shook her hand.

'Do you know, that's all I've heard since I stepped off the plane. It's getting to be a bit much.'

Doctor Rinaldi began to laugh and slipped his arm through hers. 'Well, buck up, you may have to hear it at least one more time when my friend Anwar Whabi, who is flying us to Asyut so as to cut our driving time to the clinic, sees you. This is Ahmed, his Man Friday, whom he always lends me as a Mr Fixit when I come down to Cairo. Ahmed arranged for the clinic's new Range Rover to be loaded with medical supplies and driven away last night to meet us in Asyut, and he has breakfast waiting for you in the car. Your first time in Egypt?'

'Yes.'

'Egyptians are the sweetest of all the Arabs except for a few extremist fundamentalists.'

The traffic was sparse before six o'clock in the morning but the drive was terrifying for the speed at which Doctor Rinaldi streaked through the city in Anwar Whabi's Jaguar, while in the back seat Ahmed served Eliza her breakfast spread out on a white napkin placed between them: croissants; hot coffee from a Thermos, strong, black and sweet; a mushroom omelette, no longer hot, rolled into a sausage shape which Ahmed served as finger-food, partially wrapped in a white paper napkin.

'How did you do this, Ahmed?' she asked with a smile of delight because in fact she was quite hungry as well as needing a shot of caffeine to get her going.

'Quite easy. The Nile Hilton coffee shop.'

Eliza had trouble steadying her cup, trying to see everything flying past the window, and adjusting to the heat which was already, at 5.45 in the morning, something to deal with if you had just arrived from an English summer where seventy degrees Fahrenheit and a three-day stretch of sunshine are the most that can be expected. Eliza whispered to Ahmed, 'Does he always drive like this?'

'Always. Doctor Rinaldi was a rally driver in Italy,' Ahmed whispered back.

'Are you registering a complaint against my driving, Mrs Flemming? I can assure you, you are as safe as can be. I didn't bring you all the way to Egypt to kill you.'

'You are fast and incredibly skilled but your driving is not conducive to eating breakfast.'

He laughed and admitted, 'No, I suppose not.' But he failed to slow the car. He liked her for not backing down when he put her on the spot. Instead he placed his foot down harder on the accelerator and asked, 'What hospital were you with when Cousins head hunted you?'

At that moment a line of flat carts being pulled by donkeys began crossing the intersection the Jaguar was approaching. Doctor Rinaldi gave warning to Eliza to watch her coffee cup – he was about to make a rather abrupt stop to let the traffic pass. When they were stationary he turned in his seat to face her. 'Well?'

'I was never head hunted,' she confessed.

'And you have never worked in a hospital?'

'No.'

'Then how, pray God, do you come to be here?'

'Because I was all that Doctor Cousins could get,' was the answer she gave while trying to ignore the anger and disappointment in his voice. The look of disdain in his eyes was much too evident.

'I knew when you introduced yourself you were too good to be true,' he told her.

Eliza took a long sip of her coffee, and bit into the rolled omelette she was holding in her hand. She ate with Antonio Rinaldi still glaring at her, took another sip of coffee, and having decided that she was going to start off as she meant to go on in this job and with the man she would be working directly under, told him, 'Doctor Rinaldi, I have been married to two doctors, one of them with a penchant for keeping me cut down to size. That is, the size he preferred me to be. As we are going to be working together, I suggest you do not make the same mistake my first husband did. I don't intend to stand for that from you or any man again, not in my working *or* my personal life. You've got me, now bloody well work *with* me and not against me. I've had a life-time of prima donna doctors.'

All was silent except for the sound of donkey bells and the clip-clop of their hoofs on the Tarmac as the last of the line of carts passed in front of the car. It was Antonio Rinaldi who broke the silence. 'I could do with a sip of that coffee and a bite of that omelette, maybe even share your croissant?'

They didn't smile at each other or say anything more. For a very few minutes while the intersection cleared they shared the food and became aware that they liked each other and would work well together.

A relationship had begun and they were enthusiastic about working together. Antonio turned in his seat to take the wheel again and they sped on towards their rendezvous.

EGYPT

Chapter 7

It was one of those carnal attractions that can happen at first sight. This had not happened for Eliza for many long years and now that it had it was like no other attraction she had ever felt for a man before. She was at a stage in her life where she had a history of experience behind her, had been through love and commitment; she needed no man to direct her feelings, and indeed knew to the marrow of her bones that no man would ever again take advantage of them. She was free, mistress of her own destiny.

Mario Derotti's flirtation had amused and flattered her, caught her interest in the erotic and sex for its own sake alone. The decided undercurrent of sex being lived on many different levels and always to the full: in secret, with intrigue; the more than possible illicit affairs hanging like a seductive perfume in the atmosphere of the embassy dinner party, had whetted Eliza's carnal appetite. On first seeing Antonio Rinaldi what had stirred her desire had been the aura of sexuality about the handsome doctor. Her imagination had for a moment taken flight. How delicious to be riven by such a man, how sublime to come in strong and frequent orgasms with Antonio Rinaldi. Eliza relegated such thoughts to the back of her mind so that she might forge a different kind of relationship with the man she would be working with. But with Anwar Whabi, Eliza concealed nothing.

That first gaze into each other's eyes inspired a mutual understanding, lust, a carnal togetherness. It was inevitable, it would be sublime, and no other emotion would come into it for them: not love, nor greed, not even fidelity. For them it would begin and end in freedom and sexual bliss.

The Jaguar arrived at the small private air strip, cutting through fields green with vegetation running parallel to the Nile. Eliza's first sight of Anwar Whabi was when Antonio drove to within a few feet of the six-seater Gulf Stream and screeched to a halt. Anwar Whabi nonchalantly lowered a newspaper from in front of his face and rose from a wicker chair placed under the plane's wing to keep him out of the sun.

Eliza was stunned by the physical beauty and elegance of his face. How sensual he was, and yes, there was something incredibly decadent about him: the tall and slender body, and the way it moved – slowly, like a sleek panther. He was a lovely colour: like cognac with the sun shining through it, his skin as smooth as silk. And then his gaze when Eliza had alighted from the car: eyes like dark sensuous pools, emitting looks that could liquefy a lady's soul and most certainly her heart. His nose was straight, and reminiscent, as were the sensuous lips, of ancient wall paintings. Anwar Whabi had a princely bearing.

He wore a pair of old jeans with a wide leather belt whose impressive buckle was wrought in gold and silver. He wore it like a miniature sculpture, which indeed it was, having been made for his father by Pablo Picasso and passed down to Anwar. Eliza thought that she had never seen a finer, more sexy-looking white cotton shirt. Long sleeved and rolled up to just below his elbows, it was collarless and he wore it with several of the small mother of pearl buttons undone.

When introduced, he kissed her hand. She felt as if his lips, warm and soft, were burning her flesh. She sensed herself melting from the heat of his sensuality. When Eliza was able to look away from him, a stolen glance in Antonio Rinaldi's direction revealed that he had missed nothing of that first look that passed between his friend and his new colleague. Eliza felt some embarrassment that she should have allowed her erotic side to show in public.

Anwar spoke English with a British accent, having spent five years studying at Oxford. He spoke flawless French thanks to nannies and tutors. His Italian he had learned while living with an Italian actress in Rome. All that had been teasingly revealed by Antonio Rinaldi before the three of them even boarded the plane.

Eliza's first words to Anwar were, 'Please don't say I'm not what you expected.'

'How about, what a pleasant surprise?' he asked, a smile on his lips.

'That will do. In fact, it's quite enough,' the doctor answered for Eliza, and then continued, 'I know you, Anwar. You are not to sweep Mrs Flemming off her feet and into that decadent and delicious life you like to lead. I don't want to lose her before I even get her to the hospital.'

'Whatever the distraction, Doctor Rinaldi, I don't

intend for you to lose me,' she declared rather provocatively.

Antonio Rinaldi and Anwar Whabi all but raised their eyebrows in surprise at the boldness of that little remark, and the not-too-subtle intimation that Eliza expected at some time or another to have an affair with Antonio but not one that would make an impact on her working life. It made the doctor take a closer look at Eliza and ponder for the first time on what sort of woman he would be working with. At last he acknowledged her as more than a workmate when he told her, 'I think I would prefer to call you something other than Mrs Flemming, and when were off duty – well, you must call me Antonio.'

He was the first to board the plane. He stowed Eliza's luggage safely, then strapped himself into his seat. For a few minutes more Anwar and Eliza remained on the grass runway, studying each other with slow deliberation. Anwar's delight showed openly on his face. But we are talking here about a master seducer whose greatest pleasure was the chase. To encite her to lust, lead her into an erotic world where she had hitherto never been, was his aim. An extra bonus for Anwar was a willing woman, one who was looking for adventurous sex and was great fun to play with. Once more he raised Eliza's hand and gallantly kissed it, then caressed her cheek with the back of his hand. He liked the way she trembled under his touch, the way she blushed with anticipation for what they both knew was sure to happen for them in another place, at another time. He boarded first and offered a helping hand to her so as to pull her into the plane after him.

Anwar flew them low over the Nile, following the river all the way to Asyut. Antonio closed his eyes and was fast asleep almost immediately. Not so Eliza. She was enchanted by the glorious Nile with its wide band of green vegetation to either side, spreading out into the desert. The further behind they left Cairo, the more beautiful was the countryside. Feluccas, their white sails catching the soft warm wind, sailed slowly, appearing almost to be standing still. It was as if time too was standing still and schedules were non-existent. Men in white robes and turbans, their women draped from head to toe in billowing black muslin, walked along the banks, their many children skipping along behind them. The occasional traveller rode a donkey. Women carrying metal or clay water pots or massive bundles of green grass on their heads waddled provocatively rather than walked. There was no rush, no fuss. Egypt was a place with all the time in the world where everything was according to God's will: *Inshallah*. Adults and children alike waved and shouted greetings to the plane and its passengers, clapping their hands with delight. Some shaded their eyes from the sun, gold bangles sparkling on the women's wrists. Anwar dipped his wings towards them sometimes, to one side and then to the other.

They followed the Nile for over two hundred miles into Upper Egypt and after they had landed in Asyut and Eliza and Antonio had thanked Anwar for the ride, they climb into the Range Rover, which was loaded to the roof inside and piled high on the roof rack outside with medical supplies. Only when they had been on the road for half an hour did Eliza realise how luxurious it had been to travel thus far by plane.

The ride from Asyut to Luxor was hot, dusty and bumpy, with Antonio driving at top speed, swerving in and out to pass anything on the road in front of him. Eliza sat uncomfortably squashed between cartons, her knees practically up to her chin thanks to having her feet resting on a crate containing a supply of morphine ampoules. It was more than three hundred miles to Luxor and by the time they were a third of the way she was dizzy with the heat and the dust, incredibly queasy from the rough and tumble of the ride, dehydrated, and terribly dozy. She would fall into short but deep dreamless sleeps, only to wake up feeling completely disorientated.

Eliza felt herself coming alive again, being pulled up out of the depths of one of those sleeps. Incredibly they were not moving but were parked on a narrow dirt road facing the river. The heat was beating down on the Range Rover, perspiration running in rivulets down Eliza's body. She heard voices approaching, and laughter, and tried to wake herself out of a strange and disconcerting torpor, but her body seemed unable to move. She felt as limp as the old Raggedy Ann doll she used to play with as a child back at home in Little Barrington.

Antonio appeared at the open window next to her, looking fresh and cool. Several country women smothered in black, faces half hidden and eyes black and laughing, hovered around him. He opened the door, and after removing a carton from her lap, scooped her up in his arms. 'You'll feel much better after this,' he told her, to the sound of the accompanying ladies twittering like a small flock of birds.

Before Eliza even realised what was happening, she

was on her feet and shocked into wakefulness by the first huge pot of cool water that had been emptied over her head by Antonio, who jumped back so as not to get splashed. The women took over bathing her while he watched Eliza come alive. He was clearly enjoying the sight of her nakedness showing through the clinging wet cotton. She could not understand the comments in Arabic directed to him but she did sense that they were teasing him about her and decided she couldn't care less. All she could think about was how deliciously cool she was feeling, how she seemed to be able to breathe again, be her own self. She danced around, and laughed with the joy of a child, enchanting everyone. When the water had stopped flowing, she smoothed down her hair with the palms of her hands.

Antonio went to her and presented her with what she recognised as one of her own cotton shift dresses. 'I took the liberty of opening your case and fetching something fresh for you to wear. You were in such a deep sleep, and I didn't want to waste time.'

He was not a man to complicate his life willingly but he forgot his scruples when he reached out to undo several of the bone buttons of her dress, so enchanted was he by the voluptuous sight of her full rounded breasts and erect nipples showing through the wet material which clung to her like a second skin. He was saved from his carnal feelings for her by a small boy in a tattered but clean robe who was pulling at his trouser leg, asking Antonio to return to his family's mud hut. The boy's father was calling for him. Antonio tossed the dress to one of the waiting women and instructed them to dry Eliza off and help her change. Then, turning back to Eliza, he told her,

'These are some of the clinic's patients – the sort of people you will be making contact with all the time. Let them help to dress you, they long to see your body. Your acceptance of them and their help will create a bond of sorts with them. They will be less intimidated by you, or by the nurses and doctors seeing theirs. They'll feel as if they are doing something for you. You don't, of course, have to, it's not part of the job, but it would be good public relations.'

'Antonio!'

'I'll be back in a few minutes and we'll have some lunch. Nothing special, nothing to linger over. We have still a long way to go.'

He was pleasant but matter-of-fact, obviously covering up for that moment when she had felt his long slender fingers working the buttons of her dress and a lascivious look had come into his eyes. Eliza had wanted to say something to reassure him that she liked what she was seeing in his eyes. She had wanted to indicate to him in some way that she found him an exciting and thrilling man, but the moment had passed, her chance was gone. He snatched it away from her and she could understand why.

It was a very peculiar experience, standing in high grass on the banks of the Nile, stark naked in the sun, while a flock of women cosseted her with their attention: drying her off with rough towelling none too gently, wringing out her long blonde hair and arranging it. Several of the women touched her breasts and bottom, not provocatively but curiously, making remarks of admiration. They teased her with their eyes and hand gestures and nodded in Antonio's direction. Eliza jumped back when one of the women boldly touched her very blonde triangle of pubic hair. They all twittered and lowered their eyes, behaving like children caught in a naughty act. Eliza understood nothing but got the message – they were match making. They slipped her fresh dress over her head and did up the buttons. Eliza had the most disconcerting feeling that they were playing with her as if she were a live Barbie doll. A scarf was produced: black with a row of tiny glass beads thickly sewn along the edges. It was wound around her head and tied in a turban. The women clucked their approval and looked very pleased with themselves as they walked her to the Range Rover's side mirror. She did look rather fetching, she had to admit.

The scarf was a gift. It took her some time to realise how insulting it would be for her not to accept it. Finally she felt the generosity and the sweetness of these women and was appalled at her own behaviour, so very English, embarrassed at receiving such open generosity that she knew they could ill afford. From her purse she took a pretty hand mirror, a pair of tortoiseshell combs, a lipstick, a white linen handkerchief edged in lace, and passed them out among the first of the many friends she was to make in Upper Egypt. They were kissing her hand in thanks, placing hands over hearts, their way of saying thank you.

Antonio went to her, slipped his arm through hers and told Eliza, 'You've enchanted them. They'll spread the news that the new administrator at the hospital is something special, someone to know and listen to. Then they'll brag that they have seen your pussy. Now, come and have some lunch.'

There were purple figs and slices of Parma ham and

crusty bread, a bottle of cool wine which Antonio fished from the river where he'd had it cooling on the end of a very long piece of heavy cord. They had their meal under a lean-to of palm leaves facing the river. 'I raided the Italian Embassy's stores while you were partying,' he told her, a smile on his lips.

'Antonio, I don't intend to let you down,' she told him, apropos of nothing.

'It's a hard and thrilling life doing the work we do here, Eliza. Just do the best you can, that's the way we all approach it. Make the best personal life you can for yourself. Everyone does that too. Nobody makes judgements, least of all me. But I am a hard task master, and not always the most diplomatic of people, I don't ask forgiveness for that, only understanding. It's the way to get the job done.

'The hospital and clinic are in two separate buildings but close together, connected by a roofed terrace which overlooks the river. There's a landing dock for our ferry boat and those patients who arrive at the hospital by boat from villages up or down river. You will have a small bungalow for yourself very near mine. They're a short distance from the hospital but do give a modicum of privacy. The place is very badly run for many reasons: poor administration, the nature of the people and the staff. It isn't so much that we need rigid order imposed but we need a structure, some sort of order to replace chaos. That may sound strange but once you get there you will understand. I am sometimes away for days on end when I'm making my house calls or doing my monthly visiting clinic route, travelling considerable distances. Once you're settled in, if your schedule allows, I'll take you with me. It's a great way to meet the people and see the country. I hope you can see by now that this job is going to be pretty much what you make of it.'

Eliza listened and understood that the attraction that Antonio Rinaldi and she felt for one another was going to be what she made of that too, which suited her just fine. He was not putting his cards on the table vis à vis that attraction but had cleverly skirted the issue by talking work. Not good enough, old boy, and I'm having none of that, she told herself.

'Those women were romantics, thinking the doctor and his new administrator are going to fall in love. They are wrong, Antonio. The new administrator is not looking for love. Romance, erotic idylls, yes. For the excitement and pleasure, the adventure of great sex – if the right man were to appear on the scene. But not even affairs of the heart, and affection, glorious erotic mating, would be able to keep her tied into a relationship. The new administrator wants her sexual freedom, to live that sort of life she chooses. I like to begin the way I intend to go on. Now, how does that sit with *you*, Antonio?'

There was a passionate look in his eyes, a smile of delight on his lips. He raised her hand and lowered his head to place a kiss upon it. He toyed with the beads on her turban, and then undoing several of the buttons on her dress, exposed her naked breasts. He looked at them for several seconds before he caressed them, lowered his lips to their nipples and sucked, not hungrily but lightly, sweetly, until Eliza came with the merest shudder and sigh, a faint moan of delight. He closed the buttons and brushed the side of her face with the back of his hand. 'I have the distinct feeling I will have to share you with Anwar, he made that clear to me when we said goodbye in Asyut. Is that true, would you like that?'

'Yes, if the attraction is still there, the time and place right, and it doesn't interfere with my work. Does that shock you?' she asked.

'I have shared other women with him before.'

'That isn't what I asked you, Antonio.'

'No, it doesn't shock me, it surprises me. It also intrigues me, excites my lust. The luxury of the erotic and sexual bliss with no strings attached is thrilling. Will it be an adventure for us – who knows? Time and passion govern the answer.'

With that he rose from the ground, and taking Eliza's hands in his, pulled her up and into his arms. He held her close and caressed her body through her dress. His sex was swollen and strained against his trousers. Eliza closed her eyes and savoured the feel of him pressed against her. He released her to place an arm around her shoulders and together they walked back to the Range Rover. 'We have far to go, you and I.' A smile crossed his lips and he laughed. 'I think I've just made a double entendre.'

It was a long and very hot drive to Luxor where they stopped to fill the tank with petrol and drink tiny glasses of hot, very sweet mint tea. Feeling somewhat revived, they pushed on, skirting the city and its temples. The heat and the motion of the Range Rover did their work, Eliza once again slipping in and out of sleep which she found very annoying because she did not want to miss seeing anything en route. She had fallen hopelessly in love with Egypt from the moment she looked down at the Nile from the Gulf Stream's window, and felt a passion for the place she had only felt for one other before: her beloved Tuscany.

She was nudged awake by Antonio. 'I think we must open another bottle of water, Eliza.'

He took a long drink from the bottle, and after handing it to her, surprised Eliza by beginning to speak about himself. 'I'm forty-five years old, married to a beautiful but selfish and too self-centred woman who is the mother of my four children. She lives in Florence with them where we have a house and I have a very large and prosperous practice. I spend ten months of the year here and two working in my practice. Originally I came here for a month but have been seduced by Egypt and the work that has to be done. I will not abandon this project and return for good to Italy until I am sure that we have it up and running, with the right doctors and staff to continue our work. When that is achieved, I will resume coming here for a month's work every year. I have been giving that speech now for the last five years.'

'Tell me more,' she said, placing a hand on his thigh. He took his eyes from the road to glance at it.

'That's a very dangerous act, Eliza.'

She removed her hand as fast as if she'd been burned. Antonio laughed and took her hand in his and placed it over his mouth to kiss it, without even taking his eyes off the road. Then he told her, 'How does one admit to being highly sexed without frightening you off? I don't want to. I would rather excite your interest instead. A strong libido, that's how I shall explain myself. Yes, a strong libido that is never quite sated but for the most part satisfied. The foreign women and the Alexandrines and Cairenes of the upper classes are luscious and seductive creatures. Sexual affairs are easy and never get complicated. They are romantic and intriguing, beguiling even. Not to mention adventurous, deliciously decadent, and always thrillingly erotic. I think it's the heat, the lazy soft sweetness of the way of life that is led here. It eats away at the hypocritical sexual morality of the west.'

It was all flooding back to her: the excitement of sexuality, creating adventurous sexual acts to satisfy fantasies, the sheer bliss of great fucking, wallowing in one's own lust and a lover's. Eliza had not until now realised just how much of herself she had given up for kindness, love based on friendship and affection. She was ready, so very ready, to express her own sexuality, to share it with a man such as Antonio who was being ruthlessly honest about himself and how he wanted her. And Anwar? Would he come to visit her, sweep her into an erotic affair that she suspected would be sublime? Eliza felt so young and fresh, reborn even, now that she could begin again to enjoy men, enter new worlds of sexual ecstasy.

'You're very quiet. Surely I'm not shocking or surprising you?' asked Antonio.

'Not in the least. I'm just a little distracted at the prospect of pleasure unbound.'

At El Ridisiya Bahari, a small town on the east bank of the Nile, Antonio stopped to see the local doctor and drop off a box of vaccine. They were delayed while he made two house calls and used the telephone, then they were once more on their way. Eliza was by now dazzled by the mystique of Ancient Egypt, having caught her first glimpse of the Temple of Idfu off in the distance on the other side of the river. Several miles from there they stopped at the ancient site of Gebel Serag and Eliza was, as so many others had been throughout the centuries, seduced by the Egypt of ancient times. She was astounded at the power it cast over her. She had a fleeting vision of the life she imagined was going to unfold for her here in this new and strange world: one of hard work and passion for life amidst the mysteries of the dead that seemed to linger in the very air one breathed, the silence and beauty of the desert. Eliza sensed she was catching up with a life that had run away from her. She was expecting much from this second chance.

Of course, she said none of this to Antonio. When she turned to join him he was squatting on his haunches, looking out across the Nile and smoking a large Havana cigar. There was something in the look on his face . . . it was not unlike the way she was feeling and she knew that he too had found his second chance in Egypt. They were kindred spirits.

The heat, which was still intense, quite suddenly became her friend because Eliza was giving in to it rather than fighting it. They crossed the Nile a few miles from the ancient site on an old wooden ferry boat that had been awaiting their arrival. The vessel had had cosmetic surgery to spruce it up and to accommodate two cars: today it carried only one, the overloaded Range Rover. There were several dozen people on board: poor men dressed in robes and turbans, some not looking at all well; the women in their black muslin, with no more of their face showing than their dark and exotic eyes, underlined with kohl, appeared sultry and sensuous.

Eliza stood aside as people came to greet Antonio: another doctor and two Egyptian nurses in starched white; two others in white traditional dress with heads covered; several people who had come long distances from their villages and seemed to know him and treat him as if he were a god. There was a great deal of bowing and kissing of his hands. He looked not at all embarrassed, taking it in his stride. There were several stretcher cases, all men, and a small boy who looked very ill indeed. Suddenly the glamour and beauty of Egypt, her own self-centred sexual preoccupations, seemed to assume their real proportion in the new order of Eliza's life. She suffered a momentary fear as to her own inadequacy. It passed, never to return again.

There was a kind of mad confusion on board as the ferry boat pushed off to cross the river. Eliza, who had been forgotten, watched and listened. It was all as Antonio had described it, more or less everyone doing their own thing and hoping for the best. One of the nurses was having a contretemps with several patients going to the clinic. Eliza realised that though the boat belonged to the Nile Hospital and Clinic, it was carrying people on board who were blatantly using it to cadge a ride across the river. A donkey, several chickens and a duck, a goat and some huge cartons tied with rope, gave the game away. She saw Antonio fly into a rage at one of the nurses because she could not get people to settle. Eliza went not to the nurse but a screeching old woman, smothered in black, smelling of rancid butter and garlic. She was shabby and dirty and out of control, the more so for being shoved around by one of the nurses who had at first told her the boat was full. Eliza went to the old woman and took her hand, stroking it. The woman tried to pull away several times but Eliza did not relinguish the hand. Then she stroked the woman's head and her cheek and she grew calmer. Tears rolled down her wrinkled face and Eliza took the scarf off her own head and wiped the woman's tears away, all the time talking to her, calming her with words the woman could not possibly understand while she led her to a bench. One look from her to the men sitting on it was sufficient for them reluctantly to make room for the old woman and Eliza.

Eliza called the nurse over and was much relieved that she not only understood but spoke English. She told her, 'I'm the new administrator and I never want to hear you shout at anyone ever again. You and I will have to find a better way so as not to upset the people here or ourselves.' Then she sat down next to the old woman and told her in sign language that all would be well but there was to be no more hysteria from her either. Then Eliza left her to settle another dispute on board.

As she passed Antonio, he took her by the arm and led her to a quiet spot at the railing of the boat. 'I saw how you calmed that old woman. It was impressive. Like someone who knows how to tame a troublesome horse, I half expected you to blow into her nose.'

Eliza was impressed that Antonio knew that old horse trick, delighted to learn that they had something else in common: a love of horses. That had to be so or surely he would not have recognised she was taming the old woman as she would have a distressed horse.

'It's true, I do know some taming tricks. Horses, and especially spirited ones, have always been in my life since I was a child,' she told him, assuming that he would understand such a passion: the relationship between an Englishwoman and her horse.

He made no further comment about her love of horses but instead told her, 'I liked the way you handled that situation. Look around you. Everyone is settled, impressed by your authority. How did you do that by barely taking action?'

'What I did was instinctive. There was something quite unjust about not taking the old lady on board and giving her a free ride as long as we had the room.'

Antonio smiled down at Eliza, lit the stub of his cigar and gazed silently across the water for several minutes before he left her to vanish among his patients.

The chaos was much the same when they landed on the west bank of the Nile as it had been when they embarked: the same nerve-racking and inadequate suggestions from half a dozen men while another half dozen were giving directions for getting the Range Rover safely off the ferry boat. Eliza had her first view of the hospital and clinic buildings, with a modest distance away several outbuildings. It all looked terribly impressive, more so than she'd imagined, in the hundred-degree heat, a blood red sun slipping lazily down a sky dusky with the coming of night.

Those first few weeks were not easy for Eliza. She endured eighteen-hour working days where no one had time to give her instructions, just tell her their problems. She had but one job description: sort it out, make it work – whatever *it* may be. Her nights were no more than exhausted interludes in the oppressive heat and tremendous humidity. It was 'Doctor Rinaldi' and 'Mrs Flemming' when on duty, and hardly a whisper of friendliness off. There was simply too much going on, too much readjusting to a new work ethic, a new and fascinating culture, for Eliza to deal with anything more personal. And a gruelling schedule of inoculations against polio. There were three doctors in residence and a visiting French surgeon, five trained nurses, dozens of untrained orderlies and other staff who were working for no more than bed and board and a handful of coins, and finally Eliza Flemming, to tend the relentless stream of patients that kept arriving.

The hospital was extraordinarily well equipped and its standard of medical treatment quite remarkable for a population as poor and in need as the one it catered to. The Egyptian doctors who worked at the hospital, and indeed the government itself, conducted a love-hate relationship with the institution: gratitude for the remarkable job being done, coupled with a sense of inadequacy that they could not fund or organise such a unique and successful project on their own. But in the hands of Eliza Flemming things began to ease slowly into a more workable, less hostile situation that kept bearing fruit and producing much-needed help. Every month a new medical specialist would arrive from Paris, London, New York, Rome or Dallas, and word would spread up and down the Nile by way of newspapers and posters and the people's gossip. Reluctant and superstitious patients, unable to afford medical treatment in the larger of their cities, arrived for treatment most often than not traumatised with fear, and in many cases with entire families in tow who camped out close by.

Then, quite suddenly, there appeared to be a pattern of sorts in the midst of the chaos: at last things were getting done, still in a casual manner, but done nevertheless. A kind of hush that was almost ethereal hovered over the Nile Hospital and Clinic. Things were no less busy but they were a great deal less frenetic. Eliza was actually able to sit back of an evening and look at the stars, listen to the silence and take stock of what she had accomplished since her arrival in Egypt. Quite suddenly she liked who she had become just as she had liked the girl she had been when she had run wild in Tuscany with Vittorio so many lifetimes ago.

Previously unused to admiration for her accomplishments, respect for who and what she was, Eliza found it easy to accept those things from her colleagues, and most particularly from Antonio Rinaldi. In the very nearly three months they had been working together a silent bond of affection and respect for one another had developed between them, and with it an undercurrent of sexual attraction that was exciting and put an edge on their relationship. Months of wanting each other in a carnal way, and waiting, had established an understanding between them. Friends and lovers, that was what fate had deemed right for them. Theirs was to be a one-day-at-a-time romantic and sexual idyll until the days would inevitably run out for them. It was as if written in the sands or whispered on the wind.

One midnight Eliza was sitting on the small terrace of her bungalow contemplating the stars. She was dressed in a thin white cotton nightgown with shoestring straps and a wide band of white lace that covered her breasts. Her long blonde hair, freshly washed, shone like silver in the moonlight. She had not heard him approaching so was startled when he spoke: 'Don't be frightened, it's Antonio.'

Eliza made an attempt to rise from the chaise, intending to switch on a light. 'No! The moonlight is bright enough,' he told her, and smiled as he sat down beside her and raised her hand to kiss it.

Eliza reached out to caress his cheek with the back of her hand. 'I don't think I've ever told you how handsome and sensual a man I find you. I do, you know,' she told him now.

'That's good to know. Actually I'm flattered. And look at you! I like you like this, in your nightgown. You look perfect, so delicious, and I'm ravenous.'

Eliza reached out to open the small mother of pearl buttons of his shirt. She and Antonio were gazing into each other's eyes. There was an exchange in that gaze: of sensuality, excitement, a light and delightful sense of rightness about their lustful feelings for each other. An aura of pure pleasure, a profound sense of discovery, the adventure of being sexually alive and at the top of their lives appeared like a night mist to envelop them. Antonio caressed her shoulders and fingered the lovely white lace as he slipped out of his shoes. Eliza, having removed his shirt, was slipping the snakeskin belt from the loops of his linen trousers. Sexual tension was crackling between them like lightning in the sky. They rose from the chaise together, Antonio to remove his trousers, Eliza to raise her nightgown up and over her head and drop it on the marble tiles. Together they lay down on the chaise, on their side, facing each other.

Antonio took her in his arms and held her close as he draped one of her legs over his hip. Eliza's breathing quickened from the sheer excitement of his ardour for her. 'Yes, please, yes,' she told him, very nearly breathless as he parted the soft warm outer lips of her cunt by stroking her yearning cleft with the large and handsome knob of his penis. He found the place where he wanted so very much to enter and in one powerful, but slow and tantalisingly sexy thrust, their sexual life together began.

Antonio deliberately took Eliza for the first time in this jack-knife position because he knew that that way and from behind was how to penetrate her most completely for their greater pleasure. He remained fully rampant and pulsating inside her soft warm cunt. Antonio had mastered the art of fucking and could bring great pleasure to a woman by the ways in which he moved against her cervix, the tremendously sensitive G-spot, and other places within the vagina. He felt her come as her body naturally took over, issuing a deliciously exciting but subtle pelvic motion: small circles and at the same time exquisitely sexy contractions of her own that gripped and released his penis to a beat that was as important to them at that moment as a heartbeat. Antonio was both astounded and seduced by the degree of erotic pleasure he was deriving from her sexuality.

Eliza's nipples were erect and her breasts looked dazzlingly raunchy: their fullness and shape, the large nimbus shining in the moonlight, as did her face, pink with the colour that multiple orgasm can bring to a woman's complexion. Antonio was enjoying so much of Eliza: the feel and warmth of her sex, her passion, watching her wallowing in her sexuality, her obvious lust and love for penis and penetration. He kissed her full on the lips and caressed her breasts and bit into her sensitive nipples, all the while continuing his subtle but sexy fucking. She kept coming, pent-up sexual passion flowing from her like a stream. Eliza was able to let go, to call out in a whisper laced with lust, 'Yes, oh, yes, thank you, thank you,' as tears of release and joy slipped from the corners of her eyes.

Antonio had a great deal of sexual stamina but this first time with Eliza, discovering how well matched they were in their lust and sexual freedom, was for him far more exciting than he had thought it would be. He could hold back no longer and now began to fuck her by entering and withdrawing in powerful but leisurely thrusts so that she might gain the maximum pleasure. By the time he was beating into her at a quickened pace Eliza was lost in orgasm, had slipped into a state of sexual ecstasy. Antonio recognised where she was and took his moment, joining her with a powerful and copious orgasm. Still on their sides and in each other's arms they held tight, Eliza digging her nails into the flesh of Antonio's back.

They remained lying together and dozed off until their heartbeat slowed. Both were aware that here was the beginning of what could be the happiest and most rewarding sexual life they could ever hope to expect. After some time Antonio stroked Eliza's hair and they smiled at one another. 'You are marvellous in your lust, Eliza.'

'I haven't been as I am with you for a very long time, Antonio. It was sublime. You are sublime.'

'You do know love and commitment don't come into this kind of lust we feel for each other? I wouldn't want to deceive you. I want you like this and more of this, to take you on a long and adventurous erotic journey with me, to love you as a friend, feel deep affection for you. But it's the sex, thrilling sex that goes over the edge in its abandon, that excites me the most about us. Can you live with that? Anything else would complicate our lives out here. This has been on my mind since the first day we travelled out here. That's why I haven't come to your bed before this. I had to be sure what I wanted, that I could live up to it, bide by my own rules about us. Now I must know what you want for us?'

'Take me on that erotic journey, Antonio. Let's have each other for the sexual attraction we feel for each other, and the affection and respect. If you and I have those things for as long as it lasts, we will have more than most people have in a lifetime. That'll do for me, if it will for you?'

There was something so genuine and forthright about Eliza's words. It made them aware that they were not fooling themselves about what they wanted to be and not to be to each other. There was a kind of delight, a happiness that showed in their faces, but they spoke no more of it. Instead Antonio's reply to Eliza was to kiss her breasts and to slide over her body and caress it with his before he parted her legs. He placed his face between them and with his lips and tongue teased open her most intimate lips with kisses. He took her moist, warm and satiny labia in his mouth and sucked on them, using a pointed tongue to find and excite her clitoris. He licked what tasted to him the most exquisite of elixirs – their orgasms – until his mouth was alive with the taste of sex and shared that ambrosia with Eliza in a deep and passionate kiss.

She came, once, twice more, and trembled with the sublime pleasure.

She was lost in lust again. Antonio watched her run her fingers through her hair, pull hard on it and gaze at the moon and the stars before he turned her over and arranged her on her knees.

Chapter 8

The years came and went for Eliza but time seemed somehow to be standing still. They were busy and exciting years, fulfilling years, and Eliza felt an ease, a vitality of spirit, that allowed her to live joyously once again. She seemed effervescently beautiful, subtly sensuous, in these, her mature years, strong with a quiet assertiveness that made her afraid of nothing.

It had to do with her work, how she was living, the high self-esteem so hard won, and the closer relationship that had developed between her and her children since her move to Egypt. They had made several trips to holiday with her in Upper Egypt, the Sudan and Ethiopia, had seen her working at the hospital and were amazed that their mother was running it and the clinic practically single-handed when she had never been able to make them a decent cup of cocoa. They were all, children and mother, mature enough to discuss her as the bad parent she had been, and Alexander and Olivia their father's role in separating them from her. The three children grew to accept her as having been too young, too weak, to take them over and make them her own. The pride they took in having her for their mother now could not wipe away her serious faults, they were embedded in their minds and hearts for ever, but they did manage to accept them as such and love her in spite of them.

There was, too, another reason for this joyous life that Eliza was living, which had to do with the *menage à trois* she was a part of with Antonio and Anwar Whabi. A three-way relationship had developed between the two men and Eliza. It had not been forced but rather evolved by the very nature of the people they were, the way they lived, and its being the right time and the right place for such an affair.

From that first time that Eliza met Anwar until they met again several months passed. But that was not to say that they had not spoken, they had many times, from Cairo and from various parts of the world for Anwar was a great traveller and smitten with Eliza. These were for the most part seductive conversations filled with wit, charm and promises of erotic nights. She had no doubt that as soon as time allowed he would be there to make good his promises. Eliza had been flattered, amused, and savoured the prospect of Anwar as a lover. Antonio had for months been telling her what a depraved and erotic young man was chasing after her.

He was candid with Eliza about the many times he had shared women and erotic games with Anwar. How much he, the provincial doctor, had learned from his friend and his free-wheeling lust for all things sexual. Antonio admitted it had changed his sexual life and that they, he and Eliza, were indebted to Anwar for that, because they were reaping the rewards now.

It was true. Antonio and Eliza's sex life was marvellous, full of adventurous and sometimes untamed sex games that they seemed to thrive on. But so too was their relationship outside bed. Antonio and Eliza did not live in each other's pockets, they lived lives independent of each other. He came and went in his work and personal life as he chose, sometimes with and sometimes without Eliza. She did the same. He had his wife and family. Though they were far away, they remained a mainstay in his life. Eliza understood that he'd never promised love in the marital sense of the word to her, not that that was what she had been looking for, because he loved only one woman and was committed in marriage to her and would always remain so. What they had together was something else and just as valid and important to them at this moment of time, in this place. Though they never discussed that, or that theirs was a free love that allowed them their right to have other lovers in their lives, it was accepted and, strangely, made their own relationship more intense and complete.

There was a stable in a small oasis of date palms less than a mile from the hospital. Antonio had had it built for the two Arabian stallions he kept. Most mornings he would rise at six and ride out into the desert, returning in time to begin his day at the clinic or the hospital. If he missed a morning, as soon as the sun was low enough in the sky, and if time permitted, he took his ride at dusk. The stable keeper, who lived with his family in a Bedouin tent among the palm trees at the edge of the natural spring, the reason for building the stable there, was an experienced man with horses and their breeding. His job was to tend to the two fine Arabians and keep intruders away.

In those first months, before Eliza and Antonio had become lovers, he had never mentioned the stable or his morning rides. It was one of the few private and very personal pleasures of his life at the hospital and he enjoyed keeping it for himself. The first Eliza learned of it was when she awakened him one morning with her lips. He rose to the occasion immediately, his eyes half closed, not from sleep but the bliss of oral sex and the sight of Eliza and the pleasure she too derived from her act. He came and Eliza did too as she drank to the last drop the essence of his sexual soul. Her heart racing she slipped on to her side and up the bed to rest her head upon his chest. He stroked her hair and told her how sublime she was, how lucky a man he was to have her as a lover.

It was then that he asked Eliza if it were possible for her to keep the following day free, and told her he wanted them to spend it together. That in itself was not unusual. Ever since they had become lovers, on the rare occasions they managed to take time together Antonio would take her on his house calls, or with his travelling clinic which could last a few days, or surprise her with a day trip to some magical place: an ancient ruin and a night of lovemaking under the stars. What was unusual now was a special lilt in his voice, and the expression of delight in his face.

'Where are we going?' she asked.

'It's a surprise.'

'Something special, I can tell.'

'How?'

'Because you're bursting to tell me, you can hardly contain yourself.'

He began to laugh and unwound himself from her arms and began to dress. 'A hint, just a hint,' she begged.

'All right, one hint and that's it. It's a present, one that you least expect and will adore.'

'You've bought me a present!' Eliza was quite overwhelmed at that, emotional even. He had never bought her anything, she'd never expected anything or that he would ever want to give her a gift. She had learned to accept many beautiful things – embroidered caftans, antique Roman gold, amber and diamond earrings, an ivory bracelet, a huge bottle of scent, a five-pound box of Belgian white chocolates – from the courting Anwar. That was somehow expected because of his character, the way he seduced women.

'I'll tell you no more. Just be at the dock at six tomorrow morning to meet me. I'll be coming back with it in the ferry.'

It was not Antonio's habit to report his movements to Eliza but she was not surprised to hear that he would be away the night. He was away many nights and sometimes for long periods of time. Even when he was in residence there were some days, weeks even, when they didn't spend the night having sex and slept apart.

The day's work swallowed Eliza up and thoughts of her erotic life and lover vanished from her mind. If she had been unable to relate to her children as babies and toddlers, she'd found since her arrival at the hospital that it was the adolescents and young women in their late-teens and early-twenties with whom she had a special affinity. These poor, and for the most part uneducated, women, steeped in the traditional ways and beliefs of their ancestors and trying to survive in a modern world, found a friend and mentor of sorts in the blonde foreigner who ran the hospital and clinic.

They had a confidence in her that they had in no one else, and she had the ability to deal with them and their problems justly. Eliza was a brilliant liaison officer between the medical staff and the patients.

On this particular day she was dealing with several families, all related to one another, who had come nearly ninety miles from one of the most remote and backward villages deep in the desert. Eliza felt sick with despair when the nurses reported that every one of the women had been circumcised and three were suffering from serious infection. These beautiful women, some as young as fifteen, were all married and suffering all sorts of horrifying discomfort in their sex life for having had as young children, their labia and clitoris removed, and their vagina sewn up with only the smallest of apertures left open. Their sex lives were filled with pain and *never* any prospect of sexual satisfaction.

For Eliza, who had enjoyed men and sex from a young age, and was now enjoying her sexuality to the fullest, it seemed barbaric that a custom had been designed so that women could not enjoy or reach orgasm. Not only that, it was destroying women's health, the very fabric of their life. She could listen to their heartbreaking stories and do much to prepare them psychologically to see the doctors, but she was very much aware of her delicate position as a foreigner in a strange land. She might help but had to know where to draw the line so as not to offend and cause them more grief by what she preached, which was of course no more female circumcision.

It was nearly midnight before she left her office at the hospital, having had her dinner on a tray there with two of the Egyptian doctors and a visiting Swedish gynaecologist. As she lay in bed she was thinking not about the day, which had been no more or less busy than any usual day at the hospital, but of one of the doctors and how he had praised her for her humanity, the calm with which she approached their storms, and something else, something particularly poignant: he had told her that she was blessed since quite obviously she had never experienced the pain of failure. She fell asleep realising what a long road she had travelled.

It was the habit of the hospital's ferry boat to announce its arrival by several blasts on the ship's horn. The sound made Eliza jump. She was already on the dock sitting on one of the lounge chairs, eyes closed, drifting not in thought but rather a complete state of serene emptiness. She removed the straw hat she had placed over her face to keep it from the sun and rose from her chair to walk to the end of the pier. The ferry boat was still some distance away. She shielded her eyes with her hand but could not see Antonio.

She waited for the ferry to berth. But before it did she had her first sight of Antonio, walking from aft to the prow of the boat. He waved and she waved back and thought he looked particularly handsome, suddenly somehow larger than life. He was smiling, and the air of sensuality about him took her over. She wanted him, to be *in flagrante delicto* with him, and felt shameless to realise how very sexy she was feeling, for the sexual images that flashed through her mind. She laughed aloud at herself for her passion for all things erotic she craved to experience with this man. As the boat slipped alongside the wooden dock he was walking aft and by the time that section of the deck was in view for Eliza, he was standing next to an Arabian mare, holding the black horse by the reins. The horse raised its head high, whinnied, and took several steps forward on first seeing Eliza.

She walked to the rail of the boat, her heart racing with excitement, and asked Antonio, 'Surely it's not mine? This isn't my present? Is it? No, it can't possibly be.'

Antonio was touched by how overwhelmed she was by his gift, how genuinely she could not believe that such a prize was to be hers. 'No one else's, Eliza,' he told her.

He watched with considerable pride as she led the horse from the boat on to the dock and examined her, going over her body as only a horsewoman would. There were dozens of people on the dock, by now swarming around the mare, Eliza, and Antonio. This was not exactly the correct place to express intimately to Antonio how grateful she was, how much she loved him for presenting her with such a gift. For them it was always Doctor Rinaldi and Mrs Flemming, perfect decorum in public.

'Where will we stable her?' she asked Antonio.

'Surprise number two,' he told her.

'And I'm surprise number three. You can't ride a horse without a saddle.'

Eliza swung around to see Anwar standing on deck with his Sudanese servant, wearing flowing white robes and a turban and carrying a bridle and saddle of shiny black leather embellished with delicate silver work.

At last Eliza was able to throw all caution to the wind. She embraced Anwar, tears of love and gratitude brimming in her eyes, when he approached her.

Eliza, who was wearing a pair of white linen culottes and a white shirt, walked between the two men for some distance, wanting the saddled horse to get used to her. They made a happy threesome, the men refusing to tell her where they were going or what kind of a day they had in store for her. They were a good distance from the hospital before she mounted the horse and rode while the men still walked on either side of her. Then the oasis came into view and she understood that a wider world than she had been living these last few months was opening up for her. It was there when the two Arabian stallions were brought out for Antonio and Anwar that Antonio confessed here was the place he'd selfishly kept for himself when he wanted to get away from the grind of work. Eliza later learned that Anwar was no stranger to the place either; it was he who had found it and helped to get the stable built for Antonio. The two men loved, when time allowed, to ride through the desert on expeditions to various ancient sites, sometimes with a group of Cairene friends. The horse had been bought for Eliza so that she too might join them. Anwar was a sophisticated cosmopolitan Egyptian of the upper classes but he was too a man who loved the land, its simple people, and the ancient history of his country.

It was a magical day for Eliza. They rode deep into the desert over magnificent dunes with a hot dry wind in their faces and stopped for a sumptuous lunch in a black Bedouin tent, lush inside with oriental carpets and cushions, served by two cooks and the Sudanese servant whom Eliza had seen on the boat. He had arrived by one of the hospital's Land-Rovers. They rode for a few hours in the late-afternoon and Anwar surprised Eliza when back at the Bedouin tent he kissed her goodbye and left with the Land-Rover. He was due back in Cairo that evening.

That night Antonio and Eliza's lovemaking was savagely exciting, possibly more so for having seen Anwar again. He was so incredibly sexual, he set both of them on the edge of desire all the day long. They spoke about it at one point in the night and Eliza knew that Anwar was insinuating himself further into their life.

Although the calls from him remained as frequent as they had ever been, it was several weeks later before she was to see him again and that was in Cairo where she was obliged to go for a three-day meeting with the Egyptian authorities. Anwar knew of the meeting and invited her to stay at his house.

Eliza left the hospital for Cairo on the ferry and travelled from there by car to Luxor where she took the plane. En route to the city, it was not the conferences she was going to attend that were on her mind but the three days she would have with Anwar. The sexual tension between them had been building for months. That day when they rode together with Antonio it was confirmed to her that an affair with Anwar was inevitable. In the many conversations they had subsequently had, he had been blatant about what he wanted from her, explicit but never vulgar. They had revelled, both of them, in his long and clever seduction of Eliza. He had been priming her to join him in that special place where he liked to dwell: the twilight zone of sexual ecstasy.

On arrival at the airport in Cairo, Eliza was surprised and disappointed that Anwar was not there waiting for her but had instead sent his Sudanese, Ahmed, and a driver to meet her. She was only several minutes into the city traffic before she was missing Upper Egypt and possessed by a horrible suspicion: Anwar had only been playing with her. She had not understood that and now felt a fool for the degree she had lusted after a sexual encounter with him.

In the midst of the traffic and chaos of Cairo there were pockets of sublime peace and beauty and one of these was a small stretch of green park that stretched along the bank of the Nile. Several hundred yards into this haven a pair of ornamental iron gates broke high garden walls covered in ivy and flowering vines. The house beyond was small and unpretentious by comparison to other gilded and ostentatious palaces. Its beauty was in its simplicity and serene setting. The wide veranda overlooking the Nile and surrounded by flowering gardens was where Eliza found Anwar waiting for her.

There are men in this life who possess a certain decadent beauty: sexual, charismatic, dangerous. They can be for some women an aphrodisiac, for others someone to run from. Eliza ran *to* Anwar and into his open arms. In this first passionate kiss she felt as if she were dissolving, but she was not alone. Anwar lost himself in sexual desire for Eliza. They hardly said a word as he, with his arm around her waist, walked them through the house and up the white marble staircase to his bedroom.

Eliza loved Anwar's body: smooth, honey-coloured, muscular flesh, his sex long and with girth, his scrotum large and voluptuous. She found it impossible to keep her hands from fondling him, her lips from caressing him, her tongue from licking him. She set him on fire.

He burned to have everything sexual and erotic with Eliza and knew that he would. He raised her up in his arms and she wrapped her legs around him. In one thrust he impaled her on his sex. She called out, a shout of release, pain, pleasure. He bit into her breast as hard as he could. She screamed in pain and he licked the spot and sucked hard on her nipples as he carried her thus to the bed. With hands tight around her waist, he eased her on and off his rampant penis in thrusts so exquisite to Eliza that she came in a strong orgasm. Sexual ecstasy was hers. For hours she was lost in it; Anwar's passion, his depravity, his joy in keeping her there, saw to that. Only several hours later, when exhausted from expending so much energy in orgasms, did she come out of her sexual reverie and realise where she had been, the various sexual acts he had drawn her into.

She was neither shocked nor displeased with herself or her lover, merely overwhelmed by the thrill of such sexuality. She had had oral, anal and vaginal sex before, had enjoyed the excitement of sexual toys and unguents that accompany adventurous sex, she had felt the light sting of a belt, but had never craved more of those things with such desperation as she now craved them.

And Anwar? He was enchanted by Eliza's hunger for him and his sexuality, surprised by her enthusiasm for debauchery; this cool-looking, pretty blonde was a match for him in sex, as strangely he had always known she would be. He slipped into a silk robe and left the room to return a few minutes later with a bottle of champagne and a bowl of the best Beluga caviar. 'I've sent all the servants away except Ahmed,' he told her as he fed her dollops of the delicacy by scooping the black beads on to the end of his finger and placing them in her mouth.

After several glasses of champagne and more caviar he took her in his arms and held her. They remained silent but the sexual tension was still there, for them something that spoke volumes. Anwar released Eliza and from the bedside table took a long silk chiffon scarf. He tied her wrists to the headboard of the bed while kissing her on the mouth and breasts, sucking on her nipples.

'You don't mind, do you?' he asked.

'No. But why this when you know I'm willing to submit to anything, everything, you want?'

'Because I don't want you to touch me. I want you to be totally at my will, enslaved by me for sex and sex alone. That's fair because I'm prepared to be that way for you whenever you want me to be. Strangely, I think you're the only woman I've ever said that to,' he told her, looking surprised that he should even feel that way. And once more he kissed her, only this time there was passion and a deep affection together with the lust he felt for her.

The erotic sensations Eliza experienced were overwhelming. Anwar had done well to tie her hands to the bed. Several times she wanted to run away from him and the lust he engendered in her when, with the help of beautifully carved jade objects, he penetrated her orifices and manipulated them at the same time as he was having oral sex with her.

Here was sex for Eliza at its most wild and over the top, erotic desire employed for complete and utter pleasure, to leave all else in life far in its wake. There was on that day, and for all the days and years that were to follow in Eliza and Anwar's affair, a mutual desire to go another step further down the erotic path they chose to walk together. Their affair was based on a common craving to spend their precious hours together in a world of sexual bliss where each of them in their own way would reach sexual nirvana.

Eliza was at once swept into Anwar's life, which she could only term a full-time social existence. It was rich and glamorous and sometimes interesting, more often than not amusing with its clever gossip and sensual undertones. But it was a full-time job playing that game. It was the sort of life that Julian and Dulcima Forrester had always shunned and had taught their children not to appreciate or take seriously, merely to taste it as it came and for what it was worth and then drop. It was the sort of life John, her first husband, had enjoyed and would have lived if he had not been dedicated to medicine. It was a life which Eliza had only lived before for the love of her husbands, and which she actually loathed. But it was always fun and a little naughty to eat the frosting off the cup cake. And sex with Anwar was like that; the most delicious and wicked chocolate frosting imaginable. So she did tolerate, even sometimes enjoyed, his way of life when she was obliged to.

These then were the men, Antonio and Anwar, her friends and lovers, that remained in Eliza's life for all the years she lived and worked in Egypt. It was always in the forefront of her mind that to have as uncomplicated and open-ended an affair in the freedom the three of them had chosen meant that one day it would be over. But none of them ever expected that it would end as it did, with Eliza compelled to leave Egypt, never to return.

In her years in Egypt, she came together as a whole and complete human being, finding new dimensions and happiness in her life that in the past had eluded her. Her children were at last hers; they loved and respected her not as a mother but the woman she had become, the woman she had always been but had never found before. Having found the self she had lost when she had been an eighteen year old, naive and unworldly, she was now able to sustain the great blow that was to change her life once again: the death of her mother, and at a time when her own health was deteriorating and she must leave her lovers and beloved Egypt.

Eighteen months before Dulcima died she made a journey to Egypt with Effie and Constanza. It had always been Dulcima's dream to see the pyramids of Giza and to take a cruise up the Nile. Arranged by Anwar, it was a marvellously extravagant holiday such as the Forresters had never taken. Being land rich and cash poor, their lifestyle had never allowed them that sort of luxury. It was a happy and most memorable holiday for them, not least because they all got on so well.

There was nothing sad about their farewell when the holiday came to its end. The Forresters were used to coming and going in and out of each other's lives; they had never been a family for sadness or crises. Eliza returned to Upper Egypt, her work and her lovers. In the months after Dulcima's visit there arrived as usual the marvellous letters they had always written to each other and which Eliza had shared with her lovers. Her mother wrote like a poet. Soon after her return these letters were arriving not from Little Barrington but the Villa Montecatini. She had moved there permanently, wanting to spend the remainder of her days there. How well Eliza could understand that. She often yearned to return to Tuscany herself and found it extraordinary that she had never been back since she was eighteen years old.

Close to a year after her mother's visit, the climate began to take its toll on Eliza's health. It was not so much that she had anything specifically wrong with her that needed treatment, it was a matter of the years of intense heat and dust, high humidity and hard work, exposure to a variety of diseases, all of which no longer sat well with her. Finally it became a case of leaving Egypt for the sake of her health. Still she struggled on, Antonio becoming more and more concerned about her. A leave of absence? she suggested.

Distress showed in his face when, after examining her, he told her, 'Not a solution for your lungs. Fresh clean mountain air and a different lifestyle for the rest of your days, that's the only solution.'

'Not now,' she begged.

'Before the year is out, I insist upon it.'

'Please don't tell Anwar, or anyone else for that matter. Let's just carry on as normal for as long as we can while I try to find a replacement.'

Antonio laughed but there were tears in his eyes. 'Don't bother. You are irreplaceable. And besides, the work that we've done here these last seven years has been a very thorough grounding for the Egyptian doctors and nursing staff. It's time for them to take over and run things. Who knows? In a year's time I too might be leaving Egypt, returning on a more permanent basis to my life and practice in Florence. It was always on the cards, you know.' Then he pulled her into his arms and kissed her with passion, love and admiration.

In her heart Eliza knew that Antonio was telling her that if Egypt was over for her, their long-time erotic romance was over too and it was time for them both to be moving on. Quite clearly life here without her meant the end of an era for him. It had always been inevitable that one day they would part; for them love and commitment had never governed their romance or their life together. The tears in Eliza's eyes told him what she could not find words to express: Thank you for the years you gave me, and the love. What she did manage to say was, 'Promise me you will tell no one about my health, that I intend to leave Egypt? Let's please keep it our secret until I'm ready to go. I would like for the time being for us to carry on as if nothing untoward is going to happen. And when it does, no fanfares.'

'I promise.'

Several months after Eliza knew her fate, Anwar, Antonio, and she made a two-week journey by sea plane up the Nile to its source in Ethiopia. It was part hospital business and part adventurous tourism. On their return sad news awaited them: Dulcima had died in the Villa Montecatini twelve days before Eliza's return. She had been unreachable and the funeral had been held without her. All four sisters were soon on the telephone to her assuring her that Dulcima had not suffered and had sent her love to Eliza before she died. They spoke about the funeral which was private, attended only by the villa's staff and the four sisters, no husbands or children. It was Dulcima's wish. That and to be buried next to her ancestors in the family crypt on the small island on the lake half a mile from the villa.

Eliza was distraught. She retreated for a few days: riding her mare into the desert to stay in the Bedouin tent where she mourned Dulcima. Antonio was supportive and rode out to sleep with her every night. Anwar sent Ahmed to stay with her and care for her until she was ready to return to the hospital.

Though she had lost her mother and mourned her, Eliza was able to let Dulcima go. In the desert, and on the soft warm breezes, her mother's voice seemed to whisper to her things she had taught Eliza and her sisters. 'Be brave about letting loved ones go when the time comes, it makes it easier for them and it's better for you.' 'What always makes your father and I happy is to see you girls running free, getting on with your lives, not ours. That's a great reward for us.'

When Eliza did return to the hospital, she found several letters from her sisters, all of them loving, sweet and supportive, and a large manilla envelope containing a copy of Dulcima's will. The house and all the property of Little Barrington had been left intact as one estate to be shared equally by Constanza, Clara, Effie and Dendra, on condition that it remain as one estate within the family. The Villa Montecatini, its contents and all property and the farm, were left to Eliza.

It had never occurred to her that such a prize would be hers. She was overwhelmed by Dulcima's generosity, by her having left Eliza her most precious possession. At last she had a home of her own to go to, the house and countryside she had always loved, the place where she had been happiest in love. Eliza felt quite faint to learn of it, and had to sit down. She struggled to reach a chair and very nearly toppled over, saved by a doctor who was just entering her office. He helped her.

'Eliza, you're ill, as white as a ghost!'

How could she tell him she was not ill at all? That it had taken the Villa Montecatini's being returned to her as her very own for Eliza to realise that she had never loved anything or any man, had never been loved by anything or any man, as Tuscany had loved her and she had loved it. There had been many things, places and men in her life since then but never pure unadulterated love. And certainly not here in Egypt, despite her work and her lovers. Only at that very moment did Eliza come to understand how much she'd missed being loved, and loving so completely as she had Tuscany. A whole life time of misunderstanding was coming together for her here in intriguing, beguiling Egypt.

What a long road she had had to take! The years danced before her eyes. She would not mourn all the failures, all that had gone wrong uselessly. Instead she would prepare herself and have the courage to say goodbye to all that. She was strong enough not to fool herself, never to say those unloved years were a dream. Nor would she degrade herself with empty hopes of what might be. She was long prepared and full of courage to go home to her final pleasure, to hear the real voices and the exquisite music of her beloved Tuscany, in pure heart and with a pure soul.

'Eliza, sniff this, inhale deeply,' instructed Dr Kharga as he broke open a small glass vial.

She did as she was told and was immediately revived. The colour came back into her face. She ran her fingers through her hair and undid the clasp that held it back off her face, running her fingers through it again. Then she smiled at Mirrit Kharga.

'You did give me a fright, Eliza. I want you in my consulting room *now* so I can look you over.'

'Mirrit, it's really not necessary. I promise you, I'm all right. I just had some startlingly good news that overwhelmed me. The sort of news that changes one's life for ever.'

'I would still like to look you over, Eliza.'

'No. I promise if I feel the least unwell, I will be at your door.'

Dulcima used always to tell her children, 'What you really need always comes to you at the right time.' Ever since that moment when Antonio had told Eliza that her health demanded she must leave Egypt, never to return, she had had no idea as to where she could go, what she would do, how she was going to live, if she could ever find work again. Middle-aged, without savings of any significance, no husband or a family home of her own to go to, her prospects had been grim. To begin again had seemed an even harsher prospect. To be dependent at that stage of her life on her mother or her sisters was unthinkable. In a very Forrester manner she had done what she and all the Forresters had always done: failed to dwell on what was to be but got on with living from day to day, all thoughts of the future simply drifting away. And now what Dulcima had said had come true: just when she needed it the most, she had a roof over her head, all her own, for now and for ever.

Not once had Antonio asked her what she had planned to do when she left Egypt. He had done what he had promised, put her departure out of his mind, and life continued for them as it always had since they had become lovers many years ago.

The evening after Eliza read the will was one of the evenings they were spending together. Antonio was particularly voracious for all things sexual and highly imaginative in his lust for her. There was a kind of urgency in their sex, a touch of violence, not to each other but in each of them, that put them on the edge of their sexuality. They rode that edge for a while and then slipped off it into sexual depravity that was thrilling and answered their needs. It was animalistic sex, devoid of any emotion other than the pleasure of sexual gratification at its peak, the exquisite oblivion that only exists in those split seconds of strong and powerful orgasm.

They had had that sort of sex before, many times, together and whenever they had shared their lust with Anwar. The three had become a rather extraordinary *menage à trois*, a three-cornered establishment in sex and friendship, soon after Anwar and Eliza became lovers. Eliza had the two men as lovers separately and together, and the arrangement had been handled with utmost discretion, leaving Anwar's smart and very social Cairo friends to spend years guessing about the relationship, the three of them content with the life they had created for themselves.

Now, sated and lying in each other's arms, Antonio spoke. Eliza heard a hint of anxiety in his voice, 'Something's happened, something is different about us tonight.'

'What makes you think that?' she asked, astounded he should have sensed that.

'There was an undercurrent of anger in us, hidden, transformed into a suppressed violence that manifested itself in dangerously exciting sex. I'm not complaining, mind you, it was intensely satisfying. But very revealing. So what's going on here?'

How could Eliza tell him that she adored having what they had together but that quite suddenly sex for sex's sake was no longer enough? She missed love. Belonging to herself was great but she wanted to belong to someone else, for better or for worse, just as now she belonged to the Villa Montecatani and Tuscany, for better or for worse. But that sort of love had never been what they were about, not her and Antonio, nor her and Anwar. Eliza had no inclination to end their relationship on such a note. It had been one of the best, possibly *the* best and happiest relationship she had ever had with a man, and no matter what her feelings now, she felt it deserved an honourable ending.

She unwound herself from Antonio's arms and sat up against the bed pillows. The dawn light was streaming through the windows and a bright red sun was inching its way slowly from below the horizon far in the distance. 'My mother has left me the estate in Tuscany. I now have a home to go to. I would like to leave in a few months' time – that's how long I'll need to wind up my work here and for us to make a few more excursions to places we have always promised ourselves we would visit.'

He remained silent, absorbing Eliza's news. Then, after several minutes, when he did speak, he told her,

'How extraordinary to know that when you leave here and I return to Florence, we will be so close and yet so far apart. But friends – you must promise me we will always be the best of friends?'

'Yes, always,' she told him, and slipped back into his arms again.

Eliza felt it was strange and yet not strange at all that they should have nothing more to say about the coming end of their relationship, one that had been so meaningful and incredibly happy, and so very important in her life. She could feel no sadness, only excitement that when the door closed on this part of her life, a new one would open and she would be able to step through it with pride and enthusiasm for whatever was to come.

Nothing about her departure was as easy as she'd thought it would be. It seemed that the moment she told Antonio that she was leaving Egypt, the fight went out of her. She relaxed that tight hold she had been keeping on her health problems and began to feel how much the climate was taking out of her. She managed to keep up appearances and to work as hard as ever she had, but of course Antonio had been right. A year at the most and her health would have been severely damaged. She would be leaving none too soon.

Anwar had been told about her departure when next he had flown up to visit her and Antonio. He had brought with him a beautiful young girl – there had been so many beautiful young girls over the years. He and Eliza were alone, walking together back to his plane behind Antonio and the girl. 'I'm leaving Egypt for good in three months' time,' she told him.

He was silent for several seconds and then asked, 'Is there a reason?'

'My health. It seems the climate and the work have got the best of me.'

'It doesn't have to end here, Eliza.'

'Yes, it does. In three months' time when I board that plane for Rome. We both know that. Friends, Anwar, we'll always be friends.'

'Not when we have been lovers such as you and I have been. It would be nice, but I'm not the kind of man to want something and not have it.'

'You're angry when you shouldn't be. We always knew that one day it would burn itself out, this intense sexual life we had together. Or else I would leave. Please don't be angry and spoil the time we have left together.'

It was then that Anwar stopped and pulled her close to him. Gazing into her eyes, he told her, 'I'm not angry, just telling you we can't be friends. Not the kind who send postcards or exchange calls on birthdays.' He kissed her on the lips and that sexual hold they had always had on each other was as strong as ever. 'We can only be what we are for each other, Eliza. Oh, and I have no intention of spoiling our last months together.'

The most heart-rending thing about leaving Egypt for Eliza was not the staff and the many ambulatory patients who were down at the dock to bid her farewell when she, Antonio and Anwar boarded Anwar's sea plane that would take the three of them to Cairo. She was deeply moved by that, of course, but more so by what was to follow. Once on board Anwar taxied the plane for take off, and when it rose steeply off the waters and into the air, returned to circle the hospital where the many friends she had made there waved their last farewells to her, and then the oasis where the stabled horses were brought out and led to prance around in a circle for her.

Returning to the Nile, Anwar flew the plane, not low and straight down the centre of the river as was his usual practice, but skimming in long zig-zags from the east bank to the west until way past Luxor and Asyut. Lining the banks sporadically for those hundreds of miles, and occasionally on small boats, were poor, country men, women and children in large or small groups, dressed in their best robes and turbans, the women swathed in black. The huge population whom Eliza had worked for in the last seven years. There were many there who had merely heard of who she was and what she had done. Now they took this chance of one last look at her, offering their thanks and farewells with shouts of praise and good wishes, asking for blessings on her, waving her on her way. They tossed flowers and palm fronds into the river to follow her lazily down river to Cairo and thence to Alexandria and the sea. It was then and only then that Eliza broke down in floods of tears.

The two men were moved. They had known for days that word of her departure had leaked out, and rather than a mass of people making long journeys to the hospital, had sent word around that if they wanted to see her one last time she would be travelling down the river, but never had they expected the tribute they were seeing.

By the time they flew over Cairo and followed the Nile to Giza, Upper Egypt and all the magnificent tributes seemed suddenly behind her. English calm and reserve took possession of Eliza and she was able to control her emotions enough to get her through the remainder of the day.

At Anwar's house a late lunch was served on the marble veranda overlooking the river: champagne, foie gras, lobster and crayfish in a cream sauce served with baked rice, grilled baby pigeons and small spinach soufflés, a green salad, and for pudding whole purple figs peeled and covered with crème fraîche and sprinkled with crunchy demerara sugar. Tiny cups of hot sweet black Turkish coffee followed. Anwar had done what Eliza had asked of him: kept the day of her departure from the many friends she had made in Cairo, the social whirl of farewells was something she particularly did not want. And so it was only the three of them for lunch and the three of them who were driven to the pyramids. Eliza had wanted to be with Antonio and Anwar for her last look at them and the great Sphinx of Giza.

They rode around the pyramids on camels and the last Eliza saw of her lovers was when she watched them ride away into the desert towards Sakkara and the step pyramids. For the three of them sadness, even at a time like this, the departure of a lover, was not an option. They were as happy with each other as they had always been, and there was even something joyous about their last day together. Eliza realised how much they and she celebrated life; their highly sexual lives together had always been a celebration of it.

Ahmed helped Eliza off her camel and paid the camel driver. He escorted her to the car and then got in the front seat with the chauffeur. They were headed for the airport. Eliza was leaving Egypt as she had arrived: alone and with great expectations of a new adventure.

TUSCANY

1995

Chapter 9

Five days after Amanda Dix and Eliza Flemming had tea at Amanda's house, Amanda was driving to *her* village, one of the many stone villages and towns perched on the slopes of the Tuscan hills. Only six miles from her farmhouse, the drive and the village were for Amanda two of the many perks she received for living in Tuscany. The village had, like so many other villages and towns in the area, the nearly obligatory thirteenth-century ruined Romanesque church and campanile that stood out starkly against the surrounding hills. It boasted a post office, bakery, a barber shop-cum beauty salon, a butcher, two coffee shops selling wine and spirits, two restaurants, one good, the other deserving of three stars that was quite famous, a police station and a bar-cum-discotheque. The small pretty piazza with its handsome stone fountain was where old men sat silently with nothing to compel or inspire them and where the village women, out to do their chores, greeted one another with the morning gossip. The English or other foreigners down from their villas in the hills passed the time of day at small tables under a relentless sun, saying little over an espresso or a glass of wine.

Everyone who came into the village walked or rode over a beautiful hog-backed stone bridge with arches of five different shapes and sizes that spanned a swiftly running mountain stream. The handsome, mostly abandoned stone and wooden-shuttered houses, some tilting at crazy angles on either side of the narrow cobbled streets, were at intervals spanned by remnants of elegant ruined or dilapidated arches. It was a village of few residents who mostly basked lazily under a hot sun, and where there never appeared to be more than a few people to be seen at one time except on market day, Wednesday, when the village became a place of bustle and vitality for a few hours. People came down from the surrounding villages for miles around for the fresh produce: succulent fruit, a variety of green vegetables, mounds of olives, cured meats, baskets of herbs and spices, the finest of virgin olive oils for tasting before buying, and fish caught that morning from the sea.

This was Monday and Amanda was looking forward to having her morning all to herself without intrusion of any kind, doing her errands at her leisure, having a cream and wild mushroom pasta and half bottle of the local wine for an early lunch in the shade of the village's huge ancient fig tree. Amanda was thinking that days like this were much too rare in one's life and all but praying she was not going to have her morning ruined by bumping into any of the other English in residence in the area.

She saw and enjoyed enough of them socially, but not today, thank you. Today was for her and being alone with the landscape. Ever since her tea with Eliza Flemming she had been made newly aware of how in all their years in Tuscany she and Philip were still outsiders looking in. They had somehow managed not to become part of Tuscany but were still nothing more than the English abroad. She resented what she and Philip had made of themselves in Italy.

Amanda saw Vittorio Carducci standing in the middle of the road, which was lined with statuesque poplars rustling their papery leaves: a special music of their own conducted by the soft warm breeze. He was waving at her to stop. His dilapidated old open lorry was parked at the side of the road, the bonnet up, a stream of steam rising from the radiator. It was early-morning and the day was already hot. The sun filtering through the trees shaded the secondary road that wound down the mountain to the village and cast a dappled pattern of light and shade across the poorly maintained Tarmac.

Amanda was both surprised and annoyed by the intrusion. She almost always took this road because she rarely saw another car on it. It was a scenic drive to make the heart race for the sheer beauty of it: the Tuscan hills at their best, a landscape very nearly untouched by time.

She was acutely aware of how very handsome and sexy-looking a man Vittorio was, more so than she had given him credit for before. She studied him, yes, because he was attractive: as a handsome, virile-looking man, a little common, a little too provincial for her taste and what she would consider almost rough trade, but now she was curious about him. What more than sex could he offer a woman like Eliza Flemming . . . a woman like herself? All these years that she had been watching Vittorio cut her fields she had never thought of him as more than a good-looking, possibly sexy, farmer, but having met Eliza Flemming she was disturbed to think there might possibly be more to him than she had given him credit for. Having had tea with his fiancée, she was obliged to think of Vittorio now as a man, a human being. And here he was in the middle of the road. She was irritated, felt as if he were intruding on her life. She slowed down and finally stopped a few feet away from him.

Vittorio walked round the Range Rover to speak with her through the open window. He started to explain himself, at first in Italian and then in mid-sentence suddenly switching to his very poor but understandable English. She resented that too. Amanda took pride in her ability with the Italian language. She felt the morning heat more now, or was it the warmth Vittorio exuded as he stood only inches away from her? His scent was not unlike the early-morning smell of straw, orris and roses, with a hint of warm, damp earth. Amanda very nearly closed her eyes to inhale deeply his lust for life, his perfume. She controlled herself and focused on his hands, clamped over the open window, as he continued to explain that he needed to trouble her for a ride as far as the turn off to the village. From there he could walk to Giovanni Stratsei's. Giovanni had been seeing the lorry through its many crises for years.

His hands were large and rough from years of hard work, his fingernails and the cuticles around them ragged and stained with the yellow-green of car oil. Were these hands to caress fair skin, fondle a woman? Could hands such as these excite lust in a lady? He was handsome, yes, but a sensitive lover? Amanda was transfixed by Vittorio's hands, the muscular arms and biceps, the strong shoulders – all visible because he had discarded his shirt and was standing in an undershirt that gleamed white against his dark skin. No, they were not. These were the hands of a farmer, not a lover. At last she broke her gaze and looked into his face. He was smiling broadly at her. He had caught her out in her study of him. A look passed between them and Amanda saw a sweetness in his eyes that she had seen before, a kindness, but for the first time recognised that he was sensual, a lustful man, with that special quality that some sexy men have of knowing how to be passive at the right time, in the right place, to seduce a woman they want.

She was quite shocked and disappointed that although all that was there to be seen, it was not there for her. Once more she was consumed with curiosity about the lovely Eliza and her farmer lover. Had there been other foreign women in his life? You bet there have been, she told herself, and almost laughed aloud because this interest of hers in Eliza Flemming and the farmer was not at all like her. What did it have to do with her life after all?

She smiled at Vittorio, and the moment she had creased her face into that smile, realised that she had never done that with him before. 'It's a good thing I came along, Vittorio. Hop in, I'll be happy to take you where you want to go.'

She watched him run back to the cab of his van and there slip into his shirt, take his shot gun and return to the Range Rover to slide into the seat next to her. They drove for miles without saying a word to one another. Amanda wanted to make polite conversation but simply could not think of anything to say to the man. Though she kept thinking of Eliza she could not bring herself to strike up a conversation about her with her lover, it somehow seemed a kind of betrayal. It was during that silent ride with Vittorio by her side that Amanda realised she felt something very strong yet indefinable for Eliza, saw her as an Englishwoman, a sister under the skin, who had lost her way in lust and love with an Italian farmer which had excluded her from a whole segment of friends she might otherwise have had. Including Amanda. With Eliza on her mind, and the undercurrent of raunchy maleness that Vittorio was exuding, which proved to be unnerving, it came as something of a relief when he spoke up to say, 'Here, at these crossroads, will be fine for me.' He thanked her and left the Range Rover.

Once he was gone, Vittorio and Eliza vanished from her mind and the glorious day and the ride engrossed her again. Amanda did have the quiet day she wanted when she parked the Range Rover and walked, a basket over her arm and her shopping list in hand, across the hog-backed bridge into the village. She saw not one of the foreigners she had been so loath to have to make social chatter with, did her chores, briefly acknowledged several of the villagers with a nod and a smile from under her wide-brimmed straw hat, and enjoyed her lunch and half bottle of wine. She lingered over her espresso, long after the shops had closed and the piazza emptied, everyone having gone home for lunch and a siesta. Amanda heard the sound of a closing shutter from somewhere in the recesses of the village then total silence except for the water cascading over the rim of the fountain's impressively large and elegant stone bowl.

The heat was oppressive and ate into her body and her soul. It weighted her down, rooted her to the spot where she sat. She felt stifled, barely moving a fingertip, a leg, never shifting in her chair for seemingly a long time. Then a breeze, slight and hot, the sort of intense heat that comes from the opening of an oven door, pirouetted into the piazza and shook Amanda out of her torpor long enough for her to rise to her feet and walk from the village. She was aware of her own foot steps on the cobblestones, and as she crossed over the hog-backed bridge, the sound of the rushing mountain stream.

She forsook the Range Rover for a nap in the shadow of a clump of tall cypresses down by the stream. There she fell into a deep sleep of erotic dreams. Philip was walking Eliza into their London bedroom. Eliza was naked. Her skin shone with youth and vitality. Her breasts were large and luscious and the nimbus that circled her long and thick nipples was rouged a plum colour. Her mound of Venus was shaved clean and henna-decorated with swirls and curlicues. Her waist was incredibly narrow and her hips seductive, as were her long and shapely legs and thighs that insinuated lust.

'Now here is a woman who knows how to give herself, Amanda, watch and learn,' Philip told her.

He proceeded towards the bed and took Amanda by the hand so that she accompanied them. Eliza, whose long blonde hair was piled prettily on top of her head, smiled at Amanda and told her, 'There is nothing to be frightened about,' as she seductively undressed her.

Once naked, Eliza caressed Amanda's breasts, kissed them and sucked sweetly, sensitively, on her nipples. Amanda was appalled at having a woman make love to her yet was helplessly coming in a series of short and delightful orgasms.

'Don't be afraid to die in the arms of Eros, such a death can be sweet,' Eliza told her as she caressed Amanda's body.

She felt Eliza's tongue licking her flesh. She had never known such tenderness, such excitement, never been so ready and yearning for anything, everything, sexual.

Vittorio appeared as if from nowhere and went to them. He kissed Eliza and told her how much he loved her and thanked her for his gift. Then he took Amanda by the hand and led her to the bed. There was nothing tender in the sex she had with him, it was thrillingly hard core. He was a master in lust, wringing an endless stream of orgasms from Amanda. And then, when he was through with her, he handed her over to Philip and told her, 'You get into the sexual dirt with Philip and enjoy yourself. That's where he likes to be, and is, with other women. Now, after today, we all know that's where you belong.'

The three of them, Philip, Eliza and Vittorio, now descended on her and the sex was outrageously thrilling, both men penetrating her, Eliza devouring her in tenderness. They broke down all Amanda's defences and she lost herself to their lust and found her own, the real depths of it, for the first time in her life. She died many times in her orgasms, only to rise again and see herself and sex in a new perspective. And then they were gone, all three of them, and Amanda was left on her own, seemingly with no place to go.

Her father appeared, drunk, dirty, coarse and angry,

walking alongside Vittorio's old open lorry. He was calling out in his sing-song fashion to the row upon row of terraced houses, grimy with dirt and poverty, for people's unwanted possessions. 'Your rag and bone man's here, your rag and bone man's here.' On seeing and hearing him, Amanda ran away as fast as she could, determined that he should never again catch her and beat her. She never looked back.

Amanda awakened with a start, completely disorientated and drenched in perspiration, her heart racing. She struggled to realise where she was, what she was doing there. She slowed down her heartbeat by taking deep breaths and gradually came to herself and her present surroundings, the life of today, here and now, Amanda Dix style. The dream was fast receding from her mind but what was not was her reaction to it. Memory of sexual pleasure, the shock that she should have a lesbian encounter with Eliza even in a dream, was unnerving. The excitement of sex with Vittorio, a peasant farmer no more educated or refined than her own father and family had been – and how she had revelled in it. Base, raunchy, common . . . the very sort of sex and life she had run away from so many years before.

Run away from and blocked out of her mind and her life, never considered as anything but dead. Not even to Philip had she confided whence she came, her struggle to rise above the ignorance and poverty she had been born into. How he would have hated having to hear about the ugliness she had had to crawl away from. This was the first time she had ever dreamed about her father, her past, and if doing so affected her, she wasn't aware of it. For Amanda the past was the past and dead was dead. Now that she was awake her dream seemed not so much disturbing as impossible. Almost a joke to be laughed at.

But that delicious sensation that accompanies a strong and powerful orgasm lingered with her now. She rose from the grass, and with her basket of shopping in her hand, scrambled up the embankment to walk in the shade of the laurels until she reached the Range Rover. Amanda opened the car, rolled down all the windows and spread a blanket on the seat that was by now burning, so she was at least able to sit down and drive. She switched on the ignition and was on her way home.

Philip Markham had had a glorious day alone at home. After seeing Amanda to the car, he had returned to the house to make several calls and then lock himself away in his library to work on his book on Goya. Left in London were his secretary and researcher, and his hectic life as an art dealer of some renown. He was a man who loved his life and his work and the woman he lived with, whom he considered to be his partner in life. Philip was handsome and erudite, from the English aristocracy. He was an important name in the international art market, entertaining and being entertained by a côterie of interesting people, most of whom were fabulously wealthy or representing museums that were heavily endowed financially.

As Amanda had driven away from the house, yet again Philip marvelled at how well suited to each other in love and their social and business lives they were. Though he liked to be flirtatious with the many women who chased after him, he had always been faithful to Amanda. She had met him, gone after him, entrapped him first with sex and then with her ability to give him all the freedom he needed to get on with whatever he wanted from life. More importantly, she was clever enough to hold him fast with sex, and keep him interested by her own business successes, capabilities and charm. She never intruded on him with the mundane, protected him from the common facts of life. He loved her for that and for not exposing him to those things about herself that might interfere with their stylish relationship. They did rather dwell on, were even a little smug about being the perfect couple whose standards never slipped.

They were one of those couples that were whole and complete as much when they were apart as when they were together; that was their strength. The edge to their relationship was that they never totally surrendered themselves to each other, even in sex which was when they came the closest. They were a couple who did not die for one another but instead hung on for dear life. That, and knowing their limitations and living at ease with them, rather than talking or doing anything about them, was the way of life they liked, were *comfortable* with. They never even contemplated the possibility of living without the guidelines they had set themselves for love and the good life.

Philip walked through the gardens to the kitchen where the remnants of breakfast were still on the table. He asked Maria for another cup of coffee and sat down to pick at the remaining paper thin slices of Parma ham which he rolled around a sliver of corn bread and popped into his mouth. Having seen the housekeeper had already poured a cup for herself, he invited her to sit at the table with him. Maria accepted, always enjoying the rare times she and Philip had a moment to talk. She was a little dazzled by his good looks, by what an important man he was, how good as employers he and Amanda were to those who worked for them. His Italian was excellent, much better than Amanda's, and that and his charm made their rare and brief conversations something special for the housekeeper. They chatted amicably for about ten minutes and Philip left her to go to the library where he told her he did not expect to be disturbed.

It was too glorious a morning to miss and so, instead of walking through the house to the library, a room he was extremely proud of, he chose to walk from the kitchen into the garden around the house and through the front door. He was as always distracted from thoughts of work when he gazed across the distant hills and down to the valley below. In the landscape, the Tuscan cypresses reaching for the sky, so proud, so very pure and romantic, touched the heart, tweaked the soul. There was something sinuous in these flame-shapes that always suggested to Philip they had done away with time. They undulated gently and played in the slightest of breezes. It always seemed to him as if they held secrets and kept them.

He raised a pair of binoculars that had been lying on a table on the terrace to his eyes and scanned the area, giving himself a panoramic view. Riding just below a grove of cypresses as much as a mile away he saw the pale rider, careering her white stallion along a ridge. She and her horse were a glorious sight. The horse was high-stepping, nimble, proud. And the rider? She and her horse were as if part of the landscape, like the earth and the sun, the moon and the stars. Like the cypresses, she held her secrets and thrived.

Philip placed the binoculars back on the table. Without them, Eliza and the white stallion were no more than a moving white dot on the hills. He was somehow relieved that Amanda was not here to see her pale rider. There was something about Eliza Flemming and the way she rode the Tuscan hills on her white stallion that was attractive and yet disturbing to Amanda. Even more so now that she had had tea with her and learned that Eliza was to marry the farmer, Vittorio.

Philip had deduced that Amanda was besotted with the idea of Eliza Flemming and her farmer as great lovers, the Abelard and Heloise of Tuscany. He would have liked to think of this as romantic tosh, but like Amanda he couldn't. Philip was no fool; he understood that to sacrifice all for love was a noble premise for a farmer and his upper-class English lady, for many others too, but he knew it was a dangerous prospect for those like Amanda and he who were incapable of such sacrifice. In fact, he considered it somehow obscene that any one could consider dying, giving one's life up to death, for love or sexual satisfaction. A momentary death, that split second of pure bliss in orgasm, well, that was a very different thing. The farmer and his lady posed a threat to Amanda and Philip; the odd couple's relationship was based on love alone according to what he had heard. But Philip told himself, You never miss what you have never tasted, and dismissed the couple from his mind.

It was late-afternoon when Amanda returned home and found him having a siesta in their bedroom. She very quietly peeled off her clothes, bathed and lay down naked next to him. She fell asleep. This time her sleep was dreamless but when she awakened it was Vittorio who was on her mind, not Philip or Eliza. She lay there thinking of what it must be like to be made love to by this rough and handsome, near-illiterate man, what pleasure Eliza must derive from being riven by him. She became quite excited as her imagination took flight. She rolled on to her side and then slipped on top of Philip. He had not been asleep but lying there for a long time with his eyes closed, thinking what a lucky man Farmer Carducci was.

Eliza was dead-heading the wildly overgrown wild rose bushes on the drive some distance from, but still in sight of, the main gates to the Villa Montecatini. It was close to eight o'clock in the evening and the sun was overshadowed by dusk, rushing to slay the day and meet the night. A pearly mist would soon be settling on the hills. The birds were singing now that the fierce heat of the day had passed. Eliza's long blonde hair was held back off her face in a single plait and on her head she wore a battered old straw hat, the same one Dulcima used to wear when she was gardening.

She heard the rattle of the huge iron gate and looked down the drive to see Vittorio waving goodbye to someone as he slipped through and closed it behind him. Eliza watched him walking up the centre of the long drive, bending down occasionally to retrieve a broken branch or an over-large stone, and toss it into the bushes. With his toe, he scuffed gravel and dirt into a pot hole. Always the farmer. How he loved this land, his Tuscany, the farm and the villa and its grounds. It occurred to Eliza that he was as born to it as she was, only in different circumstances.

He had not as yet seen her lost among the rose bushes just behind a cypress tree, but would eventually because she was quite visible. It gave her the opportunity to look at him. It seemed so young and foolish, childish, even that she should not be able to get enough of looking at him. But that was indeed the case. He was as much a part of her life as her own flesh and blood. She emerged from the shadows of the rose bush to make herself more visible, placed her basket on the ground, and sat down on the small wood and canvas folding seat she carried with her when she gardened, just as her mother used to do. It was an artist's seat left here by Edward Lear who had been a long-time guest in the villa in the last century. That triggered an idea. There was a portfolio of a dozen or more Lear water-colours: San Miniato al Monte, Villa San Firenze, the Villa Montecatini, from many angles, and gorgeous landscapes of the surrounding area. She would give them to Vittorio as a wedding present. When they could afford it she would have them framed for him, to be hung in the summerhouse near the lake. It had always been one of their favourite hiding places when they had been young.

Vittorio was still some distance away when he saw her. He cupped his hands around his mouth to form a megaphone of sorts and called out, 'Buona sera, Eliza,' then waved his arms, a smile of pure joy crossing his face.

She called back and watched him continue up the drive. Her mind flashed back to the first day of her return from Egypt to Italy and the villa, when *she* had walked up the drive after an absence of more than two decades. She had taken the bus from Pisa to Lucca and a taxi from there through the countryside to the villa, overwhelmed with emotion for the sheer love she felt on seeing Tuscany again. All those years when it and her home and family life there had been lost; when husbands and children, her own weakness, other priorities, had taken over her life and kept her away. It was she who pushed open the gate for the taxi and then gave the driver directions to the front door of the villa where he might leave the one small case she had travelled with. And then Eliza had walked, as Vittorio was walking now, alone up the drive, clearing it as she went, just as he was doing now, for her first time as the owner of her beloved Villa Montecatini.

The peace and contentment, the happiness that she and the family had always known there, had flooded back to Eliza, enveloping her. Though tired and in need of rest from her years of work and life in Upper Egypt, she had felt strong in herself and her heart and full of energy to begin again. The taxi had been on its way back from the villa, kicking up dust on the drive, speeding towards the still-open gate, when the driver screeched to a halt next to Eliza to tell her that there was a welcome party on their way down the drive to meet her. She changed pace and was walking swiftly up the drive, practically at a run, when a band of people waving and calling out her name came into view, the house in its dilapidated glory visible behind them.

She had told them nothing in her cable except the day of her arrival and that she was coming home at last and for ever. The staff and farm workers, whom she had known since she was a child and most of whom had lived there all their life, were in some cases now very old or just old, their children with whom she had grown up there with *their* children. Tears sparkled in their eyes. Affection for Eliza showed in their faces, and hugs and kisses bade her welcome home. Among them, lingering in the background to this brilliant reunion, had been Vittorio. They had gazed into each other's eyes and the years of separation, all that had passed for a life without each other, was there to be read in them – read and to be respected, certainly not denied. Suddenly that long period of time when Eliza thought she could not return to the villa was over. She had paid the price for not following her heart, paid for both of them. When she had walked into his arms and they had hugged each other, Eliza was a woman free from guilt and Vittorio had forgiven her.

Those first months after her return were months of convalescence, to restore her health. Eliza had not realised just how exhausted she was, and though rest and good food and the clean, clear Tuscan air put her back into peak condition, it did take time. She gradually eased herself into being the mistress of the house and assuming once more a life where she had once been happy. It had been in those months too that Eliza and Vittorio very slowly welcomed each other into their respective lives. She had had much to learn about the estate, not only how it was worked to yield the best from it but how it worked financially, and Vittorio was always at her side to teach her. It was in those months that they got to know each other again by talking about the lives that they had led since that fateful day he had seen her in John's flat in London.

Eliza had been ruthlessly honest about herself and

her marriages, her children, her years in Egypt. She portrayed those periods of her life exactly as they had been, flaws and all. Vittorio had been no less honest, and the contrast between their two lives could not have been greater. Here were two people, so different in every way, who had lived such different lives. What hope was there for them to come together? Was it possible to build a bridge across the chasm that separated them? It was, of course, there always had been one: the profound and deep love they had for each other. There were, during those first few months after Eliza's return, a few people around them who understood that, but for most people then and even more so now, years later, the alliance was inexplicable. Amanda Dix was a case in point. She could see no link and believed that any liaison between them could only be seen as a disaster in the making.

Eliza began to laugh and at the same time feel sorry for Amanda. Vittorio was now about two hundred yards away from her, picking cream-coloured roses off a bush. She watched him gather sprigs of laurel and several white wild iris. He was forming a bouquet for her. He bent down and picked some long green grass and used it to tie the flowers together so they might remain in a bunch.

As she gazed down the road at her lover, Eliza marvelled at how little Vittorio's looks had changed. She saw him still as a young man though he was middle-aged now and had some grey streaks in his hair. As he walked towards her, his offering in his hand, once more clearing twigs and stones from the drive, she was reminded of the several months that had passed before they committed themselves to a sexual life together.

Wherever they had gone there had always been women interested in Vittorio, most especially the foreign women living in and around the area. It was true there was a raw sexuality about him. He was like a tom cat always in heat, or at least that was the way he looked. And that kind of sexuality and the pride with which he walked, did rather label him. After his and Eliza's first sexual encounter, it had rather labelled her as well, for they found it impossible to keep their sensual delight in each other to themselves. They glowed with it.

Vittorio was approaching her now with his offering of flowers. He always had a happy heart, though his life at times had not been easy. His greatest asset was his strength of will and knowing how to cherish every day, no matter how bad it might be or what disappointments or tragedies might accompany it. And Vittorio had had his share of tragedies, bad times over the years: his impossible marriage to Janine, the birth of his three sons whom she had kidnapped away from him, the tragic death of his first-born, and finally the suicide of Janine, then after the return of his boys, bringing them up as a single parent. That was why everyone who knew him had a degree of admiration and respect for him. He had weathered his lot in life, the scandals and the pain Janine caused him, without complaint or bitterness. Vittorio was steadfast. Eliza saw him as essentially a simple man who knew how to live without complications. But the women he chose were more complex, drawn to him for his pure and simple qualities, his sexuality, his sense of belonging to the earth. All that was going on in Eliza's mind when Vittorio dropped to his knees at her feet and laid the bouquet in her lap. She ran her fingers through his hair and kissed him on the lips, then picked up the bouquet and pressed her face into the flowers, the better to take in their perfume.

Vittorio removed her straw hat from her head and placed it on the ground next to him. Then reaching around, he broke the band that held her plait and proceeded to unbraid it and arrange her hair around her face and over her shoulders. He gathered some of the strands and pressed them to his lips, then gave her, a more intimate kiss on the lips. 'Hello, Eliza. You look like a painting sitting here in your Tuscan garden.'

Very gently Vittorio raised the hem of her skirt and kissed it, then rolled it back, exposing her thighs. Eliza watched him as he snapped the silk strings of her bikini underpants and lowered the triangle of cream-coloured silk to expose her mound of very blonde pubic hair. He caressed it, and the crease between her thigh and the mound, and then opened her legs and caressed the inside of her thighs.

'I love you, Eliza, adore you. You are the sweet life for me,' he told her, voice husky with desire.

Placing his hands on her legs, he pulled her gently forward on the small artist's seat. Eliza leaned back and gathered several handfuls of cypress. She clung on to them to keep her balance and watched Vittorio's face as he lowered it to place his mouth upon her sex and licked, kissed, and made love to it. Once he had the taste of her in his mouth and he was assured that she had come, he carried her dew upon his lips to hers and they kissed, a kiss of tenderness and passion.

Then arm and arm together they walked up the drive to the villa, Vittorio telling her about his day, Eliza listening, always attentive to his every word. In the house he walked them into the library where he closed and locked the door and was almost immediately undressed. He bent her over the back of the sofa and raised her skirts. Eliza enjoyed being taken from behind, especially in that position. The fucking was deep and astonishingly sexy for them both. Carried away in a kind of animal lust she asked for and received the sting of the flat of his hand as he spanked the solidly fleshy orbs of her bottom. They came in a burst of orgasm and slid together in a panting heap to the floor.

Some minutes later, Vittorio asked, 'Do you think me an animal?'

'Vittorio!'

'I mean to have an answer, Eliza.'

'I have no problem answering the question, I am only astonished that you should ask that and curious as to why?'

'Today, when I was riding with Signora Dix, she couldn't speak to me. She never even made conversation about your tea party, never mentioned your name. And the way she stole glances at me . . . they were more of puzzlement than interest. Yes, I think she thinks I'm an animal, and I guess she finds the farmer and his lady a bit shocking.' All this was said with good humour.

Eliza knew him well enough to understand that what Amanda Dix thought mattered not at all to him. He had a very solid and healthy ego, a sureness of himself, and that very special Italian male arrogance, all of which he never over indulged.

Eliza pulled herself on to his lap and said, 'I think

you're looking for compliments. You know very well you are a sexual animal, by which I mean you can let go in sex, forget the moral code and enjoy sex for the sheer pleasure of it. You excite yourself and your partner to go to tremendous lengths to experience total ecstasy, without thought for your actions. You wear your sexuality like a strong cologne, that's what women are attracted to, what I am sure Amanda Dix is aware of. I think we unsettle her perfect world because we have something she and her husband are not prepared to accept: passion. Does that answer your question?'

'You're so clever about us, Eliza. I regret our lost years even though I know they were something we had to go through to get where we are now. In that car with Signora Dix, I felt a sadness for her and didn't know why. I do now. Maybe one day we can make up to her for her loss – her inability to consider throwing down her life for love.'

Chapter 10

Amanda and Philip were in Florence where he had been invited to examine what was purported to be a newly found Giotto. Controversy raged as to its authenticity. They entered the bar of the Excelsior Hotel for glasses of champagne poured into a tall flute over small white peaches. Miss Dix and Mr Markham were well known by the barman and waiters and were greeted with enthusiasm. They took a small table on the upper level of the bar. The place at this hour was always fun and always elegant because it was here that the most interesting of the scholars and travellers stopped for that first early-evening drink, and because the barman was a master of his craft. It was as much a meeting place as a bar, and it was rare not to see an internationally famous writer or successful poet, celebrated painter or connoisseur – anyone with a need to see Florence again. Florence was an addiction. You always had to have more of it. And of course there was the shopping which was paradise, be it for antiquities, jewellery, leather or bed linen. Philip always said about the Excelsior Bar, 'You wait long enough and you are sure to recognise someone you know, or at least wish you did know.'

The room was a third full by the time they arrived.

There was that lovely social buzz about the place that adds to the pleasure of drinking. It was about twenty minutes after their arrival when over the rim of Amanda's crystal flute she saw Eliza Flemming enter the room on the arm of a very handsome and distinguished-looking man, well dressed in a dark grey suit, white shirt and handsome tie, a pale pink silk handkerchief frothing just above the edge of his breast pocket. They went directly to stand at the bar. Amanda was astounded and said aloud, 'And where, pray, is Heathcliff?'

'Heathcliff? I doubt your Tuscan Heathcliff has even heard of the Excelsior Bar, never mind been here, Amanda. What are you talking about?'

Amanda turned to Philip and told him, 'I dare say you're right, but his fiancée has. The pretty blonde dressed in the black linen suit with the white lapels – she's the pale rider come off her horse. It's Eliza Flemming.'

Philip, who had never seen Eliza except through his binoculars and Amanda's eyes, looked across the room. It was at that moment that the man raised Eliza's hands and lowered his head to place a kiss upon each of them. The look that passed between them and the smiles that crossed their lips showed an obvious intimacy.

'She's far more smart-looking than you led me to believe,' said Philip.

'I suppose she dresses down for her farmer. Now I'm more curious about her than ever.'

It was at that moment that Lord Michael Fenchurch, once Ambassador to Italy, a position which he'd held for many years though now retired and living in a magnificent palazzo, joined Eliza at the bar. Like her, Lord Michael was accompanied by a man. All four greeted each other and certainly not as strangers. Amanda and Philip knew Lord Michael and his wife very well. They had often been guests at the palazzo. The Fenchurches had been, for many generations, connected with Tuscany. They were members of the old guard English in residence and very influential in Italy.

'This is getting more interesting by the minute,' said Philip.

Tables were now rapidly being taken over by new arrivals to the bar, people greeting one another and joining friends. Several of them as they passed by Eliza and her small group stopped to greet the men with her; she seemed to know none of them. An American painter living in Florence, on the way to her table where friends were waiting, stopped briefly to say hello to Amanda and Philip. It was then that they very nearly missed Eliza and her friends. They were passing the table on the way to theirs when Lord Michael saw them and stopped. Eliza of course recognised Amanda. They greeted one another warmly and Philip invited Lord Michael and his friends to join their table. There was that sociable moment of 'Why not? The more the merrier,' and chairs were brought to the table.

It was Lord Michael who made the introductions. 'Eliza, I see you already know Amanda and Philip?'

'No. Actually, I only know Amanda, we had tea together,' she answered, and offered Philip her hand. The two of them shook hands and exchanged smiles.

'Ah, then let me make the rest of the introductions, gentlemen. Amanda Dix and Philip Markham, friends of mine. Amanda, Philip, may I present Dr Antonio Rinaldi and Pietro Portinari?' Everyone stood around the small table shaking hands and exchanging greetings.

Lord Michael continued, 'Pietro is Eliza's closest neighbour and Antonio is a Florentine. Philip and Amanda have a charming place in your area, Eliza. But then, of course, you know that, you've been there for tea. I think I'm going dotty in my old age!'

'Do you often come down to Florence, Eliza?' asked Amanda.

'No, not often.'

Amanda was thinking, She doesn't give much away, when she heard Antonio say, 'Mostly when we call on her to troubleshoot for us, as she has done now. She's constantly putting me in her debt.'

'How intriguing. You mustn't leave us to guess what you have been doing here, Eliza?'

'It's always good to have a magistrate on your side, especially one who has been on the executive board of the health service,' teased Antonio.

'You make it sound as if Eliza is a woman to take sides. Very naughty of you, Antonio,' chided Lord Michael.

'How very extraordinary, Eliza. An Englishwoman being an Italian magistrate, and also having been an executive in the Italian Health Service?'

'You make it sound much more important than it was or is, Amanda. I was born here in Italy. My mother was half-Italian so I carry dual citizenship. I needed a job, got hired and did the work. Still serve as what you in England would call a circuit judge.'

'I think that's a bit of a simplification of the facts, Eliza,' said Pietro.

Now it was Antonio's turn to satisfy Amanda's curiosity. 'Luckily for me she needed a job, because when I returned to Italy several years ago and got heavily involved in the Health Service, it was an utter mess. I knew she would be the woman to get us straight here in Florence. She sorted out the entire service in Tuscany, then left us for law rather than medicine. Still, we can't complain. She troubleshoots for us when we're desperate and we can prise her away from her beloved villa.'

'I had no idea you worked, Eliza.'

'Only when finances demand. Now enough about me, what are you doing in Florence?' she asked Amanda.

It was clear to Eliza over several drinks, amusing chatter and a fascinating discussion of the painting that Philip had just viewed, that Amanda and he had been charmed by Antonio and considered him a suitable match for her. They could barely hide their disappointment when he announced he must leave them because he was meeting his wife.

Eliza watched him as he walked away from their table. The past was the past but he would always have a place in her heart for those years shared in Egypt. When they had parted that day by the pyramids, she'd honestly thought he might do as Anwar had said *he* would: never make contact again. But Antonio did make contact, not as a lover or even as a former lover but as a friend who needed her help. It was he who recommended her for the job in the Health Service, and with the help of Lord Michael pulled the right strings to make sure she got it. For Eliza the job had been a godsend. The villa had needed repairs and the revenue from the estate certainly would not stretch to them. Antonio and Eliza rarely saw each other, that was the way it had been since his return from Egypt and there was never a time when she thought that was strange. They both seemed to understand it was a way of leaving the past, something marvellous that was over, firmly in the past so that it might remain set apart and they might get on with their lives. Only once had there been a certain something in their eyes for each other that reminded them of that period in their lives, then it had vanished as quickly as it had come. They were friends who knew little about each other's emotional lives any more.

Pietro tapped Eliza on the arm. 'We must go, we've missed the early-evening rush of traffic, I hope.'

'I'll come to see you off,' offered Lord Michael.

'We'll all walk you to the car,' suggested Amanda.

Philip would have preferred to stay for another drink but had been put in an awkward position, so they rose as a group and left the bar. He was seeing more of the interest Amanda had in Eliza Flemming. She did have a certain quiet charm, a simplicity about her that got under the skin, and there was an air of sensuality about her that was mysterious. She appeared to be neither particularly wise or clever and yet she had held down very difficult jobs and from what he had heard had made a success of them. She had friends in high places. Had she lovers there as well? Was this Englishwoman, and she *was* very much an Englishwoman, really going to marry the farmer who cut their fields twice a year? Whatever for!

The doorman snapped to attention when he saw the group coming through the entrance and into the street. He was effusive in his salute, winning smiles from Pietro and Eliza with his expressions of gratitude for being allowed to drive the 1937 Rolls-Royce tourer with a drop head which had been down to the garage to be filled with petrol.

'What a marvellous car, Pietro, in such mint condition. What a lucky man you are to own such a beautiful object,' exclaimed Philip.

'You mean, what a lucky lady Eliza is. It's her car, I only run it in rallies.'

'And maintain it and all the other cars in the most perfect condition, otherwise they would be falling to bits in the barns. What fun it was for me to ride into Florence in it!' Then she turned to Pietro and kissed him on the cheek, adding, 'It was good of you to drive me today.'

There were eight or ten people around the car admiring it, a Japanese with a camera snapping away from every angle. Amanda, quite stunned that Eliza should own such a prize, felt she had to say something. It was not that she begrudged a compliment, simply that surprise had caught her out. All she managed was, 'You are a woman who surprises, Eliza.'

Eliza was nearly amused enough to say, 'Is that a compliment or a reprimand?' but thought better of it. Instead she said, possibly too pointedly, 'I imagine we will meet again.'

Amanda, Philip, Lord Michael and the band of admirers watched as Pietro drove the car away, Eliza by his side. 'Will they make it home tonight, do you think?' asked Amanda.

'They think they will, but I have my doubts,' answered Lord Michael.

'Am I to understand that Eliza Flemming has a collection of vintage cars, Michael?' asked Philip.

'Every one the family has ever purchased, and all maintained, driven and endowed by Pietro and his team of vintage car enthusiasts. Eliza could never afford to do it, and even if she could, she would not. She's a Forrester and a Montecatini, and they have a history of not bothering with their possessions. They have lived in that divine house and on that small but exquisite estate, on a shoestring for several generations. They are the most charming and eccentric of families, always have been for as long as anyone can remember. Their house is known for being a family home always with an open door and a good table. They are a family who always seem happiest in their own company. One is always welcome there but rarely invited. They have never been social animals, and especially not so with the other English families who have been living in Tuscany for many generations. They have always maintained closer relationships with the Tuscan families from the simple peasant farmer to the dukes, even the papacy. We always know where to go when we need a favour, they are known for the quiet influence they can wield without even trying. Julian Forrester was like that, Dulcima's father before him, and his father before him, and now little Eliza. It runs in the blood, I think.

'Do get yourself invited to the Villa Montecatini. You will have a splendid day, and the house . . . well, you will be astounded: genteel poverty meets eighteenth-century Italian furniture at its best. Frescos, paintings, Etruscan treasures, Greek vases, carpets, curtains, French eighteenth-century screens, seventeenth-century tapestries . . . they have no idea what they have there and wouldn't care if they did. It's just home to them. Well, we all love them for it. The Forresters have simple souls, kind hearts, and a passion for living free from stress, away from the world and the way it turns. For as long as I can remember they have lived the way they want to live, without giving a fig for what anyone else thinks, and good for them, say I. Well, I must be off. Come to dinner next week. I'll have Edwina call you.'

Lady Fenchurch did call and a week later Philip and Amanda went to dinner at their palazzo and stayed the night. The following morning Amanda was the first of the guests down for breakfast. Edwina Fenchurch was already there wearing a broad-brimmed sun hat, sitting on the terrace at the breakfast table. They greeted each other warmly and Amanda took her seat. The Fenchurches lived in rather grand style. There was no shortage of staff, all Tuscan except for Sir Michael's valet, Quimby, and the butler, Webster, who had both been serving the Fenchurches for nearly forty years. Webster poured fresh peach juice into a glass for Amanda, placed a plate on the white linen mat in front of her together with a small basket wherein nestled on a crisp lace-trimmed napkin small croissants, brioches, and pecan rolls oozing swirls of sticky maple syrup.

As Amanda and her hostess were looking out across the magnificent gardens to the hills beyond, Amanda spoke up. 'This is so different from our view at home. Ah, the charm of the Tuscan hills. Changing but always beautiful. We love our view, and now I find it even more charming because every morning I watch a woman riding a great white stallion. I have dubbed her the pale rider. She rides up and down the hills to the valley below as if she were one with her horse and they a part of the landscape. She's an Englishwoman called Eliza Flemming.'

'I could have guessed that. Her mother rode the same way. In fact Julian, Eliza's father, and all five of the Forrester girls were terrifically accomplished riders.'

'Do you know Eliza Flemming intends to marry a poor farmer? Actually the farmer who has been cutting our meadow for the last fifteen years.'

'Yes, I had heard she was engaged to Vittorio Carducci. It has been rather a long engagement, a few years now. I suppose when they are finally ready they will get to the altar,' answered Lady Fenchurch.

'You know his name!'

A wry smile crossed the older woman's lips. 'Yes, I do. Everyone who has heard of his and Eliza's love story does.'

'Have you met him, Edwina?'

'No, though I believe Michael has, several times when he has gone out on a shoot. Vittorio sometimes organises the beaters, if it's that kind of shoot. I think he even hunted with him once. Yes, I remember now, Michael said he was a fine shot. I did know his wife.'

'I had no idea he had been married?'

'A tragic affair for all concerned.'

It was just then that Webster arrived followed by two maids, middle-aged and dressed in black uniforms with pretty white organza aprons. He stood to the side while they served Amanda with eggs poached on a bed of spinach, in a *pancetta*, shallot, wild mushroom and cream sauce. Lady Edwina was served a plate of scrambled eggs.

'I must confess that I am puzzled how a woman like Eliza can make such a lowly marriage. What might they have in common? How will they be able to share a life? Frankly, it disturbs me. I can't imagine that she will go through with it. And the wife? A tragic affair? What happened there?' pressed Amanda.

Edwina Fenchurch suddenly looked embarrassed, and in French, which she knew Amanda spoke fluently and the butler and two maids did not understand, told her, 'My dear, not in front of the domestics. Later, if we must.' Amanda noted a tone of annoyance in her voice. Why? she wondered. Over a peasant farmer and his wife?

The chance to speak again did not come until after breakfast when the Fenchurches were walking Amanda and Philip to their car. Amanda took Edwina by the arm and, walking her away from the men said, 'Edwina, about Vittorio and the wife you knew – do briefly fill me in. I would so like to know. Vittorio has been nothing but the farmer who cut my meadows for all these years, and now suddenly he appears to be far more than that.'

'On the contrary, Vittorio Carducci is and will never be more than that. That's his power: being a handsome, unambitious man, content with his birthright. A farmer who has a love of the land and is prepared to eke out a living from it all his life. That's what attracts the women that have fallen in love with him, some of whom have been destroyed by loving and wanting to change him. His wife was the most tragic example of that. She never understood how strong he was. Amanda, your interest in all this surprises me, though I suppose you might just as well hear about her and poor Vittorio from me as from anyone else. It's common knowledge in these parts, which was why I didn't want to discuss it in front of the maids. You see, for the locals Vittorio Carducci is a rather romantic figure.'

It was at that moment that Philip called out for Amanda to hurry along, they were due a good distance away for lunch with more friends. Edwina Fenchurch smiled and started walking back to the car, Amanda placed a hand on her arm. The two women gazed into each other's eyes, then Edwina slipped her arm through Amanda's and called over her shoulder, 'Just a few minutes, Philip, I want to show Amanda my white roses.'

'Thank you, Edwina.'

'What is this strong interest in Vittorio, Amanda? That's blunt but I mean to be blunt. There is nothing there for you, my dear. I can assure you I am right about that.'

'Edwina! No, no. It's not him, it's *them*. I'm repelled at the idea that a woman such as Eliza should give herself over to a marriage with all the limitations that this one will surely impose on her.'

Lady Edwina actually raised her eyebrows. She had never realised before how truly insensitive to real beauty and intolerant of pure love Amanda was. And as everyone else knew, there was real beauty in Eliza and Vittorio, it was that which people saw in each of them and were drawn to. Quite obviously Vittorio and Eliza's story was a blow to the very foundations of Amanda's own life and love. Now Edwina felt compelled to tell her about Vittorio's wife, something that should settle her curiosity and make her back off and leave Eliza and Vittorio to get on with their lives. It would not do to have another woman come between them once more.

Surely everyone can rise to a love story? she thought. Even a tragic one if it ultimately has a happy ending, as she dearly hoped this one would. She told Amanda, 'Janine le Donneur had many lovers in her day but only one husband, a well-kept secret, and he was Vittorio Carducci.'

'Le Donneur the writer! That brilliant, talented woman, sophisticated, beautiful, an intellectual, one of the extreme right-wing French writers? Oh, please, surely not?'

'Surely yes, Amanda. I know the story because I knew her. My nephew married her sister. She had a house some ten miles from the Villa Montecatini. When Vittorio was sixteen he started doing odd jobs for her there. She was a difficult and very beautiful woman with a strong libido that she exercised with discretion. Tuscany was her hideaway where she liked to seclude herself for most of the year when she was writing. She took Vittorio on as a young and secret lover, despite or maybe because there was a large difference in their ages. They suited each other's sexual needs, and for years it went on because where else would a poor Tuscan boy get sex without complications?

'But she made the fatal mistake older women often make. When he wanted his freedom, she found he was already a part of her life. She refused to let him go. Janine was a devious woman. She had a grand reputation to uphold in the literary world which she kept alive by never allowing her personal life to become public. She truly cared for and loved nothing but writing. But she held the one trump card that she knew would keep Vittorio in her life. He married her when, at the age of forty-two, she gave him a son. Then at forty-four, twin sons.

'It was all a grave mistake. For her nothing was the same once the children were born. They infringed on her life with Vittorio and on her work. She deserted him when the twins were only a month old, kidnapped them actually and returned to France, never to return to Tuscany. She took a house in Grasse, and her children were brought up there by their grandmother. Janine closed the Tuscany house and divorced Vittorio, tricked him in fact, by declaring that she would give him back his sons if he did nothing to hinder a divorce and kept their marriage and their having children a secret. He believed her, to his detriment.'

'She got her divorce and kept the children!' exclaimed Amanda.

'Exactly. Vittorio hadn't the money nor was he clever enough to fight her. Eliza was his first love and he lost her, he lost the woman he never loved but married, he lost his children, then he lost his first-born in a tragic boating accident off St Tropez. As you and the rest of the world know, Janine le Donneur, when she died several years ago, burned all her personal papers except for a letter she left to her sons, telling them that Vittorio was their father.'

Amanda was at last silenced on the subject. Edwina Fenchurch took some satisfaction in that. She had known Eliza since she was a child and felt she had that same sweet innocence and purity of heart she had always had, in sharp contrast to the more hardened Amanda, who, Edwina imagined, would never feel able to lay down her life for love – a state of mind that, for Eliza, was as natural as the sun rising every morning. Edwina slipped her arm through her guest's and together they walked towards the men who were patiently waiting for them.

Off in the distance, a grey mist was climbing the hills. It was sure to be raining on their crest but no rain was falling this far away. It was dry and hot, and the Villa Montecatini was waiting for the sun to break through the clouds. A wind seemed to be blowing in from the north-west. Dark clouds were hanging low but bright light behind them etched an edge, a shimmering glow, around their voluptuous shapes. The threatened rain storm would blow itself away, the sun would not be long in coming to burn off the mist. In an hour's time it would be all bright blue skies, the humidity would have vanished, and then the glory of all glories: a hot late-summer day in Tuscany.

Eliza was on the terrace waiting for Vittorio to bring the horses around, a pair of picnic baskets connected by a leather strap, waiting at her feet. These would soon be slung over her horse, Braganza. Today they were to ride across the Montecatini estate, to check out the vineyards and orchards, the olive groves and farm yards; to speak to the farm hands, ride into several villages and have a drink with the pickers who would soon be coming to the farm for the harvesting. Afterwards they would make the pilgrimage they tended to make every few months, to gather wild flowers for the mausoleum where Dulcima Forrester lay interred with her ancestors on the small island in the lake. They would be home just before dark.

These visits round the estate were always happy and easy going, whether it was a good, just fair, or even a bad season for the farm. This was an abundantly good one. Vittorio and Eliza were close to the land and the people who worked on it with them. It was a profit-sharing enterprise between landowner, tenant farmer and the workforce that had been going on for ten generations. The Montecatini farm was unique in the area and the envy of less liberal and generous landowners. Over the years the system had worked for the Montecatinis, maybe not enough to make them rich but certainly to keep the estate going and self-sufficient. The local farming community gave a certain amount of respect to Vittorio Carducci since he and his family had for generations been running the farm, but in the few years since Eliza's return she had become equally important in their lives for the work she had done in the Health Service and as a local magistrate, and not least because she was a Montecatini, half-Italian and mistress of the farm and the villa. Everyone waited in hope that the promised wedding between the farmer and the magistrate would finally come off.

Eliza heard the clip-clop of the horses' hooves before she saw Vittorio come into view, riding his horse and leading hers. This morning she was riding the Arabian mare that Antonio had bought her years before in Egypt. A month after her return to Tuscany the horse had arrived with a note signed by him and Anwar. It merely said, 'Lest you forget.'

Eliza mounted Braganza after handing Vittorio the picnic basket and together they rode down a bridle path along the edge of the garden then struck out alongside a field blue with flowering flax.

They had made several stops and had had talks with the field hands and the dairy man, had coffee with a half dozen people who ran the dairy and the cheese house. Over glasses of wine and slabs of fresh buffalo mozzarella laid on chunks of rough granary bread, they listened to the cheese man's idea to expand their output. Eliza was quite stunned at the difference in her earnings over the last few years, which had all been poured into saving the roof and buying equipment for the farm.

Once mounted again on Braganza, riding next to Vittorio, she told him, 'The farm is so much better and more prosperous than when we were children, and I know it's all due to you. We owe you so much, Vittorio. Father always said, "Leave it to the Carduccis and we will always have the Villa Montecatini." And he was never wrong.'

'In the last of your mother's years here she always told me, "Vittorio, save the Villa Montecatini for Eliza. She'll be back, and when she is, together you will keep it always safe for our families."'

'Vittorio! You've never told me that before.'

'No, I haven't.'

They rode in silence for some distance before Eliza spoke again. 'Have you noticed, Vittorio, in the last year the family has been drifting in and out of the house again, as in the old days when we were children? The cast of characters may have changed but they come in and out in a celebration of life and Tuscany. Effie,

Constanza, Clara, Dendra . . . sometimes just their children. Then there's Samantha and her father, and now Olivia is asking when she can come with some of her friends. And I'm so thrilled that your two boys have taken to coming over, wanting to stay with us rather than in the house Janine left them. I know how much having them back means to you. The house is full of the lives and comings and goings of family, yours and mine. It's what we've wanted ever since we've been together.'

'We've all come a long way. But maybe not so far, if you know what I mean?'

'Well, I think I do, darling.'

'Have you noticed that no one asks any longer when we're going to marry?' he asked Eliza.

'Yes, I have actually. It sometimes bothers me.'

'Why?'

'Because I think they assume we will not marry. I would hate to think we were becoming a joke with this long engagement.'

Vittorio began to laugh. 'Are you proposing to me again, Eliza?'

'Yes, dammit, I believe I am.'

He laughed even louder and looked very happy. 'Name the date!' he told her.

'You do mean it? We said we would wait to marry until we were certain we could live with each other, accept our differences, the years and the other lives we have lived without each other. Is that time really over? You're sure about this? You won't leave me at the altar?'

He pulled up his horse and leaned over to take the reins of Eliza's from her hands. She smiled but there were tears in her eyes. Vittorio dismounted and led the two horses out of the sun and under a huge old apple tree, laden with ripening fruit tinged red. There he tied the horses to a bough and, taking Eliza by the hands, helped her to dismount from Braganza.

Vittorio removed the wide-brimmed straw hat from her hair. He pulled the tortoiseshell hairpins from the French twist at the nape of her neck and tossed them into the grass. Tears began running from Eliza's eyes. He licked them away with the tip of his tongue as he unbuttoned the white silk shirt she was wearing and pulled its tails out from under the waistband of her riding breeches. He caressed her breasts and licked the beads of perspiration from between them. Then he moved his lips from her breasts to her mouth and kissed her passionately. Finally he told her in a voice husky with emotion, 'I've waited since you were seven years old to commit myself to you in love and before God. Why would I leave you at the altar?'

The tears were fast flowing from her eyes now, he caressed her hair and kissed her again and told her, 'I love you, Eliza. All the feelings I have ever had in my life were to make me ready for you, they begin and end with you. Loving you is like nothing else I have ever known. All the women I have had in my life were for my own selfish needs except for you. For you, right from when we were children, it was an unselfish love that came from the heart. What I have always felt for you was a grown-up passion and love, absolute and thrilling. Leave you at the altar? I have waited several lifetimes for you to come back to me, to love me as I have always loved you. These last years with you by my side have been the happiest of my life. There has not been a morning when I have awakened you with a kiss that I have not asked myself: "Today, will it be today that we know we are ready to make that final vow?" Leave you at the altar? I would sooner die.'

They were married five days later in the lovely hill town of Barga, at the very top of the town in its celebrated cathedral. The view from the cathedral terrace with its panoramic vista of roof tops and the surrounding hills clad in bright green velvet and bare mountains raked with white marble seemed to Eliza and Vittorio to epitomise the Tuscany they were born in and loved beyond measure. That was why they had chosen to be married there.

The blond stone exterior of the cathedral with its square façade discreetly decorated with a shallow pattern of charming reliefs and two leering lions on the side of the campanile that was incorporated into the church, glistened with an aura of ancient Tuscany under the bright morning sun on the day they were married. Eliza and Vittorio, wanting to keep their wedding a happy and very personal affair, had been extraordinarily casual about announcing it. But like all happy and surprising events, word spread like wildfire. When they had arrived together in one of the family's vintage Rolls-Royces driven by Pietro Portinari whom Eliza had chosen to give her away, the terrace was filled with a varied group of friends and associates they had never expected to see.

Eliza actually found it overwhelming. She'd never dreamed that people would want to be there to see them wed. Invitations, mostly by telephone, had been issued to say that Eliza and Vittorio would be having open house, and for people to spread the word that everyone was welcome to come that day for a celebration at the villa, but they had mentioned to only a few the place and the time of the wedding. Most of the five days between their decision to marry and the actual day of the ceremony had been spent organising their wedding feast: long trestle tables, chairs, musicians and paper lanterns had to be procured. Room had not been a problem, it was to be held in the gardens, the weather posing no threat to their plans, and the Villa Montecatini staff were masters at conducting open-ended parties and casual arrangements.

The wedding of the farmer and the magistrate was a far greater event, and to many a curiosity, than either the bridegroom or the bride had imagined it would be. So many people, for so many years in the background of their lives, wanted to be in on the celebration and to wish them well. It was a measure of respect they had never expected. After the initial shock of seeing the crowd on the terrace in front of the cathedral, an even greater enthusiasm and gratitude than they were already feeling for their wedding day took over and they rose to the grand occasion that friends and even strangers made out of it.

All of Vittorio's family was there, including his two sons; most of Eliza's Italian branch of the family who had played with her and Vittorio when they were children appeared, but none of her children or her sisters. They had been told about the event but Eliza had said that it was going to be a small, very private affair, to be celebrated at a later date each time any of them arrived for a visit to the villa.

Eliza and Vittorio married in grand style in the

cathedral with its red marble pillars, each one supported by a carved dwarf and a pairs of lions grinning over a conquered dragon, its polychrome wood statue of St Christopher and the glorious oval window. They took their vows among the friends, acquaintances, and many strangers who admired them for conquering all for love, in an ancient church heavily scented with incense. A choir sang Gregorian chants. Eliza, dressed in a clinging 1920s cream-coloured silk crêpe-de-chine dress with a two-foot-long train, and wearing a very sheer veil, just long enough to cover her eyes, and embroidered with a fine almost invisible lace pattern that covered her hair, which had been dressed high on her head with twists to form a crown, walked to the altar on the arm of Pietro Portinari, feeling in her heart like the young girl in love with Vittorio she had always been.

Everything except the stockings that she wore had been found packed away in trunks and cupboards in the villa. She wore her grandmother's wedding dress, her mother's veil, Vittorio wed her with a diamond band that her great-grandfather had once given her great-grandmother. Even her shoes, cream-coloured satin embroidered with rose buds, had belonged to a great-aunt. She was wed in the sight of her ancestors and when she walked away from the altar as Vittorio Carducci's wife, she sensed their approval. They could rest secure in her happiness and the knowledge that the villa was safe and in the family for many generations to come. She was carrying one more secret: a love child.

Chapter 11

It was several weeks after Eliza married Vittorio that Amanda Dix saw her again. She was sitting alone in the piazza of the same village that had the Wednesday market, drinking a glass of wine. The sun was playing on her blonde hair and she looked incredibly pretty and at ease with the world. The two women greeted one other and Eliza asked Amanda to join her. They talked about the weather, and how limited the shopping was in the village, and Eliza confessed she bought very little in the shops here or anywhere because they were self-sufficient by way of the farm, even curing their own meat. The two women enjoyed themselves and Amanda suggested that if they were going to be in the village the following week on market day, they should have lunch together. They did.

It was nearly a year before the two women were to meet again and that was by chance in Barga. Once again they chatted amiably. Eliza went home and told Vittorio that she liked Amanda Dix, but probably they got on because they were so very different from one another and could never be real friends. Another time Amanda and Eliza met by chance at the hog-backed bridge. They walked into the village together and did their shopping. Both women began to look forward to these meetings, and the more they saw each other, the more interested they became in each other's lives. They were almost voyeuristic about them. Eliza realised that Amanda never mentioned Vittorio, or the fact that they now had a son, though Eliza always asked after Philip. A friendship developed between them: one that can happen between women who meet over cups of coffee or a drink in the village café, who walk through the open market on market day but never infringe on personal lives or relationships.

Amanda finally came to understand that it was their Englishness that they had in common, that they liked each other as human beings, but because they had chosen such very different lives for themselves, they could never be more than casual friends. She never again seemed able to equate the pale rider with Eliza once they began having their meetings. Soon after these meetings began she stopping watching her on her morning rides on the white stallion. They were a reminder of another Eliza, set apart from the woman she chatted with.

The more Amanda grew to know and like Eliza, the more she resented her wasting her life on a dull farmer. But when Vittorio came, as he always had, to cut the meadow, Amanda found it very nearly impossible to tear herself away from the window. She watched him, stripped to the waist, handsome, muscular, erotic as hell. She was never quite sure if it was sexual fascination because of the women he had had or if she really wanted to be fucked by him. All she was certain of was that when he left the meadow, she was voraciously hungry for sex, as wild and thrilling as she could get it with Philip.

Amanda and he were aware of her bizarre love-hate feelings, for both Eliza and Vittorio, over the few years since they had met. They caused a dissatisfaction that had never been evident before. Philip did not like it, Amanda too disapproved of this blemish on their perfect world.

One day, apropos of nothing, she said, 'Philip, I cannot make sense of Eliza's choosing Vittorio. How can they be happy together, how can they be so content with their lives? She's constantly having to step down to his level, I find it degrading, pathetic, that she should be so weak.'

'Maybe she has never been above his level, maybe circumstances dragged her up the hill and she never wanted to be there? Vittorio is a more than a nice guy. He looks to be a passionate man, probably a terrific lover, and for Eliza, if maybe not you, Amanda, that's enough.'

'But she's laying down her life for him, Philip.'

'Maybe that's how it works for them. Maybe he is laying down his life every minute of every day for her, Amanda. It does happen, you know, love for love's sake and nothing more. One partner happily sacrificing all for another. Not for the likes of you and I, Amanda, but possibly for them.'

'They're interfering with our life, Philip!'

'No, Amanda, just showing us up for what we are and are not to each other. They're a painful reminder of something we can never have. But don't despair. I am sure we are an equally painful reminder to Eliza of a life she could never succeed in.'

'Now what does *that* mean?'

Philip recognised real anguish in Amanda's voice.

He did not often see the vulnerable side of her, she hid it very well. He went to her and raised her by her arms from the chair where she was sitting. He stroked her cheek with the back of his hand. 'A life where security, success, fame and fortune, style and beauty, are equally as important as love and sex. A life that is tempered, organised for survival of the fittest, not simple-minded farmers and sweet passionate dreamers like your friend Eliza.'

Amanda kissed Philip on the mouth. Her lips were trembling with real passion and love for him. He was always there for her in those moments when she really needed him. And she *had* needed him. She was envious of Eliza and what she had, how much she could give. Only in the night was she Eliza's equal and she had almost forgotten that. Only in the night, in the throes of glorious sexual bliss, could she abandon herself and her careful, well-organised life, submit totally to the god Eros and her lover. Only in the night could she die for love of Philip.

In the months since Amanda and Eliza had been seeing each other, a sincere affection crept into Amanda's feelings for Eliza and Vittorio, whom she barely knew and rarely saw, each of them had learned bits and pieces of the other's life. But the more they learned, the more it set them poles apart. They had a strong but strange friendship that demanded of them respect and indifference. Amanda imagined that it was a friendship that would last all their lives and never change. But she was wrong in that.

The beginning of the end came when the two women stepped outside the boundaries they had drawn in their relationship: Amanda's decision never to become involved by actually seeing with her own eyes the life Eliza lived with Vittorio, Eliza's never to see her friend socially except during their quiet meetings for coffee, lunch or a drink, in a public place, after which each would wend their own way home.

There was a chance meeting between Eliza and Amanda, this time in Siena quite far from where they lived. Amanda and Philip were sitting out at a café table in the piazza facing the Palazzo Pubblico. They were with four friends, their house guests, talking about the Palio – the painted prize for which ten riders gallop bareback around the great Campo of Siena where they were at that moment sitting. They were all laughing at Philip and Amanda's description of the crowds and the air of hysteria, fun and danger that accompanies the race that is all over in ninety seconds, when Eliza and two young men, very tall and very handsome, came into view weaving in and out of the tables, looking for an empty one. Philip and Eliza saw each other just at the same time. He rose from his chair and all eyes at the table followed his gaze. Amanda was at first surprised and then both pleased and not so pleased to see her. Her not-so-pleased feelings were only because she found it disconcerting to see Eliza outside the little world where they were able to be friends.

Eliza looked very attractive, flanked by the two young men. She appeared to be more sensuous, more exciting than usual, dressed in a flesh-coloured silk blouse with dropped shoulders and balloon sleeves that buttoned tight to her wrists. A skirt cut on the bias hung in voluptuous folds down to her ankles.

Made of flesh-coloured suede, it was belted by a three-inch-deep coral-coloured patent leather belt. Her long hair fell in a tumble of soft waves around her face. Amanda rose from her chair and the two women greeted each other. Amanda quickly introduced her friends to Eliza who was then obliged to introduce her companions.

'Boys, these are neighbours of ours, Amanda Dix and Philip Markham. Amanda, Philip, I would like you to meet Hervé and Michel le Donneur, Vittorio's sons.'

Here was another part of Eliza's life being played out in front of them. Quite suddenly Philip could understand from where Amanda's anxiety about Eliza and Vittorio derived. She was something very quietly special with a soft, sensuous, submissiveness about her that intrigued a man. The handsome young men in their early-twenties were identical twins and the absolute image of their father, only more polished, very French.

As Eliza walked away from Amanda and Philip's table she was aware that they thought of her as an oddity, someone who should have stayed home with her farmer husband, who should not have two such handsome and cultivated sons. For shame, Amanda. For shame, Philip, she thought. Several times she looked over at them and their friends, the sort of people she had known when married to John and Robert, the sort of people her sisters had for friends. She marvelled at how easy it had been to give them up in favour of being in love and married to Vittorio. She had a sense that a miracle must have taken place to have delivered her from the life that Amanda and

Philip thrived on to the place and the man she loved above all else.

The following day, after their return from Siena, Hervé and Michel arrived in time for dinner at the Villa Montecatini. There were several of the farm workers there talking local politics with Vittorio, the usual Montecatini house staff, and two pretty young girls from the village who were Dulcima's godchildren. An aroma of roast veal, and a *pancetta* and asparagus cream sauce in the massive bowl of fettucine being passed around the table, hung like a strong kitchen perfume in the air. There was laughter and good wine being drunk – this was the atmosphere that had always prevailed in the Montecatini kitchen for as long as Eliza could remember. She took considerable pride in the fact that since her arrival as the new mistress of the villa nothing had changed in the running of the house, nor had it when she had married Vittorio. It was the same casual, generous hospitality that was offered to every guest.

Eliza looked down the table at Vittorio who was sitting between his two boys. It was a wonderful sight to see. Hervé and Michel were still getting used to Vittorio as their father, Eliza as their step-mother, and to Tuscany. Vittorio took his sons and their family predicament in his stride: that was, calmly, looking for the positive, happy side of it, and choosing not to deal with the poison and pain their mother had so ruthlessly dealt him by never speaking ill of her. Eliza could see them, every week they were with their father, slowly and surely falling that little bit more in love with him. Strangely these two boys who had never had an understanding of Italy, nor a love of country life or the land, discovered once they took over Janine's house that they had a natural affinity with farming, husbandry, and a respect for the father who was less educated, cultured and ambitious than they.

How Eliza loved her husband. And as she watched him at table, laughing and chatting with his sons, she realised why she loved him so very much, why he had been the only true love of her life. He was a man who never tore her down. He had always made her feel confident, more than she was. Vittorio had always made her feel more, rather than less, of everything and he was the only man that had ever done that.

More people dropped in just as they were beginning dinner: Pietro Portinari and several of his house guests, friends from Rome and Madrid who wanted to go to the barn to see the cars. But the aroma of the Montecatini kitchen seduced them to the table and they too stayed to dine. For generations, the charm of visiting the villa had always been the same: a cross-section of people from all walks of life, an unstructured household enjoying themselves. After dinner most people did go to the barns, and from there they drifted back into the house. Slowly the villa came to life as lamps in the hall, library, dining room, drawing room, and the small sitting room that had always been called the morning room, were switched on and people drifted through them. In the music room, a small oval apartment behind the hall, Hervé played the piano – Cole Porter, Rodgers and Hart, Jerome Kern – and Michel sang the show tunes in French and charmed everyone. It was too late for the two girls from the village to go home so they slept over in one of the many guest rooms. It was a happy evening and everyone left much too drunk and much too late.

Finally alone, Eliza and Vittorio walked through the house, turning off lights, closing windows. The last stop was the kitchen there they found Francesca the cook and Paolo the gardener sitting at the kitchen table, he playing the accordion very softly, she singing a Tuscan folk song while she shelled a huge basket of bean pods. Eliza was about to step forward into the room to demand that she stop working and go to bed when Vittorio stopped her first with a hand on her shoulder, then a nod of his head, and took her silently away from the kitchen door.

'They're enjoying themselves,' was all he said.

They went arm-in-arm upstairs, first to check on their son Julian, which they did every night before they went to bed. A cousin of Vittorio's, a plump and very pretty girl who'd needed a home, had been taken in by Eliza and Vittorio to be nanny to their unborn child. Weeks before Julian was born Beatrice had proved to be a happy addition to the household. There she was, asleep in her bed in the large room that had for generations served as the nursery. Eliza tiptoed first to Beatrice, to cover her, she always kicked her bedcovers off, and then walked across the room to stand next to Vittorio who was bending over the crib doing the same for his son. As usual Julian was sound asleep. Mother and father kissed their son, and as silently as possible left the nursery.

At last they undressed and went to bed. Naked, lying on their sides and in each other's arms, they kissed and caressed each other. Vittorio said, 'To have courage to live is everything, Eliza. Look what it has brought us.

Our children, all six of them, and you and I are to be the custodians of the place we love the most in the world for the rest of our lives. How blessed we are. Tonight was such a good time. You were, as you always are, marvellous, a great hostess, all charm and beauty, the light in a sometimes dark world. Thank you, my heart, my life.'

There was love and passion, admiration and respect, in his every word. He kissed her, and between kisses repeated her name again and again. And then lust took over. *Her* lust for her husband. She draped herself over Vittorio's body in such a way that he could caress her back and bottom, toy with the crevice between its cheeks, fondle her orifices with searching fingers, excite the bud of pleasure hidden between her most intimate, warm and already moist lips while she took him, rampant and throbbing, deep in her throat. Such exquisite oral sex caused him very nearly to weep for the sexual bliss it produced for him. They came together in a shatteringly powerful orgasm and rubbed their lips, the skin of their faces, with the elixir that such sex can produce. They tasted of each other in their kiss and once more came before they fell asleep, exhausted by the joy of being one with each other.

The next morning they were in the bath. It was their habit to wash each other with a large sponge and a creamy almond-scented liquid soap made on the estate from their own almond trees. Eliza was scrubbing Vittorio's back when he said, 'Your friend Signora Dix, why do you always meet her in town, never ask her back here for your English tea party or a meal? She asked you to tea.'

The question took Eliza by surprise. How could she

explain that she wouldn't feel comfortable about doing either of those things? Then she would have to explain to him that she sensed socialising with Amanda Dix and Philip Markham in any way other than according to the limits of the two women's friendship was something that would not work. First and foremost Vittorio would not understand her. And she certainly would not go on to explain that the scandalous alliance between an English gentlewoman and an Italian farmer was a stumbling block to a closer friendship with the couple. What she did say was, 'Well, I must one day.'

'Good. When?' he asked, sweet enthusiasm in his voice.

'I hadn't thought,' she answered.

'Next week. I'm going over there to cut the meadow today, I can ask them for you.'

'Why is this so important to you, Vittorio?' she asked as she kissed the back of his neck and squeezed the water-logged sponge over his shoulders to wash the soap away.

'Because she's one of the only English ladies like yourself who has become a friend you enjoy meeting. It doesn't exactly worry me but I do sometimes think you have given up so much of your English ways and friends to marry and make a life here with me. I don't want you to miss them and be discontent and maybe even . . .'

'Stop right there, Vittorio. I have given up nothing. I miss nothing. You forget, we have my sisters and all their families, other English friends that we have known all our lives who drop in on us frequently. All those English holiday meals and treats I make when I cook – this is an Anglo-Italian house. We've known each other practically all our lives, and have you ever known a Forrester to live in any way but the way they want to? Now, will it make you happy if I ask them to a grand and very English dinner?'

'Well, not too English but I don't mind grand. And I will help you, and so will Francesca.'

He had turned himself around in the bath to face her. How young and happy he looked to be doing this for her. All his life he had been doing everything for love of her. The least she could do was carry off a dinner for Amanda and Philip for him. There was nothing for it; it would be *their* invitation, not hers. She would make him a part of it and began by asking him, 'Would you mind stopping in and inviting them for dinner any day that's convenient for them next week? They are to arrive at five for drinks. That will give them time to see the gardens and the orchards if they like, even time to walk down to the lake and see the stables.'

Vittorio was thrilled. He took her in his arms and kissed her, caressed her breasts, all shimmery and slippery smooth as the puffs of steam swirled up and around them from the hot bathwater. Eliza was filled with a sense of joy at being able to make him happy. That was after all what they were all about, what they had always been about, and nothing more. How had she not understood that when she had been a young woman, and other people and the outside world had declared love not enough?

Philip and Amanda, Philip's publisher and his researcher, and Amanda's assistant, just back from a day in Lucca, entered the kitchen with bags of shopping for Maria. Amanda and Phillip were surprised to see Vittorio sitting at their kitchen table having coffee with her. They had forgotten that he would be there all day cutting the fields.

Vittorio rose as soon as they entered and relieved Amanda of the shopping she was carrying. It was quite obvious to her and Philip that their house guests found him impressive and attractive. There seemed about him that day an aura of delight, a sense of joy, which combined with his unusually rough and handsome dark good looks was very winning. Philip felt obliged to introduce him to his guests. 'These are friends who are staying with us. And this, everyone, is Vittorio, the farmer who cuts our meadow.'

Vittorio acknowledged them with a broad smile and a nod of his head, and then turned directly to Amanda and said, 'Eliza asked me if I would, on her behalf, invite you and Mr Markham to come to dinner at the Villa Monetcatini.'

Amanda kept her surprise well hidden when she answered, 'This evening? Oh, dear, that's rather impossible. You see, it's our guests' last evening here and we have made plans. But do thank Eliza very much.'

'Oh, that's no problem. The invitation is extended for any evening of your choice next week,' he told her, beaming with delight and then waiting for her to choose the date.

Everyone standing around, watching and listening, flummoxed Amanda. She found it impossible to find a way to reject the invitation in their presence without making an issue of it. Feeling utterly defeated and put upon, she managed to answer, 'Thursday would be good, unless Philip has something on that I don't know about?'

There it was. She had tossed the ball in to his court. He could get them out of the evening with some dignity. He was a man who knew how to handle awkward situations and get what was best for them in the most dignified manner. She very nearly sighed with relief.

Amanda was therefore stunned when she heard him say, 'Thursday will be fine, and we thank Eliza very much for the invitation.'

Vittorio told them the time, and the plan suggested by Eliza. He was gone almost at a run in his enthusiasm to get away. Almost immediately their guests wanted to know about him and Eliza. Much later Amanda's only comment about Philip's accepting the invitation was issued when they were alone in their room dressing for dinner.

'You couldn't resist seeing the palazzo. Is that why we will be subjected to an evening that will probably be awkward for all of us, embarrassing even? Honestly, Philip, how could you? An evening with the farmer who cuts our meadow. I don't mean to sound like a snob but in the fifteen or more years he has been doing the fields he has hardly spent fifteen minutes speaking to us.'

'Yes, I suppose the chance of seeing the palazzo was why I accepted. Michael and Edwina said it was a rare invitation, *if* ever extended, so be flattered it was issued to us. After all, she is your friend, and friends do go to one another's houses.'

'You know very well we're not that kind of friends, and so does Eliza. I can't imagine what has prompted this invitation. It's not going to be any easier for her than it is for us. Well, just don't expect too much.

Eliza has told me it's a very casual lifestyle at the Villa Montecatini.'

'Amanda, you do understand that this dinner invitation is quite an honour for us? In all the years we've had this house, it's only the third time we've been invited by one of our Tuscan neighbours to dine. I realise only now how little we have fitted into the community. Granted we probably set a certain amount of isolation upon ourselves. It could be either very boring or a tremendous surprise, or both. Let's not think about it, just go.'

Philip was of course right. What was there to think about? And so she put it and any expectations of the forthcoming evening out of her mind, as did he, until they arrived at the closed entrance to the Villa Montecatini.

The massive iron gates hung on chipped stone pediments bearing twisted vines and ivy and were capped by what once must have been handsome crouching stone leopards, now worn away by the centuries and the weather. Looking through the bars up the avenue of cypress trees and overgrown shrubs, wild flowers and flowering bushes, many of them heavy with scorched roses, they were enchanted before they even opened the gates.

Amanda slipped into the driver's seat of the Range Rover to drive it through the gates being opened by Philip. She sat silent, staring up the drive, while he closed them with a clang. All day the heat had been oppressive. Now though the sun was still hot and high in the sky, there was a warm but pleasant late-summer breeze ruffling the leaves of the rose bushes and shrubs, making the cypresses sway their length sensuously, as if they were seducing Amanda and Philip to go forward and be embraced by the Villa Montecatini.

Back in the driver's seat again Philip sat for some minutes, just taking it all in silently before he turned to Amanda and said, 'Impressive for its decadent beauty. Jesus, is it ever! This only comes with time, centuries of it, and secrets, past souls. I can almost hear their laughter. I had no idea!'

'Nor I.'

He put the Range Rover into gear and drove slowly up the gracefully winding drive.

'That perfume – mint and roses, a hint of something like frankincense. The leftover scent of those who have passed on, having lived and loved here. God, what a romantic place,' said Amanda.

The sky was a bright blue and seemed to widen as they drove up the incline along the avenue, to the summer song of the breeze in the trees and the sound of small animals scurrying through the undergrowth. It was more a passage through something mysterious, simple and lovely, than a three-quarter-mile drive before one was able to get a first glimpse of the house. Small by palazzo standards, it was a fifteenth-century classical building, and like the drive, not groomed to impress. However, it *was* impressive, with the look of being well lived in, a very much loved place and home.

The house was set high on a hill and the views in consequence sensationally beautiful, especially by contrast to the very English lawns and formal garden. Philip stopped the Range Rover close to the front door which stood open as were all the windows on the ground floor. The severe façade was softened by dozens upon dozens of terracotta-potted trees and flowering plants, looking thirsty and worn down from days of heat and burning sun. Several period Chinese bamboo tables under white canvas umbrellas of considerable size and a scattering of wooden chairs, all askew, of which no two matched, a handsome and elegant French Empire chaise with an open book lying on it, gave the impression of having only just been evacuated by a household that had been lazing in the afternoon heat.

Amanda and Philip were looking down at the tennis court and a croquet lawn when they heard someone approaching the front door of the palazzo through the house. Assuming it was either Eliza or Vittorio, they turned to greet whoever it was. They were further surprised that it should be neither of them but an elderly houseman dressed in smart black and grey pinstripe trousers and a white collarless jacket with epaulettes on the shoulders and cuffs embroidered with slim bands of gold thread. He spoke only in Italian and suggested that they sit down at one of the tables and he would fetch Madam Signora Carducci as soon as he had poured them a Pimms. Then, passing each of them a small white linen napkin, trimmed in an exquisite two-inch band of ecru-coloured lace, and a large silver goblet, perfectly chilled, containing a paper thin slice of orange, a wedge of apple, a large sprig of fresh mint and a roundel of cucumber, he departed.

'I simply cannot think of the Eliza Flemming I know over coffee and drinks in village cafés as Signora Carducci – and all this given over to a farmer lover, no matter how nice he appears to be. If we had not accepted this invitation, I could have kept my illusions about Eliza. Born to all this and settling for Vittorio – what kind of a life is that!'

'Your inability to love on the scale that Eliza can is showing again, Amanda. Give it a rest and face up to your friend's life,' said Philip, at the same time feeling a bit inadequate himself about his own limitations in the love stakes.

Eliza's daughter Samantha appeared with the twins who introduced her to Amanda and Philip and promptly left them, to head down to the lawn for a game of croquet. They were just recovering from finding that Eliza had a grown-up daughter when Beatrice wheeled a magnificent 1920s pram through the front door. It was empty because walking directly behind her was Eliza carrying her son. She handed the baby to the nanny, and turning to Amanda and Philip, said with a welcoming smile, 'He's Vittorio's and mine. We named him Julian after my father. Sorry I wasn't here to greet you, welcome to our home.'

An hour passed before Vittorio found them down by the lake and joined them, nearly two hours more before the four of them returned to the villa. It was quite obvious to Eliza that Amanda and Philip could not quite cope with the house and the way she and Vittorio lived in it, never mind the fact that *he* lived in it at all. Adopting a 'their problem, not ours' attitude allowed her the luxury of not giving a damn and enjoying herself.

In the hall was a large console table whose gilt pheasants and other game birds beneath its *fleur de pêche* marble top were held together with a piece of clothes line and a pink ribbon. It was choc-a-bloc with Ming vases, dead roses in Tang bronze bowls, a lamp with its torn and yellowed silk shade atilt, a stack of newspapers, a tennis racquet and a fishing rod. There were besides dozens more beautiful things used in the family's everyday lives, assembled without a collector's eye or any consideration for their value. The house and its contents simply overwhelmed Eliza's guests, so much so they had to say something.

'Have you any idea the treasures you have here or their value?' asked a concerned Philip.

'Vaguely, but not really. What does it matter? The family never sells anything anyway. It's all just part of our lives. Do you sell off bits and pieces of your lives or your ancestors'? Some do but my family never does.'

'But if you sold off only a few things, you could restore the house and all the other objects here.'

'We do restore but on a limited scale because of money. We never seem to have enough to do major things, but we soldier on.'

'Would you like to see more of the house?' asked Vittorio. They did want to, very much. The last stop they made was the long dining table in the kitchen where they found about eight people sitting drinking wine and waiting for dinner. When Eliza bade everyone to have a happy meal, Amanda realised they were not dining with them.

Eliza, seeing the confused look on Philip's face, told him, 'No, no. Vittorio suggested we dine alone, just the four of us, in the small dining room. It has all the pomp and circumstance of a proper English dinner to make you feel at home.'

'Do you always follow his directives?' asked Amanda.

'Well, I hadn't thought about it, but I guess for the

most part I do. You see, they always seem to benefit me in some way. Come, we can go through the library.'

The small dining room was enchanting in spite of the eighteenth-century silver Chinese wallpaper of slim blossoming cherry trees and exotic birds that was in places blistering off the walls, stained by water damage and damp. They dined on a round Queen Anne table with one leg wrapped in white wadding and tied with a soft leather belt, and sitting on Chippendale chairs, one with a back patched with Scotch tape. The rock crystal chandelier dribbling clusters of carved fruits in miniature and holding cream-coloured candles cast the perfect light over the Meissen dinnerware and French crystal goblets.

Vittorio, all the time he had been with them, had hardly said a word to either Amanda or Philip – not that he wasn't pleasant or hospitable, because he was both of those things, merely that he was quiet, enjoying himself, watching Eliza's every move, listening to her every word with the same pride he had shown when he first introduced her to Amanda.

For Philip and Amanda he was hard work, yet to be admired for the way he supported Eliza, loved her openly. Even the way they called each other 'Bunny', as cutesy as it was, seemed acceptable. It was clear that Vittorio was not really there for them but for his wife, that she should have the best of visits, a lovely day with her English friends. His adoration of Eliza, though held in bounds, expressed itself in his every gesture. Amanda was profoundly affected by them as a couple, and the eccentric manner in which they lived in the Villa Montecatini: a house of infinite beauty filled with heritage and family treasures yet treated as if it were no more than a farmer's cottage.

They were at table for three hours, dining on an outstanding meal of eight courses served by Giacomo and Amiata, who doubled in the house as cleaner and waitress. That evening Amanda was confronted not by the simple, charming friend she had made so casually but by Eliza: a beautiful, erudite woman who had elevated herself through the professional classes, acquiring education and culture far beyond her husband or his friends. She had never tossed those things away to settle for lust and love with a farmer, as Amanda had assumed. She had instead retained them, to give as part of herself to her farmer, in exchange for unconditional love on both sides.

Dining in this eccentric, shabby house that seemed to stand still in time, enjoying a perfect meal of pigeon pâté; poached quail's eggs covered with a light hollandaise sauce on a bed of mushroom purée, which sat in a pastry boat that melted in the mouth; a cold creamed-crab soup decorated with snippets of fresh chives; pan-fried trout in butter with crunchy almonds; a lemon sorbet; rib of beef, served rare, with horse-radish sauce, miniature roast potatoes and a scooped-out artichoke basket of miniature green vegetables; a platter of soft cheeses served with paper-thin biscuits; and for pudding, the finest crême brulée either of the guests had ever eaten, was an occasion that neither Amanda nor Philip would ever forget.

Vittorio Carducci's table manners were as rough and ready as the rest of his personality, but though he clanged his plates and cutlery and shovelled his food, and spoke with his mouth full the rare times that he did speak, it seemed no more bizarre than the entire social event already was.

The meal over, demitasse cups of coffee having been served with home-made chocolate truffles, and port having been drunk, the evening was at an end. Eliza and Vittorio, holding hands, walked their guests to their Range Rover. If there had been any awkward moment during Amanda and Philip's entire visit it was when they were thanking their hosts profusely for a most lovely afternoon and extraordinary meal and saying goodnight.

The men shook hands, Philip kissed Eliza on the cheek, Eliza and Amanda clasped hands for a moment. The yellow light cast from massive iron lanterns to either side of the entrance was sufficient for the two women to read what was going on in the gaze passing between them. Just as Eliza had guessed, this was not goodnight but goodbye. The boundaries of their friendship had been breached, the two had lost the casual tie that had bound them together. Eliza had forfeited her English friend, but she was no longer a woman who fretted over loss. She had lost and found so much in her life she had come to terms with it as part of the grander pattern.

LONDON

Epilogue

One very grey and cold rainy November afternoon, umbrella up and carried low and tilted over her face to keep the gusting wind from drenching her, while rushing down Bond Street Amanda Dix crashed into Eliza Carducci. The two women were delighted to see each other again after so long a time.

Several days after the dinner party Eliza had given for them at the Villa Montecatini, she had received a letter of thanks from Amanda in which she said that she and Philip were returning to London. For years the women exchanged Christmas cards and Vittorio twice a year cut their meadows but Amanda and Philip's villa remained empty, locked and shuttered.

The two women decided they would have tea and rushed through the wet streets to the Ritz. The years had been good to both of them and they praised each other for how well they looked, spoke about life in Tuscany and in London, asked after each other's friends.

Finally, just as they were about to leave, Eliza asked why Amanda and Philip had not returned to the villa. Amanda told her they had realised that the Tuscany years were over for them. Most of their friends were now in the South of France and the lifestyle there suited them better.

While standing behind the doorman who was calling separate taxis for them, Amanda told Eliza that the dinner party at her house was an evening she and Philip never talked about but would always remember. 'One day,' she declared, 'when we have given up the insincerity of the life we thrive on, we'll go back to the villa and have you and Vittorio to dinner.' Then, sad-faced, she dashed away without her taxi, tears trickling down her cheeks because both of them knew that would never happen.

Eliza took the taxi to the British Museum and there, standing on the steps under a large black silk umbrella, waiting for her, was Vittorio. They kissed and he presented her with a bunch of violets.

Going Too Far

Catherine Alliott

From the bestselling author of The Old Girl Network;
'[An] addictive cocktail of wit, frivolity and madcap romance' Time Out

'You've gone all fat and complacent because you've got your man, haven't you?'

There are some things only your best friend can tell you but this outrageous suggestion is met with indignation from Polly Penhalligan, who is recently married, trying for a baby and blissfully happy in her beautiful manor farmhouse in Cornwall. At least, she was, until Pippa's unfortunate remark forces her to realise that her idyllic life of gorging on chocolate biscuits, counting her seemingly endless blessings and not getting dressed until lunchtime could be having a few unwelcome side-effects.

So Polly decides to razz things up a bit – and agrees to allow her home to be used as a location for a commercial. Having a glamorous film crew around should certainly put something of a bomb under rural life, shouldn't it? But even before the cameras are set up and the stars released from their kennels, Polly's life and marriage have been turned upside down. This time, it seems, she's gone too far . . .

0 7472 4607 6

HEADLINE

Splash

Val Corbett, Joyce Hopkirk, Eve Pollard

'Bold, bubbly and deliciously bitchy. From three women who have seen and probably done it all'
Michael Dobbs, author of *House of Cards*

Katya, Liz and Joanna have been friends for years; closer even than sisters, they have always shared everything – except men. They have always supported each other on their way to the best jobs in a world dominated by men, acquiring the trappings and luxuries of authority that are the envy of other women. Nothing could drive them apart – or could it?

Now they're coping with new pressures. Katya is breaking all her own rules, for her new lover is married and she won't tell even her closest friends who it is. As the Television News Personality of the Year, Katya is a front page story waiting to happen – and the news, much more sensational than mere adultery, is beginning to break. It's just the story Liz needs for Page One to clinch her appointment as first woman editor of a British national daily newspaper. Their friend Joanna, editor of a glossy women's magazine, argues no story is worth destroying a friendship for – but how can Liz resist the splash of the year?

SPLASH is the story of power struggles between men and women, of unexpected love and the hurt of betrayal. Above all, it is the story of a friendship. No woman who has ever had – or been – a friend should miss it.

0 7472 4889 3

HEADLINE